PIPELINE

A Novel

Hugh Harris

PIPELINE

Copyright © Hugh Harris, 2018 *All rights reserved.*
ISBN 9781719982795

This novel is a work of fiction. Names, descriptions, entities, and incidents included in the story are products of the author's imagination. Any resemblance to actual persons, events, and entities is entirely coincidental.

Scripture quotations are from the New Revised Standard Version of the Bible.
Cherokee text to "Amazing Grace" from United Methodist Hymnal

WORDQUILT BOOKS
North Chesterfield, Virginia

WORDQUILT BOOKS

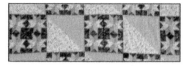

By Hugh Harris

Fiction

PIPELINE: A Novel

The Dinkel Island Series—
FORGIVEN
Return of BLISS
Secrets at Lighthouse Point

Nonfiction

When Love Prevails
Tag-along Talk: Wordquilts Blogs
NPH: Journey into Dementia and Out Again
Co-authored with Sharon French Harris

To Sharon, for her love that has enriched my life, her help in acquiring information about pipelines, and her patience during the long hours I spent living in the story I tell in these pages.

Pipeline: *"a line of pipe with pumps, valves, and control devices for conveying liquids, gases, or finely divided solids."*
Protest: *"a complaint, objection, or display of unwillingness usually to an idea or a course of action."*
　　　　　　　　–Merriam Webster

◆ ◆ ◆

"But seek the welfare of the city where I have sent you in exile, and pray to the Lord on its behalf, for in its welfare you will find your own welfare." (Jeremiah 29:7 NRSV)

ONE

Billy Upshur stumbled into the bathroom on a bleak February morning, rubbed his eyes and squinted against the glare from the window. Tousled brown hair and a whiskered face greeted him in the mirror. He grabbed the washstand, shook his head as though unsure where he was, then splashed cold water on his forehead.

"Oh, Lord, help me."

Uncertainty and anticipation bounced around within him like an electrical charge shooting back and forth between two alternating poles. He was inside a brick bungalow located on the main road just inside a rural Virginia mountain village called Strong's Creek.

Until four weeks ago the place had only been a notation in some computer file at work. Now it was to be his home. He showered, wrapped a towel around himself, then stepped into the bedroom. An open suitcase was on the bed waiting to be unpacked. Another sat on the floor.

He started at the sudden sound of laughter coming from the hall. A strange man stepped into the doorway, obviously amused by what he saw. Shock and anger flared within Billy.

"What the...how'd you get in here"

The man was clad in a faded flannel shirt, worn work pants, and a shabby down jacket. A dirty baseball cap bearing the New York Yankees logo was pulled down over dark, shaggy hair. He looked like he hadn't shaved in a couple of days. Pulling the stub of a stale cigar out of his mouth, he scowled. "Man, if you ain't a sight!"

Billy started to move toward him. The man held up his hands, palms outward. He spoke with a twangy drawl. "Now don't go gettin' flustered. It ain't nobody here but me 'n you." He stepped away from the door frame. "It's my job to check this here house rug'lar like, to make sure everthin's okay."

He studied Billy. "So, you be the new preacher?"

Billy ignored the question. "You can just get yourself right back outa here. And, you can tell whoever sent you that I don't need your help."

"That'd be Mistah Bendah down to th' Emporium. He done sent me."

"Well, I'll have a talk with Mr. Bender! How did you get in here?"

"With m'key, of course." He put the cigar back in his mouth, reached into his pocket and produce a metal ring full of keys.

"So, you have a key to this house where I'm supposed to live. I'd like for you to give me that key on your way out."

"Can't do that," he said, returning the keys to his pocket. "It's Bender's key."

"In that case, I'll have the locks changed. Now, I want you out of here."

"Okay, okay. I don't know what all the fuss is about. Like I said, I'm jest doin' m'job."

The stranger turned and was gone as suddenly as he had appeared. Billy heard the front door close and realized he didn't know the man's name. He finished dressing then called Oscar Bender, a local merchant who was chairman of the trustees for the churches of Strong's Creek Wesleyan Brethren Circuit. After several rings he was greeted by a gruff, emotionless voice.

"Bender here."

"Mr. Bender, this is Pastor Upshur...."

The man's voice brightened a bit. "Oh, Upshur. Heard you was moved in. Is there somethin' I can help ya with?"

"For starters, I was shocked to find some guy who says he works for you standing in my bedroom laughing at me when I stepped out of the shower this morning. I'd like to know what that was all about."

"Oh, don't worry 'bout him. That's Zeke. He works for me. I'm sure he was just checkin' things out—probably didn't know you was in there."

"Well, he knows now. I asked him to give me his key, and he wouldn't. Said it belongs to you."

"That's right. Since we don't have no pars'nage, that's one o' my rental units I'm lettin' the church use."

"I understand all that."

"So, what's your problem? Zeke has a key so's he can do maintenance. You don't have to worry 'bout him."

"Uh, Mr. Bender....'

"Oscar's the name."

"Okay, Oscar—I might be new in the ministry, but I know the denominational rules for parsonages, and this is improper. I want...."

"Hold on! I told you this ain't no pars'nage—it's one o' my rental houses."

"I understand that, but I was also told the parsonage rules still apply, and I want them followed."

There was a pause, then a cough. Bender came back on the phone, his tone of voice much cooler. "Okay, I'll check that out with the district supervisor. And to show you I'm not such a bad guy, I'll tell Zeke not to go into that house. Will that make you feel better?"

"Thanks. I'd appreciate it."

At thirty-one, Billy was a college graduate who, up until now, had worked in the Richmond office of a state utility contractor, EverMore Energy, that was involved with acquisition of private property on which to build a natural gas pipeline expansion. He hadn't been involved with the actual acquisitions which had often become volatile issues. He had just been what the company informally called a "go-fer," a clerk in the central office. Being out of that intense work environment now felt strange.

Suddenly he remembered his employee ID card, which he was supposed to turn in when he left. Had he done that? He went into the study and rifled through some as-yet-unpacked boxes without finding it. He shrugged. *Guess I did!*

Integrity was important to Billy. He had grown up in a family where honesty and respect had been drilled into him—yet sometimes he could be scatterbrained. He thought about the change he was trying to embrace. During a week-long spiritual life retreat two years ago he had felt a deeper sense of God than he'd ever known. It became so personal that by the end of the week he had responded to an invitation for people who felt they were being called to ordained ministry.

That had launched him into a two-year process of committee meetings, studies to qualify as a lay pastor, and finally assignment as student pastor at Strong's Creek. He was to serve the two active churches on weekends, attend school during the week, and be available for emergencies at any time. He would serve full-time during the summer months, as well as during the interim time until fall classes began.

It was normal practice for rural churches to provide a house, or parsonage, for their pastor. The Strong's Creek Circuit had always met that requirement until recent years when maintenance costs overwhelmed the declining congregations. For the past five years a retired pastor served the circuit, working out of his own home thirty miles away. The situation changed when he suffered a fatal heart attack.

Billy needed housing, so Oscar Bender offered to help out. He wasn't sure what he had expected, but the condition of the house came as a shock. Oscar had done nothing to spruce up the place. It was basically clean, but sparsely furnished. Faded beige walls seemed to cry out for a fresh coat of paint. Billy felt so let down when he arrived the night before that he simply dumped his belongings and collapsed into a fitful sleep.

He knew he needed to unpack a few boxes of personal things he'd stacked in the living room, but somehow couldn't bring himself to do it. Everything felt jumbled and confusing. What was he supposed to be doing? Why hadn't someone at least met him and offered some assistance? He didn't begin to know how to organize either his work or his living space. Somehow, it all felt temporary.

Walking into the kitchen he spied an old coffee maker with a smudged label, "Mr. Coffee." There were dried stains on both the appliance and the counter. *Somebody must have left this behind—or else they just didn't want it. I can see why they wouldn't.* He picked it up, examined it and set it back down. *Wonder if it works?* He plugged it into a nearby socket, hit "start," and saw a red light come on. *Guess so.*

He unplugged it, rummaged through the cabinets and found some dish detergent and frayed towels. After washing it, he rummaged some more and came up with a tin containing coffee. *Wonder how fresh this is?* He couldn't find filters.

"Improvise," he told himself. A roll of paper towels attached under the cabinet brought forth an "Aha!" He tore off one panel, folded it and placed it in the coffee maker. After guessing how much coffee to add, he plugged the machine back in and turned it on. It gurgled and coughed as it came to life.

While the coffee brewed, Billy walked through the house, opening the plastic window shades and taking a look outside. Barren trees and a nondescript yard created a sense of isolation. It was cold in the house and he shivered. A thermostat on the wall indicated it was sixty degrees. He turned the knob to a higher temperature, but nothing happened.

Pulling on a light coat he sank into an old recliner, closing his eyes with his hands to his temples. A truck rumbled down the narrow street thirty feet away, causing the window panes to chatter with vibration. He leaned back.

"Lord, I ain't ready for this. Sorry. Thought I was."

The coffee maker stopped gurgling and he wondered if his makeshift filter had worked. The glass carafe showed that it had. Billy searched the cabinets for a cup. Nothing there but a few plastic utensils, paper plates, and Styrofoam cups. He filled one with coffee then looked in the fridge for milk. It was empty. No sugar anywhere in sight. He decided to drink it black, but when he took a sip, the hot liquid had an unpleasant bite to it.

"Ugh!"

The coffee splashed onto the counter as he set the cup down harshly. He pulled off another paper towel and mopped up his spill. There was no trash can, so he set it on the counter. In exasperation, he tossed the coffee into the sink and headed out to a small diner he'd noticed on the village's main street.

♦ ♦ ♦

Driving into the parking lot Billy took in the setting. A large sign broadcast, "Clete's Happy Place." There was a quaintness about the dingy building set against the backdrop of a grove of cedar trees. Across the front were long-neglected flag stone planting boxes beneath a façade of streaked windows interspersed with faded blue metal panels. Dried, bushy plants suggested attractive vegetation had once occupied the boxes. Long, stringy vines overflowed onto the weedy gravel parking lot. Dilapidated latticework framed the entrance. Billy wondered how long it had been since someone had administered a dose of tender loving care to the place.

Stepping inside he saw a long counter with bar stools. Behind it was an array of equipment, posters a chalk menu advertising the specials of the day, and a long mirror with a slogan printed across it: *Happy Food Makes a Happy Day.* A door with a small, round window gave entry to the kitchen.

Billy gazed around the room, taking in booths with tables set apart by high, straight-backed benches. He decided to sit at the counter. Almost simultaneously a gruff looking man with a white non-descript cap appeared from the kitchen door. He wore a faded plaid shirt and a smudged apron with the name "Clete" stenciled under a faded yellow smiley face. Clete shoved a cup of coffee toward him.

"What'll ya have?"

"Coffee first," said Billy as he pulled the cup toward him and studied the menu. He looked up into Clete's grinning face. "How about two eggs over medium with sausage links."

"You got it! Toast with that?"

"No, thanks."

Clete disappeared into the kitchen and Billy swung around on his stool. Two guys drinking coffee were engrossed in conversation farther down the counter, about fifteen feet away. Several booths had customers who were being tended by a middle-aged waitress wearing an apron with the same smiley face on it with the name, "Evie" stenciled under it. Directly behind him were three rough looking men dressed in tattered jeans and grungy denim shirts. One man pointed in Billy's direction and for a few moments it felt like everyone was staring at him.

Billy turned his gaze away as his food arrived. He could see the men in the mirror directly beneath the TV. They put their heads together, muttered something, then broke out laughing. One of them wore a dirty baseball cap turned backwards. High cheek bones and the cut of his jaw suggested he might be Native American. The other two had thick beards and one had a pony tail. They quickly devoured their biscuits and gravy, got up jostling with each other and laughing as they glanced his way, then left.

The men had set Billy's nerves on edge, feeding anxiety that had been firing up since his encounter with Zeke. *Shake it off*, he told himself. *This is a different place from what you're used to. Once you get to know folks, things won't seem so bad. Don't make a big thing out of small stuff.*

Nobody seemed to notice the drama Billy felt. Clete brought his breakfast. The eggs were okay, and the sausage tasted pretty good. He gulped it down and finished his coffee, then paid his bill. He wasn't anxious to go back to the dingy house just yet. He'd noticed a fireplace, but no wood, so he knew he had to find a solution to the heat situation. That was not a task he was thrilled about tackling.

Stepping out of the building, Billy noticed the sun had begun to warm the atmosphere. He felt refreshed as he breathed in the mountain air. *Ah! Maybe I should drive out and find that small church—get a feel for the countryside.* The Strong's Creek Circuit had two active churches, one in town and one at a place called Frog Hollow.

Pulling out onto the highway he felt his spirits rise. Some cattle grazing in a field caught his eye. A flock of small black birds darted between the trees. Wooded, rolling hills featured scattered farms and a small housing development that looked fairly new. Mountainous ridges seemed to hide and then reappear ahead of him. People waved as he drove by...a man putting something in his mailbox, and a pickup truck driver. Maybe this wasn't such a bad place after all.

TWO

Along a straight stretch of highway two miles out of town a dirty faded blue van with muddy windows that had been following him suddenly zoomed past, disappearing around the next curve. *Hope you get where you're going in one piece,* Billy thought. The van was out of sight by the time he rounded the curve himself.

Billy glanced at a hand-drawn map on the seat beside him. It had been in an envelope given to him by Dr. Fletch Waverley, supervising pastor for the Alleghany District. "You'll need this," Waverley had told him. "I drew it because Frog Hollow is pinched in between some ridges and I wasn't able to get a fix on it with my GPS. I don't want you to start out not being able to find your way."

Three miles later he came to a bridge with a sign that read, "Strong's Creek." His map told him to turn onto a road he saw just ahead of the bridge. As he turned he saw another sign, "Frog Hollow Three Miles." *That would be about right. Frog Hollow Church is supposed to be seven miles from town. So far, so good.*

The road ran alongside the creek which seemed to be about thirty feet wide, its banks lined with wild grasses and trees. Rope bridges with wood planks periodically crossed to small rustic cottages with numerous outbuildings. He didn't see any people stirring around, but the houses did look as though they were occupied.

Good night, this is like a time warp...like stepping back into history. A rusty old washing machine adorned the front porch of one house. Several others had worn out children's toys in view. Nearly every yard had chickens meandering around. Even though it was winter, clothing hung on stretched lines. Billy had never seen anything like it.

A mile later the paved road made a sharp turn away from the creek. A sign said Frog Hollow was up a gravel road straight ahead. Billy paused, checked the map, then set out on the rugged byway. He soon realized there were no longer any cottages across the creek, which now was narrower and featured a sharp bank breaking off from the road. To his right, trees gave way to steep, rocky cliffs and scrubby brush. He felt a shiver of uncertainty. *I don't think I'm gonna like commin' up here.*

He drove a mile or so farther, then as he came around a curve an old battered van was parked so it blocked the narrow roadway. Billy recognized it as the same one that had sped past him earlier.

"What the heck?" he muttered, slamming on the brakes and skidding to a stop. A creepy sensation ran up the back of his neck. He sat for a moment, looking for someone who might belong to the vehicle, wondering what this was about. Instinct told him to turn around and leave, but he overrode that impulse, stepping from his Honda Civic to check out the situation. *Maybe somebody's sick in there. Maybe that's why the driver sped past me out on the highway.* The windows were so muddy he couldn't see inside.

Walking up beside the van he called out, "Are you okay in there?"

There was no answer. Billy took a few more steps and suddenly three figures emerged from the brush just in front of him. It was the same guys he'd seen in the diner. One of them carried a tire iron, and another had a baseball bat. They stepped toward him.

Billy froze in shock.

"Well, well, look who done come to visit," said the man with the pony tail.

The other men laughed and Billy now saw that one of them had a rifle. Fear surged within him and he instinctively bolted for his car. The crack of the rifle created a spidered pattern in the glass on the door he'd left open. Billy stopped in his tracks.

"Y'all ain't gonna run off now, is yah? Don't y'all know that ain't neighborly?"

"Naw, he ain't got no manners. Maybe we oughta teach 'im some."

The men guffawed with laughter. Panicky thoughts hammered inside Billy's head. *What have I gotten into? These guys are gonna kill me...gotta get out of here.*

His back was to the men. A hand suddenly grasped his shoulder and spun him around. A fist crashed into his jaw. Pain shot through his mouth and up the side of his face. He felt sharp gravel biting into his knees as he fell to the ground.

"Ain't yore mama never tol' ya to be po-lite? Why you tryin' to run away from us? We's jest a welcomin' committee."

"Hey, Rev'ner...why don't y'all ask that god o'yourn to hep ya out righ-chere?"

Holding his hand against his aching jaw, Billy rose to his feet, not sure what to expect next. The man with the baseball bat stepped closer with a mean look in his eye.

"Easy there, Burly...God'll git ya. Thet thar's his boy."

"Ohhh. Maybe I oughta crawl on the ground in front of 'im."

They all whooped with laughter. In a panic, Billy started to turn toward his car. From the corner of his eye he saw the man who looked to be Native American raise his rifle again.

"Git 'im, Beanpole," barked the man with the pony tail.

"This here's fo y'all takin' away Mama Jean's house."

The words were like a slap in the face with a sudden gush of courage. *Mama Jean's house?* Billy stopped and turned towards the men. "I...I don't know what you're talking about," he stammered. "What house? Who are you? What do you want with me?"

Everything froze. The men glared at him for a moment. Billy kept his eyes on the man with the pony tail. *They think I'm somebody else.* He tried to force a smile, looking for a way around the impasse.

The leader's face was hard, hostile. He gestured toward Billy and shouted, "Beanpole!"

Billy lunged for his car. He hit the driver's seat, pulled the door shut and started the engine almost in one motion. Throwing it in reverse he turned hard right, slammed on the brakes, shifted into drive while turning the wheels hard to the left. In a spray of gravel and dust he zoomed away on the narrow road.

The rifle cracked behind him, but the shot barely grazed his car. Breathing hard, sweating profusely and aching all over, Billy tore down the narrow road with only one thing on his mind—getting as far away from Strong's Creek as he could.

THREE

At the main highway Billy turned left and headed back toward town, frantic to get someplace where he could plant his feet on solid ground with people he trusted. Beside him the window with its spidered pattern from Beanpole's rifle shot threatened to crumble with each bump in the road. He hoped it would hold together. The crack of the rifle still rang in his mind. Briefly he thought he'd stop at the rental house and pick up some personal belongings, but the specter of Zeke, plus what he'd just been through, drove him to keep going. He breezed through town nonstop, instinctively headed for the home of his adopted family in Healing Waters, West Virginia.

Darkness began to enshroud the landscape with deep shadows as he entered the George Washington National Forest. His headlights clicked on automatically. There was almost no traffic on the road, which suited him fine, except it did create a sense of isolation. Turning on the radio he found a local station where Tennessee Ernie Ford was singing his signature piece, "Sixteen Tons." The song triggered a mixture of emotions. Billy was heading into coal country, which is what the song was about. His family name, Upshur, derived from Upshur County, near the town of Elkins. Ironically, he was looking for comfort in a place that could be every bit as unnerving as what he'd experienced on Frog Hollow Road.

Rounding a curve Billy noticed a wide section along the shoulder and pulled over. Turning off the engine he leaned forward with his head in his folded arms, then sobbed uncontrollably for several minutes. As his inner turmoil subsided he brushed the sleeve of his lightweight jacket across his eyes and blinked a few times. *I need to get out and stretch.* Opening the door almost made him change his mind. A sharp blast of cold air sent a shiver down his spine. He pulled his jacket tighter. *Should have stopped to get my heavy coat!*

Across the highway a rocky alcove afforded a fading view of the mountainous terrain where ridges of denuded trees danced to the harsh whistle of the wind. Billy breathed in deeply, absorbing the timeless drama of nature's evening shutdown. Fear and anger sank into the background, replaced just for a moment, with calm rationality.

"What am I doing here?" he muttered.

His mind replied, *Running away!*

Fear and anger resurfaced.

"That's crazy," Billy yelled at the trees. "God, where are you? You got me into this...what's it all about. Speak to me!"

The wind whistled and tree branches chattered, but he did not perceive the voice of God. Time warped for a moment as he clenched his fists and shut his eyes. The judgmental wind rattled his bones. He shuddered and bolted back to the car where he started the engine, turning the heat on high. Billy sat immobilized for a moment. The sound of a passing truck nudged him forward. *Life goes on,* he told himself as he pulled back onto the road.

◆ ◆ ◆

Lottie and Clint Upshur were Billy's aunt and uncle, and their home was the only one he could remember. He did have some recollections of the day when his world fell apart...twenty-seven years ago. Everybody said his mom and dad had married too young. He'd heard stories about how they were free spirits, unbridled by time, space or responsibility. Nobody in the family could understand them. When Billy came along, things did change...for a while. Then one day when he was three his dad mysteriously disappeared. No one knew where he went, or why. His mother took it hard.

Billy remembered the morning she packed his clothes and took him to her sister Lottie's small house on a crowded street. She practically dragged him up onto the porch, sat him in a chair, then rang the doorbell. When there was no answer she pointed her finger in his face.

"Now you sit there, ya hear me?"

He could still feel the fear that gripped him as she turned, ran back to the car and drove away. He never saw her again.

It was a warm spring day and the sun crept onto the porch as Billy sat in fear of what might happen next. He didn't really know his aunt Lottie, which made his anxiety worse. Then her cat that had been observing from the yard, came up and began rubbing its furry back against his leg. Tears rolled down Billy's cheeks. He pulled the cat onto his lap. It didn't resist and soon boy and cat were sleeping in the sun's warmth.

That was how Lottie found them when she returned from the market a little later. Billy remembered how she cried with him when he told her what his mom had done. A lasting spiritual bond formed between them. She and Clint adopted Billy and raised him as their own. They became his Mom and Pop.

Clint worked long, hard hours. It was work that turned many men tough and sour, but not Clint. He and Lottie were people of faith who prayed daily and took their Christian teachings to heart. They were active in their church. Sometimes when it seemed there wasn't enough money to keep them going, Clint would say, "Trust the Lord. The Lord will provide." No matter what crisis they faced, things always seemed to work out. Billy grew up in that mold.

Ernie Ford's song on the car radio touched a nerve inside Billy because all of this happened in a mining town, part of the Elkins Coalfield. Clint was a coal miner. The song pulled Billy's inner rage back up. "I guess I got soft workin' in that office in Richmond," he sputtered. Slamming his hand against the steering wheel his emotions exploded again. "God! Where are you? Did you really call me? Or am I just some weirdo who imagines things too big to be real?"

Rage, once vented, receded again. Guilt moved into its place. "I should have stood my ground back there!" he spit out. He thought of Clint's manner of natural leadership. He remembered when Clint was promoted to a shift foreman and it brought a new kind of stress into the family. What had stayed with him was the way Clint never let it get the best of him. Many of his men were hot tempered and immoderate. Drugs and alcohol besieged them. Others became sick with black lung disease. Clint had to deal with it all.

"Pop always prayed, no matter what," Billy muttered.

Memories from his teenage years crowded into his mind. He and Welby, Clint and Lottie's son, became true brothers. They hunted, played sports, and went to the church's teen club together. After high school, Clint had saved enough money to help each boy get a start on college, or whatever they wanted to do. He wanted them to escape the mines. Billy chose college, and Welby joined the Air Force. Like his dad, Welby had a natural way with people. *Boy, wish I'd had Welby with me up at Frog Hollow! Things would have been different I expect.*

Billy caught himself. *Lord, I had you right there. Why didn't I trust you?*

♦ ♦ ♦

It was late when Billy drove up the lane to the house in Healing Waters. He loved this place, although he'd never lived there. He had visited on occasion. An aging uncle that Clint hardly knew had unexpectedly left the property to him, along with a tidy sum of money. The inheritance had enabled him to retire from the mine and move away from the house and town owned by the coal company. He and Lottie praised God for this gift that had opened a whole new world to them.

The two-story house loomed in the darkness as an oasis might to someone lost in the desert. Light glowed from the living room and upstairs windows. Billy parked next to Clint's GMC Yukon, then walked to the back door, harsh cold air biting into his face. There seemed to be a touch of moisture with it. The door was unlocked so he quietly opened it and stepped inside. He heaved a sigh...*Home!* Stepping into the kitchen he heard the TV on in the living room.

Clint stirred. "You need somethin' outside, Lottie? I didn't hear you come downstairs."

Billy heard the recliner clank as Clint got up. "Sorry to come in so late, Pop. It's me, Billy."

"Billy!" Clint appeared in the doorway. "What in tarnation you doin' here, Son? Did Lottie know you was comin'?"

"No, I didn't know it myself. Something happened, and I needed to get away. I'll tell you all about it later." He and Clint embraced as they heard Lottie's footsteps on the stairs.

"Is that Billy I hear?" Lottie, who had turned 58 the previous fall, was known for her sharp wit and bouncy disposition. She was slightly stout with greying hair that framed a face marked by twinkle lines and engaging blue eyes. She came into the room wearing a casual housedress and the apron she'd probably had on all day.

"Land sakes, what you doin' comin' in here late at night like this?" She threw her arms around Billy and kissed his cheek. "I declare, you're gittin' too big to hug proper."

Billy returned the hug, and she stepped back with her hands on her hips. "Why didn't you tell us you was comin'?"

"I'll fill you in on stuff tomorrow," he said with a smile. Neither Lottie nor Clint pushed him.

"Didn't ya bring some clothes with ya?" asked Clint, looking behind Billy toward the back door. "I don't see no suitcase or nothin'."

"No, like I said, I really left in a hurry...I'll explain it all tomorrow. Figured I could find some of Welby's old civies that would fit me. We always could wear each other's stuff."

"Indeed you can," said Lottie. "The bed's even made up in his old room, or I can make one up in another room. Oh, I just bought some new toothbrushes on sale at the Dollar Tree. They're in the bathroom closet...listen to me go on! You know where everything is."

Billy gave her a hug. "Sure do!"

Lottie stepped away and motioned toward the table. "Let me get ya somethin' to eat. Bet you ain't had no decent supper. What can I fix ya?"

"Believe it or not, I did stop at a restaurant."

Lottie smiled. "Well, it's cold outside, and you always did like hot chocolate on a cold night. I'll fix some o' that...oh, and I just happened to bake a caramel cake today." She reached for the cake pan and a knife. "Get a plate off the sideboard. How big a slice do ya want?"

Billy remembered the routine. Reaching for the plates and forks he said, "Don't you want a slice, too?"

She winked playfully. "Maybe I'll have one later."

He picked up two plates, and two forks. "I'll take whatever size Pop wants.

"Now hold on here you two. Don't go gittin' carried away. I want some o' this left for tomorrow."

They all laughed as she served the cake and hot chocolate, then sat down with them. Billy heaved a sigh of relief as guilt, anger, fear, and confusion melted from his spirit. He was home!

FOUR

The next morning Billy slept late. He awoke to the aroma of bacon and eggs wafting through the house. Lottie's voice drifted up from the kitchen. She was talking to someone on the phone. Hearing her laugh made him feel almost like a kid again. Lottie had helped him find pajamas that fit, and Clint loaned him a razor. Before he turned in the three of them prayed. Sitting on the edge of the bed he stretched and yawned, then got up and went down the hall to the bathroom.

He still had a lot going on in his mind, but he felt grounded. As he shaved he talked to himself in the mirror. "Look at you! You're not a kid anymore. You're a grown man. You have a calling, and you let some backwoods people get under your skin—running away. That was just plain stupid! You need to get yourself together. Get a grip!"

In the shower he turned up the heat and inhaled deeply, clearing his head. *Lord, forgive me for my fears and weakness. Help me get a better start today. Show me what I need to do.* He dried off, went back to his room and dressed. The words of the man called Beanpole suddenly charged into his mind, "You done took Mama Jean's house."

He sat down on the bed and smacked the palm of his hand against his forehead. *Mama Jean's house...of course! It's that gas pipeline!* He felt sick at his stomach. *Strong's Creek is right in the path of that project.* The pieces clicked together. He had seen paperwork about the various locations the pipeline project affected, and he'd seen reports about peoples' reactivity. He had thought of those protests as more or less isolated things that would pass with time. *I guess those guys had to take a settlement for their property that they didn't want.... But why did they attack me?*

He felt a mixture of both relief and alarm. The incident at Frog Hollow suddenly made sense, but it raised the question of how they knew he had worked for EverMore. He needed time to process the situation—to regain a sense of balance. *Guess I oughta talk to Pop about this.* He finished dressing and went downstairs for breakfast.

Lottie turned from the stove as he walked into the kitchen. "Well, look who's up! You sure was worn out last night! Looks like you're feelin' a mite better today." She handed him a cup of coffee. "How 'bout some bacon, eggs and grits?"

The warmth of family connection brought a smile to his face. "That's just what I need! Nothin' like your cookin' to start off the day, Mom."

"And them eggs ain't store bought, neither—come right fresh from the hen house mornin'," said Clint. "Sorry I can't say the same about the bacon, though." He chuckled as he spoke.

"It's good to be home." Billy put cream and sugar in his coffee and stirred it. "If you've got some time, Pop, I'd like to tell you about what happened yesterday—the reason why I came here so unexpectedly...and I do apologize for that."

"No apology needed, Sonny. Time! I got plenty of that these days."

"Now, now—don't forget that firewood you was gonna bust up today," said Lottie.

Clint put his hand to his forehead. "Oh, no...just when I thought I had nothin' to do." He laughed, reached over and gave Billy a pat on the back. "Tell ya what...you look like that city livin's done made you soft, boy. How 'bout me and you bustin' up them logs together?"

"Sure, just soon as I get fueled up here, I'll challenge you. Betcha I can split more logs than you can in half-an-hour. Whaddya say?"

"Are you sure ya wanna take me on?"

"You're the one oughta be worryin' about that! I'm not as soft as you think."

"You're on! Just bein' younger don't mean ya can get the best o'me."

They finished eating, put on some heavy work clothes and went out into the back yard. Dense clouds were building in the sky and last night's sharp breeze still cut through the air. A pile of thick fireplace length logs lay waiting to be split where a large tree had once stood. Billy could see they had been there for some time. Weeds had grown up around them, and the wood looked dry and faded. He pulled a log off the pile and lugged it over toward a chopping block. It hit the ground with a thud.

"What is this? Oak?... Looks pretty seasoned."

"Yeah. Big ole tree came down last year in a storm. Been sittin' here agin' for over a year now. Oughta be just about right for the fireplace."

"Wow! This stuff's gonna be hard to split."

They set to work and after twenty minutes Billy began to feel the strain. It had been some time since he'd done anything this strenuous.

"Pop, you could save a lotta work if you rented a log splitter."

"So, what's wrong with a little work?" Clint stiff-armed him. "Like I say, you're gettin' soft."

Billy grinned as he stopped to rest, leaning on the handle of his ax. "Reckon I gotta admit it. Looks like you're gonna win on this one."

Clint stopped, too. They walked over to the shelter of a tool shed and sat down on an old wooden bench against a plank fence under a cedar tree. "This here looks like a pretty big storm movin' in. We're gonna need this wood."

Clint lit up one of the pipes he sometimes smoked. Under his heavy coat was a body he kept tuned with exercise and a moderate lifestyle. At age 62 he was often mistaken for being a dozen years younger. His hairline had receded over the years, greying at the temples. He had a strong jaw, moderate mustache, dark eyes and thick eyebrows. A smile curled naturally at the corners of his mouth, so people usually took him to be in a good mood. He traded on that impression but was capable of being tough when necessary. Billy had always admired him.

Clint puffed a smoke ring into the air. "So, tell me what's goin' on back there in Virginia."

Billy shuffled his feet and heaved a sigh, then went through the whole story about moving into the house and the incident on Frog Hollow Road. Clint puffed thoughtfully, making eye contact as he listened.

"So, ya ran away from that mess." He tapped the spent pipe out on his boot, put it in his pocket and said with one eyebrow raised, "That ain't like you, Sonny. You're tougher than that."

"Yeah...." Billy felt his face turn red with embarrassment. "That's not the way you raised me, Pop. It's not my usual way of handlin' stuff. I guess the rifle made the difference. I'd never run into that before."

Clint slapped him on the shoulder. "Everybody has times like that when they hit a wall, or just fall back in the face of a challenge. I've had 'em. Never told ya 'bout the guy pulled a pistol on me once when I was tryin' to calm down a bunch of riled up miners. I know how it feels to stand on the wrong end of a gun."

"So, what did you do?" said Billy, shocked.

"Near's I recollect, I just stood there and stared 'im down. Kept lookin' 'im in the eye. He got nervous, but instead o' pullin' the trigger, he broke. Believe it or not, he dropped the gun."

Billy's jaw dropped open. "Just like that? Ya mean you stared him down?"

"Well, yes and no. Ya see, I knew my men. I knew him. I knew he was hard pressed, but he weren't no killer. Somebody else, it might a gone a different way."

Billy shrugged his shoulders. "Trouble is, I don't know those guys who attacked me." He paused, but Clint just nodded without saying anything. "But, I guess I did something like what you're talkin' about, at least for a minute or two, once they told me what was going on."

"You mean about that woman's house?"

"Yeah...all I could think of was they had mistaken me for somebody else. I think I've figured that out now, but...what can I do about it?"

"Sounds like you're plannin' to go back."

"Yeah, I don't think I ever intended not to, I just wasn't thinkin' straight when it all happened."

"Of course not. You want a suggestion?"

"Sure!"

"Seems to me you got two things you gotta do first off...I mean after ya square things with them church people who ain't gonna be real happy with ya."

Billy tried to anticipate his next words. "Two things?"

"Yep, it's plain as the nose on yer face...ya gotta get to know them guys, and ya gotta find out about that house thing, who that woman is and what's goin' on with 'er. And *pray!* They ain't gonna let ya pray with 'em first off, but you can start prayin' fer 'em now...and for yourself!"

Billy nodded. "Yeah...I think I'll go back Monday morning, if y'all don't mind me stayin' around. I'm not ready to face church folks quite yet. Still got a lot to talk out with God."

Clint nodded. "Good idea. Maybe you'd also better check in with somebody to see if you've still got that job."

Billy took a deep breath. "Yeah, you're right."

The two men went back to work and finished the wood pile by late afternoon. They shared stories and talked some more about the Strong's Creek situation.

♦ ♦ ♦

Billy called his district supervisor Friday evening. Fletch Waverley answered, "William, I'm glad you called. Been wondering what's going on over there. Sunday's coming up quickly and the folks at Strong's Creek are upset that you haven't settled in there yet." Billy sensed a critical edge in his voice. "Where are you?"

Billy swallowed his nervousness and went through the whole scenario. "I don't know what got into me. I just felt like getting completely away from everything, so I came home...."

"Home? So, you're back in Richmond?"

"No, I mean home to West Virginia—Healing Waters. That's where I am now."

Fletch mumbled something and Billy could hear papers being shuffled in the background. "Healing Waters...yes, I see that on your record. I guess I'd forgotten you came from West Virginia."

"Yes, Sir...that's where I am now. I'm not sure what to do next."

"Did you call the police? Why didn't you tell somebody what happened?"

Billy felt a flush of shame. "No...I just didn't think. I needed to get away."

"Well you should have called me. We could have worked on this situation together. Now we've gotta do a lot of catch-up to try to get things back in order."

Back in order, Billy thought. *That's all bureaucrats live for—keeping stuff in order. Same way it was at my old job.* "Yes, sir. I would appreciate your help."

There was a pause. "Okay, how long will it take you to get back here?"

"On a good day, maybe three hours. But we've got a storm building up here, so I don't know how that will affect things."

"Yes, we have the same forecast here. I'm going to put you down for Monday afternoon, say at two o'clock, if you can make it. If not, keep me informed and we'll change the time. The main thing is to move forward from where things are now."

"So..." Billy hesitated. "Do I...I mean...do you still want me to serve there?"

"Of course." Fletch paused. "We'll get to the bottom of this. No need to jump off the ship.... I'm going to call the sheriff's office and report the incident. Ordinarily I'd find a lay speaker to go out and do your services Sunday, but under the circumstances I'll do that myself. I'll give the sheriff your cell number in case he wants to talk with you. I'll see you when you get back."

"Thank you, Sir. I won't let you down."

Fletch prayed with him over the phone, and Billy hung up, then told Clint and Lottie his plans. When he went to bed he read from the Psalms and thought about David's struggles and faith. One of his favorites was Psalm 23. The words of verse four seemed to jump out at him, *"Even though I walk through the darkest valley, I fear no evil."*

"Fear no evil! That's exactly what I do fear. Evil." He read on, *"for you are with me; your rod and your staff—they comfort me."*

O Lord, I need to feel the comfort of your presence, and the strength only you can give me. Take my fears from me. I don't know what lies ahead, but I want to trust you so deeply that fear can't take me down.

Billy set the Bible down. The words of that fourth verse continued to ring in his mind. He tried to picture the Frog Hollow incident as though he were an observer, unseen, not attached to the situation. He pictured himself—bolting into his car.

An insight forged its way into his consciousness. *The guy with the rifle—Beanpole. He never meant to shoot me. He just wanted to scare me. He's lived in those hills all his life—could probably hit anything he wanted to.*

He lay on the pillow with his eyes closed. *Beanpole's the one who is scared. All those guys are scared. Of what?* He tried to imagine what the natural gas pipeline extension must mean to simple people who only wanted to be left alone, to live in peace.

Is that what's going on? What they need from me is support. Clint's right. I need to get to know them, to connect with them. Lord, show me how to do this ministry. Show me how to turn this threatening valley of fear into a place flowing with your blessings.

He turned out the light and fell into a restful sleep.

FIVE

On Friday, the day after Billy left Strong's Creek, the weather turned sharply colder. An intense storm system was moving in from the west, and reports from West Virginia indicated a snowstorm would develop rapidly. Carrie Glossner, head of the Strong's Creek Wesleyan Brethren Woman's Association, was concerned when she heard the forecast. A retired social worker who had never married, she had lived at Strong's Creek all her life, knew almost everyone, and was deferred to by most. Her high expectations were well-known, as was her impatience when people didn't measure up. She knew somebody hadn't measured up to the accepted way of greeting a new pastor.

When she learned that nobody had welcomed the new pastor, or prepared supper for him when he arrived Wednesday evening, she was livid. As far as she could determine, nobody but Oscar Bender had spoken to him…and that had been on Thursday morning. *Whatever happened to old fashioned hospitality? Ya jest gotta stay on folks to git 'em to do anything anymore.* A storm moving in meant the churches owed it to Pastor Upshur to see that he had everything he needed. She called Oscar and charged right in.

"Oscar, what's got into your head? You're in charge of seeing to the new preacher's housing needs, and far's I can see you haven't done anything outside of providing one of your rentals for him...."

"Now, Carrie, hold on here. Don't get yer blood pressure up. I did talk to 'im. Told 'im we was glad to have 'im...I did. Even sent Zeke Stoner over there to check if he needed anythin'."

"Oh, that's great! Zeke probably scared the stuffing out of him. You men!"

"I'm sure he's doin' okay. The good Lord'll look after 'im."

"Well that might be, but we've got to do our part, too. It's our duty to see that he gets settled in here...and now there's a big storm coming in. I should have known better than to count on you. If you want to get something done right, you have to do it yourself."

"Now, Carrie, I'm sure he's alright. Ain't heard nothin' to th' contrary."

That comment didn't set well with Carrie. She had a dental appointment that morning, and then her weekly book club meeting, so she ended the conversation. Right after lunch she drove up to the rental house. With the window shades half-closed, it looked empty. She decided to leave the pastor a note on the door asking him to call her about some food she and the women were fixing for his supper.

She parked in front of the house and walked up to the door. A creepy feeling crawled up the back of her neck and she realized the door was slightly ajar. "That's strange," she muttered to herself. "Either he was in a heap of a hurry this morning, or somebody's been in here."

She decided to check further. Cautiously pushing on the door, she tried to see inside as it opened. Stopping in the doorway she called, "Anybody in here? Hellooo!"

Not a sound. She stepped inside. The room felt cold. Carrie called Oscar on her phone. "I'm over at the preacher's house, and somethin's fishy. The heat ain't even turned on. I want you to come over here and help me check this place out."

Oscar stammered about how busy he was and said he'd send Zeke.

"I didn't ask you to send Zeke," she snapped. "I want *you* over here. Somethin' don't seem right."

Oscar had learned not to argue with Carrie. Everybody knew that was a losing proposition. He arrived within five minutes.

"So, what's all the fuss about, Carrie? I 'spect the man's out visitin' and learnin' the community—like he's s'posed to."

"It don't feel right. For one thing, the heat should be on. It's cold as ice in here."

"I can tell that!" barked Oscar. "You checked on anything else? Maybe the thermostat's busted."

"No! That's why I called you."

They walked through the house, found the boxes Billy had left in the living room and study. They could see he had slept in the bed, and it was obvious he had used the bathroom. "Now look here," said Carrie. "He's got a suitcase open on the bed, and another one sitting over there...and his shaving stuff and all is in the bathroom. It looks like he got up and just walked away. What do you make of that?"

"That's his personal stuff. Don't mean nothin'. Ain't everybody as neat and proper about stuff as you are. I'll see about the heat and just let things be."

Carrie was not about to "let things be" when she sensed something wasn't right. They found the mess in the kitchen where he'd jury rigged the coffee maker, then spilled coffee on the counter. There was no food in the refrigerator, no clothes hanging in the bedroom closet—nothing to suggest the pastor was settling in.

"I'll have to admit, this don't look right," said Oscar. "Actually, I know he was here yesterday morning. Like I said, Zeke come by, but he and the preacher didn't get along. I told Zeke to stay away."

"Zeke! I don't trust him. He's not even part of our church, much less a trustee."

Oscar bristled. "Well, this is my house, and he's my maintenance man. I told him to check on things, and then I told him to leave the preacher alone."

"Let's get this straight. If you loan this house to the churches, then it's ours to manage as long as we have a preacher living in it."

Oscar leaned his head back and surveyed the ceiling. "Yeah, yeah, yeah. I know.... Ya try to do something to help out, and ya get caught in all them rules."

Carrie ignored the comment. "I think somethin's mighty wrong." She pulled out her cell phone and dialed. "Let me speak to Cam."

"Whatcha callin the sheriff for?"

"Because that's what you do when somebody's in trouble, and somehow I think our new preacher's in some kind of trouble. I can feel it in my bones."

"If that don't beat all." Oscar smacked the palm of his hand against his forehead. "He'll be back. Jest out doin' his job."

"Oh, Cam, this is Carrie. Look, I don't want to get anybody stirred up, but me 'n Oscar's over here at the new preacher's place, and things don't look quite right. Wonder if you'd come over and check it out for us?" She paused to listen. "That's right...the one on the highway just outside of town. Okay." She turned the phone off.

"He's coming right over."

Within minutes Cam Bordain pulled up. He had been the county sheriff for the last five years. A tall, muscular man in his forties, he wore a uniform jacket with a fur collar, and his usual wide-brimmed hat. He had dark eyes, a heavy mustache, and short hair that was beginning to grey at the temples. With his glock strapped to his waist he made a formidable, no-nonsense impression. Carrie met him at the door and invited him inside.

Cam nodded toward Oscar as he spoke to Carrie. "What seems to be the problem?"

Carrie told him why she had come to the house, how she had found the door ajar, the heat off, and no clothes in the closet to suggest Billy was settling in. "Actually, I just have a gut feeling that something isn't right."

"Ma'am, I respect your gut feeling, but I have to have more to go on."

Carrie explained the whole scenario about Billy being young and new, and Oscar confirmed everything he knew about the situation.

Cam listened, then said, "With all due respects, I don't see anything here that suggests he's not comin' back. Maybe he went back to Richmond for more of his belongin's. I don't know why he would've turned the heat off, but maybe he just didn't know how the thermostat works. From what you say, y'all ain't done much to help him get started yet."

Oscar excused himself. "I've gotta get back to the store. Don't look like y'all need me now." Cam told him he'd call if he needed him, and then turned to Carrie.

"Here's what I'd suggest. You said you brought some food over. Just put that in the kitchen and leave him a note. Check on him tomorrow and if there's a problem then, call me. Meanwhile, I'll keep an ear out. If I hear of something strange goin' on, I'll check into it and let you know. Okay?"

Carrie agreed, and they left the house. She locked the door from the inside on her way out. When she got home she called her friend in Frog Hollow, Earlene Josef, and told her about the whole thing.

"I'd agree with Cam," said Earlene. "He has probably gone back to get some more of his belongings." When she hung up Carrie decided maybe they were right and she was getting upset over nothing. She tucked it into the back of her mind.

SIX

The storm moved into Healing Waters with a vengeance on Saturday. Clint and Billy ran to the store for a few things Lottie needed that morning. They spent the afternoon playing checkers and watching a basketball game. Billy even took a nap. Sleet rattled against the window pane as he went to bed that evening. By morning it had been replaced by large snowflakes. Looking out at the fallow garden plot behind the tool shed the snow appeared to have accumulated nearly a foot. Bulky objects masqueraded as smooth, miniature hills and valleys. He shivered as the thermometer on the window frame said it was seven degrees.

Hot water gurgling in baseboard pipes created a sense of grounding. Billy yawned and stretched. *The heavens declare the glory of God, and the earth shows forth his handiwork.* The words seemed to flow naturally into his consciousness. *Behold, God makes all things new.* He spent a few meditative moments in prayer that wrapped him within a quilted assurance that all would be well. *One step at a time.*

Downstairs Clint looked up from the roaring blaze he was tending in the living room fireplace. "Hey, Sonny, how'd ya sleep last night?"

Billy yawned again. "Great. No town noises to keep me awake."

Lottie called from the kitchen, "Breakfast in five minutes."

The two men went into the kitchen. "Anything we can do to help?"

"Just get yourselves some coffee."

"Division of labor," commented Clint with a chuckle. "I chop the wood and stoke the fire, she cooks." Putting his hand beside his mouth he whispered, "Just between you and me, I wouldn't want it t'other way around."

Laughing, Lottie turned from the stove wagging a finger at Billy. "One o' these days you'll get hitched and find out how that works."

Billy laughed. "Yeah, guess so."

"Surprised a handsome guy like you ain't done that already." Lottie opened the oven door and pulled out a pan of fresh biscuits. "Maybe the Good Lord'll take care o' that when ya git settled pastorin' them churches."

"Oh, I don't know about that. So far I've never found anybody who'd measure up to you."

"And you won't," added Clint with a wink.

"Y'all git y'selves over there and set down afore this food gets cold."

Obediently the men took their coffee to the table and Lottie served a breakfast fit for royalty. When she sat down they joined hands and bowed their heads while Clint offered a blessing. "For providin' us with a warm home and good food, we give you thanks, Lord. Amen."

They bantered small talk around the table while they ate. Billy thought about the churches at Strong's Creek. "Wonder if those folks back there on the charge are snowed outa church today?"

Clint looked surprised at the comment. "Snowed outa church? I guess if they're out in the woods they might be. Our church'll be open for all who can git there. We don't never shut it down."

"That's right! You've got four-wheel drive, don't you?"

"Sure do. Wouldn't live out here without it. Say, you might wanna git y'self somethin' to drive that'll be better fit for country weather, Sonny. That little Honda don't look too stout."

"Guess you're right. Hadn't thought about that."

"I'm wonderin' if you'll even be able to git back there for that meetin' y'all set up tomorrow. Dependin' when this thing ends, they might not git them roads opened up that quick."

Billy shrugged. "I guess the Lord will take care of that."

After breakfast they dressed warmly and trudged out to Clint's Yukon. A fencepost-mounted snow gauge said they had sixteen inches on the ground. A look at the sky said there was more to come. Clint started the engine and Lottie climbed in while he and Billy shoveled snow away from the wheels.

"You gonna put chains on?"

"Got 'em in the back if I need 'em. I hate them things, but there's nothing like 'em for traction, I gotta admit. Got the plow mounted on the tractor up in the shed. When we get back I might see if I can push some of this outa the driveway so's we can git that little car o' yours outa here in the mornin'."

"I appreciate that," said Billy as they climbed into the SUV and Clint shifted into four-wheel drive. All they needed was the start where they'd shoveled the snow.

The Yukon gained traction and they moved toward the road with no trouble. Even though the highway had been plowed, there was a lot of snow and ice packed on it, but they arrived at church with little delay.

"This here stuff's deeper than I thought," Clint remarked as they drove up. Someone had already pushed much of the snow back in the parking lot. A highway dump truck equipped with snow blade and a load of salt sat empty just inside the entrance.

"Wow! I'm impressed! You've even got the highway department workin' for your church."

Clint chuckled. "Looks that way, don't it?"

As they stomped snow off their feet entering the building, a man bundled up and carrying a coffee thermos was just exiting.

"You got an early start," said Clint. "We 'preciate it. Looks like you got a long day ahead."

"I jest come by to open things up for y'all. Gotta git back out there. We're tryin' to keep up with the main roads. Say a prayer fer us."

The pastor walked in on the conversation. "We'll be praying for ya." Since he lived next door to the church it was never a problem for him to be there, but the weather appeared to be keeping a large part of his flock away. Billy counted fifteen people in all. It was his first visit to the church. Billy's occasional visits with Clint and Lottie since they moved to Healing Waters had always been brief. He'd never gone to church with them. He took in the interactions among the people, imagining that he might soon have a leadership role in just such situations. When Clint introduced Billy to the pastor, he asked how many people he thought would be attending.

"Hard to tell. On a good day we have a hundred or so. Doubt if we'll get mor'n a fraction of that today."

A few more people came, and everybody milled about warming up with coffee and fellowship. Finally, the pastor raised his voice. "We're gonna be few in number but great in spirit today. Y'all come on up to the front of the sanctuary. Mabel called and said she's snowed in, so we'll hafta sing without the piano today."

"Make a joyful noise," said one of the parishioners as they gathered around.

"Amen!"

They sang heartily. *"Standing on the promises of Christ my king, through eternal ages let his praises ring."* Their enthusiasm created an atmosphere that said all was well, storm or not. After a few more songs, the preacher read a scripture lesson and delivered a message of encouragement. He called them to a time of prayer before ending the service.

"Lord, we thank you for the snow—we know it brings balance to the land, but could ya bring it to a close pretty soon? We don't want folks gettin' hurt or sick from it."

"Yes, Lord," several people responded.

The pastor continued his prayer, naming several people who had special needs, then he paused. "Is there anybody else we need to pray for this mornin'?"

Clint spoke up. "Sure is, preacher. My son here had hisself a bit of a rough time the other day, but the Lord was with him. Just wanna ask ya to pray for him to get back over to Virginia safe, and for the Lord to bless his ministry."

There was a rumble of "amens" in the group. People seemed to take that in with no need for explanations.

The pastor concluded his prayer, then pronounced the benediction. As people bundled up to leave, he spoke to Billy.

"Your daddy said you was startin' in the ministry. If you don't mind, I'd like to pray with ya about that at the altar."

Billy thanked him and shared his call, and what had happened at Frog Hollow. They knelt at the altar. The pastor placed his hand on Billy's head, and prayed for God to anoint him. "Lord, I feel some heaviness over there at Strong's Creek. Equip your servant with wisdom and strength to be your servant, to do your will. Take him victoriously through whatever challenges he faces. We renounce all forces of evil that may oppose him, in the name of Jesus Christ. Amen."

During the prayer Billy felt a surge of warmth that started at the top of his head and spread through his body until he felt it in his toes. Then a deep sense of calm rested upon him. He felt totally relaxed, filled with deep joy.

"Thanks for the prayer," he said as they left the church. The pastor nodded with a knowing smile. As they got into the Yukon and headed back to the house Billy felt totally at peace and ready to get back to his churches.

"Thank you, Lord," he whispered as Clint drove them home.

SEVEN

Life slowed to a crawl at Strong's Creek on Saturday when the storm moved through causing near blizzard conditions and fifteen inches of snowfall...with no end in sight. Sheriff Cam Bordain had answered a call in Strong's Creek and was heading back to Peakview. Driving out Main Street he glanced across miniature mountains of plowed snow. Something caught his eye. He turned around and went back, looking more carefully.

The front door to the Wesleyan Brethren rental house was wide open, and it appeared there was a light on in the front room. Something didn't seem right. He recalled his conversations with Fletch Waverley and Carrie Glossner. *Hmm, maybe that preacher did come back like I said he would.*

He started to move on, then took another look. Not only was the door open, but there was no smoke coming from the chimney. Most people had fires going during weather like this. There was also no car in the driveway, although he reasoned that it could be around behind the house. *That open door bothers me. Think I'll check to make sure the guy's okay.* He nudged his four-wheel-drive Ford Interceptor SUV over the snow bank into the yard, then climbed out and trudged toward the house. He noticed depressions in the snow that could have come from driving a car around back. *He must've gotten in before the snow got too bad.*

Approaching the open door, Cam listened for sounds from inside. Nothing. He checked his watch—2:30 p.m. He rang the bell and scuffed the snow with his feet. The cold- wind-driven air caused him to shiver despite his heavy coat. There was no answer. He knocked loudly and called out, "Hello! Anybody here? This is Sheriff Bordain."

Still no answer.

He called in to his dispatcher. "Is Rafe still working that accident north of Strong's Creek?"

"Uh, he just left there. Everything's cleared up."

"Okay, I'm at that rental house of Oscar Bender's that the Wesleyan Brethren Church is usin' for the preacher who was reported to have disappeared. Place is s'posed to be empty, but the door's hangin' open and nobody responds from inside. I'm goin' to walk around to the back and check the place out a little more. I want Rafe with me when I go inside."

"Ten four."

Cam made his way around the house through snow that was blowing off the roof and beginning to drift out from the structure. There was no car, but snow patterns indicated a sizeable vehicle had been there for a while, then driven out to the street past a large tree in the front yard. Cam saw right away that the back door had been forced open. He walked up the three steps and examined the damaged door frame. It looked like somebody had used a crowbar on it. That's when Rafe pulled in behind the Interceptor and checked in with Cam.

"Rafe, I'm not sure what we've got here. This back door's been jimmied. I'm going in here now and I want you to come in through the front. I don't think anybody's in there but be prepared."

"Ten four."

Cam stepped into a mud room with empty utility shelves and a few coat hooks along one wall. Splinters of wood from the door frame were on the floor along with a dirty, crumpled up utility rug. A door to his right opened into the kitchen where it was obvious someone had rifled through the cabinets and drawers. An overhead light fixture was on, and a coffee maker was on its side with dried coffee staining the counter where it had spilled. A trash can had been emptied onto the floor and the contents scattered.

He called to Rafe in the front room. "This place is a mess...somebody's been looking for something. What you got in there?"

"Same thing."

Cam stepped into the living room. A lamp had been knocked over, and pillows from the couch had been tossed on the floor.

"Looks like a robbery" said Rafe. "Although, I can't imagine what would have been in here of any value."

"I don't know. Can't take anything for granted."

The two men walked through the rest of the house. Billy hadn't brought much with him, but what was there had been thoroughly ransacked...especially in the office. Torn boxes, scattered papers, books—everything thrown about.

Rafe took off his cap and scratched his head. "If this don't beat all. I wonder if the perp got what he was lookin' for?"

"Yeah...what makes it more interestin' is this ain't the first incident at this house." Cam related the call he'd received from Carrie Glossner two days earlier, and the mysterious disappearance of the preacher.

"I didn't give this too much thought then, but later I did a quick record check out of curiosity. The preacher's name is William Upshur. He has no record...seems okay. Worked in Richmond 'til he came here." He rubbed his chin. "I'm gonna call Glossner and Bender over here and see if I can find out more from them."

When Cam called Carrie, she expressed her concern but didn't want to go out into the storm. He asked her a few questions and then hung up as Oscar arrived, huffing and stomping snow off his shoes. He gestured at the weather outside. "This better be good, Bordain, callin' me over here in this mess."

"Well, we got a breakin' and enterin' here and possible robbery, and you own the place. To top it off, the preacher who's 'sposed to be livin' here has disappeared. Since it's your property, I called you over."

Oscar was steamed about the broken door frame and the general condition of things. He fumed as they walked through the house.

"Darned if I know anything about this mess. I gotta pay to clean all this up—I'll get the church to pay for it. It's all their fault."

"What do you mean, *their fault?* I just talked to Carrie Glossner and she says it don't make no sense to her. She just got a call from the Wesleyan Brethren district supervisor who said he's talked to the preacher and he's comin' back soon's the roads are clear. Seems like he's in some town over in West Virginia."

"Good. What's he doin' there?"

"She didn't know but said that's where he's from. Said they'll be havin' a meetin' this week to clear up everything."

"Yeah, well clearin' up everythin' is gonna include payin' fer this mess."

"Oh, come on, Oscar," said Rafe, who'd been leaning against a door frame watching the interaction between the two men. "What's this gonna cost you—a new door frame and some clean-up?"

Oscar bristled. "Ain't gonna cost me nothin'. Either the church or the preacher'll pay for it. But it don't make no sense...none of it."

"Agreed," said Cam. "Fortunately, we can get all our questions answered this week. This kinda takes the edge off things. Once we talk to the preacher you'll have a chance to place charges, if that's what you want to do. Meanwhile, me an' Rafe's gonna leave you to close up and secure your property."

Oscar grumbled. "Yeah, yeah...well, thanks for callin' me anyway." He shook his head. "Try to do somethin' good for somebody and look what you get."

Cam was starting toward the door. He paused and looked back toward Oscar. "If you're talkin' about rentin' this house to the church, that was a good thing. This ain't their fault. We'll find out this week whether or not it's Upshur's fault."

♦ ♦ ♦

By early Sunday morning the snow threatened to block roads and topple power lines. Only a hardy few would venture out past their woodpiles. Fletch Waverley had planned to lead the services and help them deal with their plight. Now that opportunity was lost.

Frog Hollow Church with its remote location was a small family-oriented congregation consisting mostly of older people. Few active members lived close enough to go to church in a snowstorm.

Main Street Church, however, was a more established congregation located in the village at a major intersection with Village Way, diagonally across from the local bank. It was conspicuous for its corner entrance and square bell tower. An adjacent parking lot was used by the community during the week, and by the church on Sundays. Services were never closed due to weather. It was assumed that if people could get there, they would.

Oscar Bender sent his man Zeke over to the church to clean away as much snow and ice as possible. Zeke complained, but dutifully complied. He hadn't been working long when Grant Mackabee, the church's lay leader, showed up with his snow blower.

"Want some help?" Grant hollered toward Zeke.

"Naw...I got it."

"You sure? Brought my snow blower. Workin' together we can make a quick job of this."

"Well, Mr. Bender's payin' me to clean up the whole thing m'self."

Grant smiled and extended an open hand toward Zeke. "I figured he did. Just so you don't lose out, I'll be glad to pay you anything you might lose by my workin' with ya."

Zeke stopped shoveling and studied Grant for a minute. "Ya will, eh? How I do know ya still gonna feel that way when we're done?"

Grant put his hand on Zeke's shoulder. "What's Oscar payin' you?"

Zeke shifted his feet but didn't answer.

"Ten dollars an hour?"

Zeke had an expression like a sudden insight had taken hold of his brain. He looked Grant in the eye. "More like fifteen."

"Okay, let's say I save ya two hours of work. That'd be thirty dollars." Grant pulled off his glove and reached inside his coat for his wallet. He pulled it out and counted three ten-dollar bills, then extended them toward Zeke. "Here, I'll pay ya in advance. We got a deal?"

Zeke looked like he'd just won the lottery. "Okay, Mr. Mackabee. You payin' in advance, I'll work wi' ya." He pocketed the money and grabbed his shovel. "Gittin' cold ou'chere—reckon we better git t' work."

With that he picked up his shovel and started in. Grant suggested a plan that would coordinate their efforts, and within an hour they had the entire parking lot and walkways clean. Even as they worked, cars began to pull in. When they were finished the two men joined a small group of people who were warming up inside with Carrie's freshly brewed coffee.

Oscar walked up to Zeke. "I see ya had some help out there. You know I'm only paying for what you done yourself."

Overhearing, Grant stepped in. "I just offered to help out. You know I love to use that snow blower. Me an' Zeke worked that out."

Oscar pulled out some bills and handed them to Zeke. "Humph. Next time ya talk t' me before ya go settin' up any deals."

"Yessir." Zeke pocketed the money, said he had other work to do, and left.

Oscar was tuned up for conflict now. "So, where's this here preacher we 'sposed to have? Thought that supervisor was comin' in this mornin' to straighten things out."

"Hold your horses, Oscar. He's snowed in just like a lotta folks. We'll get along okay today, and after this here storm's over, we'll figure stuff out."

Oscar grumbled and turned away.

By eleven o'clock nearly thirty people were present, including the organist, Holly Jinks and her husband, Bernie. Grant gathered some folding chairs and placed them around the piano. Holly began to play as he called people together.

"I'm so glad to see y'all were able to get out this mornin'. We don't have no preacher today, but we can still praise the Lord."

One of the people in the back said, "Yeah, what's goin' on with the new preacher?"

"I'm wonderin' the same thing, and I'm afraid I don't have an answer for you. I'm sure once this storm's over we'll get to the bottom of things. When I talked to Dr. Waverley this mornin', he said he's been in touch with Pastor Upshur."

"So, what happened?"

"Is he comin' back?"

"Hold on. I don't know any details. I just know Dr. Waverley said he thought things could be worked out."

"Well, okay then," said Carrie. "You just let me know when he's comin' back, and I'll see the Women's Association has a proper welcome for 'im this time."

That seemed to satisfy the curiosities in the crowd. Holly struck up the chords of a familiar hymn, and they all settled down to worship. Grant shared a meditation he'd found in a devotional book, they took up an offering, and said a prayer for everyone's safety during the storm. To end the service, he prayed for the new preacher, but he wasn't sure that had done much to calm the situation.

"Glad y'all came today. Be safe goin' home," said Grant as he ushered people out. One of the church members wasn't to be consoled.

"You think this storm's bad, just you wait for the one that's brewin' over this preacher runnin' off."

"I hear you, but there is another side to things. Let's just wait 'til we know the whole story...and in the meantime, do me a favor and pray about it. Okay?"

The man grumbled, "Okay," and left the church.

Grant locked the door and headed for his car. *Lord, help us,* he breathed.

EIGHT

By Monday morning the storm had ended, and people at Strong's Creek began to move about. One place they went was Coop's Pit Stop, a popular watering hole on the western edge of the village. A landmark, it was a colorful, rustic holdover from post-World War II days, built around an old cottage style gas station that had been popular back then. Bunk Cooper ran the combination country store, gas station and auto repair shop. It was where you went if you wanted to feel the pulse beat of local life.

Bunk stoked the fire in a large wood stove at the center of the store, adding two more logs. He took off his utility gloves, set them on the woodpile, and looked up as the door alarm rattled to announce a customer. Zeke Stoner stomped into the shop.

"Ho, man--I'm gettin' tired o' this here weather." He shook his head as he walked over to warm his hands at the stove. "Got me some froze up pipes. What ya got I can patch 'em with 'till this cold spell's over?"

Bunk didn't run a hardware store, but he did have lots of fix-it stuff in his inventory. There had been a time when he'd done some plumbing.

"Hmmm, best thing'd be to replace them pipes if they's busted."

"Yeah, but it's hard to reach 'em in that crawl space. I'm afraid to light a torch to thaw 'em out. Place I'm talkin' about is that house Oscar done rented to the preacher."

"Oh, I know the place. They ain't much crawl space under there. Them pipes is so close to the floor it seems like the heat from upstairs should keep 'em from freezin'."

"That's th' trouble." Zeke rubbed his hands vigorously over the stove. "Ain't nobody in that house, and the heat was turned off. Thermostat didn't work, and nobody thought about seein' if the main switch was turned on. I went over to check on that when the new preacher arrived, but he run me off."

"You don't say. Guess he was in too much hurry to think about the heat. I heard he high-tailed it when he left town."

"I'd of checked the house after 'im if I'd known he'd gone off like that. Oscar told me to stay away from there, so that's what I done."

"Ahh, so where you been—up there in Rooster Holler drinkin' a little 'shine? Shoot, seems like ever'body 'cept you knew about it."

"Waddaya mean 'where've I been?' Been cleanin' snow off stuff all over town. Besides, can't get up to the holler right now."

Bunk slapped him on the back with a chuckle, then stepped away from the stove and dug through stuff on some shelves behind the counter. After a considerable amount of racket and mumbling he produced a container of putty and some tape.

"How bad's the break? Is it in more'n one place?"

"They's a coupl'a cracks. I'll know better wunst it's thawed out. Them pipes gonna need replacin', but right now I just wanna fix it so's they don't leak. What'cha got there?"

Bunk showed him the putty. "This here'll seal them busted places, then be sure to wrap 'em good. Oughta hold till ya can do better. Spring ain't too far off."

"Okay. Put it on Oscar's bill." As he spoke, the door opened again. Cam Bordain stepped inside.

Bunk looked up. "Hey, Cam, what's goin on? Seen ya go by, and later on them boys from the firehouse came roarin' up toward Crowfoot Knob. Almost didn't make the turn." He winked at Zeke as if to say anybody should know you couldn't get up there just yet.

Cam caught the interaction between the two. "Guess you missed that plow that went up there ahead of us. Ole' Miz Fields had a heart attack, but she was gone by the time we could get the crew in there." Cam stepped over to the coffee counter and poured a cup. "This weather'll freeze yer insides." He came over to the stove.

"Can you believe ole Zeke here didn't know that preacher's done skipped outa town?" said Bunk.

Cam shot a harsh look toward Zeke. "What you been up to? Ever'body knew about that." He laughed and turned playful. "Maybe you run 'im off. One look at you and he'd have wanted to get as far away from Strong's Creek as he could."

Zeke grumbled and walked toward the door. "Yeah, you th' one prob'ly run 'im off. I got work to do. See y'all later."

"No hard feelin's," Cam called after him.

Zeke slammed the door.

The two men laughed, and Bunk decided to pump Cam for some juicy tidbits. "So, you got any idea where that preacher went in such a hurry—why he pulled out so fast?"

"If I did, I couldn't tell you." Cam slapped Bunk on the shoulder. "Shoot, he didn't hurt nobody or commit no crime. Ain't none 'o my business where he went."

As he started out the door he stopped and turned back toward Bunk with a more serious expression on his face. "Listen, it's always possible somethin' else is goin' on. If you hear somethin' about that preacher I want you to call my office. I told the folks at the church that he probably went back to Richmond to get some stuff...maybe got snowed in. Still, I've got a gut feelin' there could be more to the story than we been hearin'."

"Ain't heard nothing so far," Bunk said. "Lotsa folks'll be comin' in here for gas and supplies now the storm's over, so I'll keep an ear out. Let ya know if somethin' turns up."

"You do that."

Cam went out to his Ford Interceptor and headed back into the village where he stopped at the diner. Evie was wiping off the tables and putting things back in order after the lunch crowd had left.

"Hey, Evie, is Clete around?"

"He just went to the bank. Be back soon unless he stops off someplace and gets to talkin'. Somethin' I can help ya with?"

Cam walked over to where she was working, and she stopped. "What was all that mess o' sirens about earlier? Terrible time to have to go out on a call."

"Oh, that was Miz Fields...she had a heart attack. Didn't make it, I'm afraid."

"Been expectin' that. How many is that now? She shoulda been livin' with somebody who could take care of her."

"I dunno—lost count. Listen, I'm tryin' to find out about that new preacher in town. He ain't been in here, has he?"

"Matter of fact, he was here...what was it," she counted on her fingers, "three, four...I guess Thursday mornin'. Didn't talk much to anybody, but I noticed his car when he left...got one o' them little Hondas same color as my brother's Chevy—*red*."

"He didn't come back in later that day, did he?"

"No, but I noticed that same car goin' forty-leven miles an hour out toward the highway later. I was takin' my break. Didn't seem fittin' for a preacher to drive like that."

Cam laughed. "So, how are preacher's 'sposed to drive?"

"You know what I mean. My friend Gertrude lives out on the main highway. She told me she saw that same car bustin' a gasket headin' toward the mountain just a while after that. Then I heard people from the church talkin' in here at lunch...said he done left town. What do ya make of that?"

"Don't know that I make anything out of it. Man's got a right to drive out of town in any direction he wants. Sounds to me like y'all ain't got enough to do if ya go around tryin' to figure out where somebody's goin' when they drive outa town."

Evie put her hands on her hips. "Cam Bordain, you got a lotta nerve talkin' to me like that." She sputtered, "You know I work my tail off around here and...."

Cam threw his head back and laughed. "Okay, okay, you're right. I didn't mean nothin' personal." He put his hat on and turned toward the door."

"So, you gonna come in here and get me all stirred up and then walk out the door. Just like a man."

Cam paused. "Do me a favor? You hear anything more about that preacher, let me know? I ain't sayin' they's anything wrong, but ain't sayin' they ain't neither." He gave her a wave.

"Yeah, I will. Now you git on outa here."

♦ ♦ ♦

In Healing Waters Billy awoke early Monday morning, anxious to see if he could get back to Strong's Creek. Clint's support coupled with the prayers at church had pushed his fears into the background. Glancing at the alarm clock he saw it was almost seven o'clock. He'd slept later than he'd intended. Opening the window shades, he stepped back at the brightness of the morning sun casting long light patches across the landscape. The snow might have stopped, but he saw the temperature was still very cold...18 degrees on the outdoor thermometer.

Humph," he muttered to himself. "If it stays cold like this that sun's just gonna make things worse tonight." He picked up his Bible and sat down in a wingback chair, closed his eyes, flicked through the pages, then opened them to see where his fingers had stopped. He began reading the fifth chapter of Romans. Certain words jumped off the page like they were meant just for him... *"suffering produces endurance, and endurance produces character, and character produces hope, and hope does not disappoint us, because God's love has been poured into our hearts...."*

"Yes," exclaimed Billy as he closed the book and his eyes. *That's what Pop's been remindin' me. I feel stronger already. Thank you, Lord.*

As soon as he'd shaved and dressed he charged downstairs. Clint was dressed in his heavy coat and hat, headed for the door. "Hey, Pop, you goin' out for more firewood?"

Clint turned and smiled. "Good mornin', Sonny. No, I had an idea durin' the night. I'm goin' out to the shed and get the old Jeep Wrangler fired up. Ain't used it fer a spell."

Billy was puzzled. The snow blade was on the tractor and the GMC was heavier. "Why? I mean, seems like you wouldn't need it with your Yukon."

"I don't," said Clint, "but you will. Tell ya about it later. You get yourself some breakfast, then come on out to the shed."

Kitchen aromas overcame Billy's puzzlement as Clint left. He turned toward the kitchen. "Mornin', Mom. Pop just went out to the shed to see about the Wrangler. What's that all about?"

Lottie had a fresh batch of biscuits on a plate as she turned toward the table. She laughed. "You never know what he's up to. I'm sure he'll tell you all about it. What do ya want with these biscuits?"

"Some of your damson preserves. He sat down, and his thoughts turned to the Wrangler. It was a 2010 model that had been Welby's car. When he went into the Air Force, Clint bought it from him and kept it as a back-up vehicle. He knew Lottie had used it some. She interrupted his thoughts as she served his breakfast. "You fixin' to go back today?"

"Yep. Way I figure it, this sun's gonna start meltin' the snow, but tonight the roads are gonna ice up again. Guess I'll leave in the next hour or so."

Lottie walked around beside him, leaned down and gave him a hug. "You be careful out there, hon. Let the Lord be your guide and keeper."

"I will," Billy assured her. He finished his breakfast, put on his heavy clothes and Lottie gave him some coffee to take to the shed. Clint had the doors open and the engine running and was cleaning the windows when he stepped inside. He took in the rugged burgundy Rubicon model with dark trim and a three-piece modular hard top. The spare tire was mounted on the rear tailgate.

"She's low on gas, Sonny, so you'll need to fill 'er up soon as you can."

"What are you saying? You want me to take this back to Virginia?"

"Yep, for two reasons. First is that busted window on your little car. I know a guy who can fix that for cost, and it won't have to come outa yer insurance. I expect it would have to come from your deductible, right?"

"Yeah, guess it would. Hadn't thought about that yet."

"Same with that crease along the side. Plus, this Jeep has four-wheel drive and it'll serve you better travelin' in the snow."

Billy felt overwhelmed. He knew Clint was right. "But, don't you need it?"

"Haven't used it more'n takin' it out for a spin once in a while to keep it in shape."

"Well, I don't know what to say...thanks."

"That's all you need to say. I have a feelin' this Jeep will be better where you're going to be servin' anyway. Might be we could work us out a swap down the road."

They got the car out of the shed and Billy tried out the four-wheel drive as he pulled it down to the house. Lottie had packed him a lunch and a thermos of hot coffee. He thanked them both and after a prayer and hugs, he drove out the lane, then headed back toward Virginia. It was just a few minutes before noon.

NINE

The trip back to Strong's Creek went surprisingly well. Driving the Wrangler was totally different from his small car. For one thing, he sat higher which gave him better vision of road conditions. The 3.8-liter V-6 engine provided all the power he needed. Clint had been right about gas mileage being much lower than his Honda, but other features made up for that. According to the odometer the vehicle hadn't been used heavily. It was seven years old with just under 100,000 miles on it.

The roads had mostly been cleared, sanded and salted. He took it easy, paced himself with rest stops, and arrived back in Strong's Creek without incident as night fell. He decided to stop at the diner for supper. The place looked much different with the snow covering many of its rough features, although the parking lot had been churned into a slushy mess. There didn't seem to be too many folks there for supper, which pleased Billy. He had thought a lot all day about facing peoples' curiosity and wasn't quite ready to plunge into that, or so he thought.

The warmth inside the diner was augmented by the buzz of good natured conversations among patrons. A sign said, "Please Seat Yourself," so Billy decided to sit at a booth with a window looking out into the parking lot. "Can I get you somethin' to drink?" said Evie, handing him a menu.

Billy looked up and smiled. "A good hot cup of coffee would be nice. I've been travelin' all day. I'd like a few minutes to decide what I want."

As they made eye contact Evie seemed to stiffen and grow nervous. "I'll be right back with the coffee." Her tone of voice had flattened. "Take your time lookin' over the menu."

She turned and walked behind the counter just as Clete came out of the kitchen. The two of them spoke quietly for a moment, then Clete went back into the kitchen and Evie poured the coffee. Was it his imagination, or did the atmosphere in the room seem to change? People stopped talking and he was aware they were looking at him. *I guess the word's out about me leavin' town last week. I haven't met many folks...don't know how they could recognize me.*

It was puzzling, but he decided he'd have to get used to that and sent a silent prayer request for God's help. A few conversations resumed in hushed tones and several people paid their bills and left. Billy ordered country steak, mashed potatoes with gravy, and green beans. While waiting for his order he looked out at the parking lot where an SUV pulled up with county sheriff's department markings. A tall man wearing a leather uniform jacket with a fur collar and a wide-brimmed hat stepped out, then walked toward the diner. When he entered, Evie tossed him a friendly greeting. They were out of Billy's line of vision, so he didn't see her also nod her head in his direction and mouth, "that's him."

Billy was enjoying the warmth of the coffee when Cam came over to his booth. "Mind if I sit here?" He took off his hat and opened his jacket as he slid into the seat.

That's strange, thought Billy as he reached across the table to shake hands. "Sure, help yourself. I'm Billy Upshur...the new Wesleyan Brethren pastor for the Strong's Creek Circuit...that is, I will be. I haven't gotten started yet."

The sheriff flashed him a disarming smile and shook his hand. "Actually, I know who you are, that's why I sat here. I'm Cam Bordain, the county sheriff."

Evie walked up with Billy's order. "Can I get you somethin' too, Cam?"

"You know, I've had a hankerin' for a slice of Clete's apple pie...and I could use some coffee, too." As she left the table, Cam looked back at Billy, who stumbled over his words.

"Uh, how...how do you know who I am?" He felt nervous, but not threatened.

"Well, there's been a little trouble over at the house the church rented for you, and we discovered you seemed to have disappeared when I answered the call."

Billy was shocked. He stopped eating and leaned toward Cam, picturing Zeke Stoner standing in his bedroom doorway and wondering if he was part of it. "Trouble? Like, what kind of trouble.?"

Sheriff Bordain studied Billy as he spoke. "Listen, Rev. Upshur, you're not in any trouble with me, if that's what you're thinkin'. When the storm started the other day, I noticed lights on in that house and the door standing partly open...and no smoke comin' from the chimney, so I stopped to see if everything was all right.

That's when I discovered somebody had broken in and rummaged through stuff like they was lookin' for somethin.'"

Billy felt a cold chill run down his back. He knew his face must have turned pale. "A break-in? Good Lord, what's that about?"

"That's what I was hopin' you could tell me."

Billy realized his hot meal was cooling faster than he was eating it. "I don't know about that...but I'm glad we're having this talk because there is something I need to tell you about."

Cam raised his eyebrows. "Oh?"

Evie brought Cam's pie and coffee but didn't linger. Cam stirred some cream in the cup, then took a bite of his pie. "I think we've both got a lot to discuss, and this ain't exactly the place to do it. I know you've been away someplace, and from your reactions, I don't think you've been back to the house yet...right?"

"Yep. Just comin' in from my folks' place in West Virginia."

"Oh, really? Where 'bouts?"

"Healing Waters," said Billy.

"Heard of it. Ain't never been there that I can recall. Look, let's finish eatin' and I'll follow you over to the house and we can talk more there."

"Sounds good to me," said Billy as he finished his last few bites. "I'm driving that Wrangler that's all full of salt and grime out there."

Cam nodded. "Noticed that when I pulled in. I'll be right behind you." They finished eating, paid their bills, and left.

♦ ♦ ♦

As he pulled up to the house, Billy noticed what appeared to be tire tracks partially hidden in lumpy snow drifts. Cam parked behind him and they trudged their way up to the front door. It was locked and the house dark. Billy unlocked the door and hit the light switch as they entered.

"Man, it's cold as an iceberg in here. I remember it was cold last week when I first got here, but it wasn't this bad," said Billy. He tried the thermostat and heard the furnace come on. "That's funny. When I tried it the night I got here, nothing happened. That's one of the things I meant to find out about."

"I noticed some dry fire logs in the mud room off the kitchen when we were in here the other day," said Cam. "If we light a few of those we can warm things up faster." He helped Billy bring in the logs and they soon had a roaring blaze going in the fireplace. Then they sat down to talk.

Once he got started, Billy had a hard time holding back. He mentioned the incident with Zeke, saying as an afterthought, "Guess I shoulda listened to him...he probably could have shown me how to turn the furnace on."

"Probably, but Zeke's a strange guy. I know he fixed a water leak under the house, and probably turned on the furnace at the same time. He's okay."

"Yeah. It was dumb to let him bother me...especially with the real trouble I ran into after that."

Cam took notes and asked questions as Billy recounted the Frog Hollow incident. "I don't know what got into me runnin' away like that. Guess it was the rifle shots mostly. Pop kept my car to get the bullet hole in the glass fixed...I kinda like this Wrangler, though. Might swap with him."

Cam checked the time. It was nearly nine o'clock. "I've got what I need for my report. I'll be back in touch, and if you run into more problems, you call me, got it?"

"I will. You can count on it." He took Cam's card with the contact information, then locked the door after he left. The house was empty, but unseen spirits of discord pulsated in the shadows. Billy turned the couch around to face the fireplace and made his bed on it. Then he prayed. *Thank you, Lord, for bringing me back here where I belong. Thank you for Sheriff Bordain. Show me how to get started with my ministry.* Despite all he'd been through, he managed to sleep soundly.

TEN

Billy shook himself awake on Tuesday morning, his sleep suddenly interrupted by the jingle on his cell phone.

"Hello."

"Pastor Upshur?"

"Yes."

"Pastor, my name is Carrie Glossner. I'm in charge of the Women's Association for the Strong's Creek Circuit. Hope I'm not calling you too early."

His watch told him it was 8:30 a.m. "No..." he stifled a yawn then cleared his throat. "What can I do for you?"

"Actually, it's the other way around. I called to see what we can do for you. Sorry you had to miss your first Sunday, what with the weather and all. I came by the house Thursday, but you weren't there."

"I really do apologize for that. Sheriff Bordain mentioned your name when he told me about a break-in that happened here while I was gone."

"Oh, so you've met Cam...good. He said you'd probably gone back to Richmond and would return soon. Some of us weren't sure...it was awkward not knowing where you were or why you left so unexpectedly...."

She seemed to leave her words hanging in the air. Billy cleared his throat. "Yes ma'am. I understand people are curious about my absence. I want to get some of the church leaders together this week to explain what happened."

"So, is your absence somehow related to the break-in...I mean, since you've been talking to Cam?"

"I don't know yet."

"What does that mean?"

The conversation stalled awkwardly for a moment. "Okay," said Carrie, "we can talk about it later. The reason I called was to apologize for not having the house in better condition and someone there to greet you when you arrived. Now that you're back some of us ladies want to come by and do a little house cleaning, if that suits you. We'd like to come by as early as possible today."

"Well, sure, that would be fine. I just need to eat some breakfast. Why don't y'all come about ten o'clock?"

"Okay. We left some food in the refrigerator for you. Did you see my note?"

Billy felt embarrassed that he hadn't even thought about anything except the disarray in the house. "Uh, no, I came in late last night and really haven't noticed. But...thanks for your thoughtfulness. I appreciate it."

After he hung up Billy went into the kitchen where he saw the note on the refrigerator door. Inside he found eggs, bacon, a half-gallon of milk, a container of orange juice, and a large plate of sandwiches covered with plastic wrap. There was also a two-liter bottle of Pepsi Cola. Billy closed the fridge and opened the door of a cabinet next to it. He remembered how empty the place had been on Thursday.

Now the cabinet contained paper plates, bowls, cups, napkins, plastic silverware, a bag of chips, a box of raison bran, and a loaf of bread. There was even a small box of sugar, a container of coffee and a box of filters. Billy closed the cabinet door and noticed something he hadn't seen—a new coffee maker. He felt overwhelmed. *Wow. This is incredible. I wish I'd had these things last Thursday mornin'—and some heat in the house. I probably wouldn't have gone to the diner or had that experience up in Frog Hollow.*

He started the coffee maker, then went back to the bathroom where he shaved and cleaned up. He'd hardly dressed and eaten a bowl of cereal when the doorbell rang. It was Sheriff Bordain. Billy invited him inside.

"Looks like you're gettin' things under control," said Cam as he stepped into the kitchen where Billy offered him a cup of coffee.

"Found some food and stuff the women from the church left for me. A Mrs. Glossner and some other ladies are comin' over to help clean up the place."

Cam glanced around approvingly and nodded. "Glad to hear that. Now, I've been goin' over what you told me about your experience on Frog Hollow Road. I think I know who those guys might be."

"Already? How'd you figure that out so fast?"

Cam laughed. "Remember, this is a small town. Everybody pretty much knows everybody else around here. You said you used to work for EverMore Energy, and that's the company tryin' to take local land for the natural gas pipeline. I got to thinkin', folks around here have some pretty strong feelin's about that, especially a bunch of guys who call themselves the Frog Hollow Boys. Frog Hollow lies between two ridges up in one of the most remote areas in Limestone County. The pipeline's comin' right through there and they've been puttin' up quite a fuss."

Billy nodded. "I can understand that."

"Their leader is a guy name of Gus Wheeler. I don't know everybody who's involved, but I do know the most visible ones along with Gus are Burly Branson, and a Cherokee guy named Waya, which means 'wolf,' I think. Folks around here call 'im 'Beanpole.'"

"Yes! I heard the older guy with the pony tail call the others by those names. I thought at the time the guy who shot at me looked Native American. They also mentioned something about Mama Jean's house. Do you have any idea what that was about?"

"Mama Jean's House...that's like their war cry, so to speak."

"War cry?"

"Yeah. The first place EverMore took under eminent domain was a small house that had been there for decades. It was the home of an old Cherokee woman who was reputed to be a healer. She gave advice and spoke chants over people. When they were sick she took care of 'em. She was always there for weddin's, funerals...and child birth. She was like a mid-wife. Everybody up there took it hard when they took her property."

"So, what happened to her?"

"Oh, she's still there in the hollow, but some people think her power was broken by losin' that house. I'm not sure who, but one of the families took her in. I think she stays at the house during the day—they ain't tore it down yet. Like I say, that's a pretty closed community. They don't take much to outsiders to begin with, and this just made it worse."

"That helps me a lot. Thanks. My guess is somebody found out I worked for EverMore Energy in Richmond. That probably wouldn't be too hard to do. So, my guess is they took out some anger on me. I think they just wanted to scare me."

"You might be right, but intentionally shooting at or toward someone is a crime in this state, even if nobody is killed or injured. It also happens to be against the law to discharge a weapon on or across a public street, as well as to discharge a weapon at a motor vehicle. So, based on your report, I'm gonna pay them Frog Hollow Boys a visit."

Billy was startled. He hadn't thought of Beanpole shooting toward him as a crime since he wasn't hit, even though his car had been damaged. "Guess I shoulda reported this right away. Wish I had the car here so you could see the damage."

"That would have made it easier to follow up. I'm not gonna arrest anybody right now...just want *them* to know *I* know about it. The weather's supposed to warm up and a lot of this snow will melt. As soon as I can, I plan to examine the site where they ambushed you. There might be a couple of shell casings lyin' around." Cam finished his coffee and put his cup on the table. "I'd really like for you to go along and show me exactly where it all happened."

Billy thought about that a moment. "Yeah, I'll do that. Also, I'm sure Pop hasn't done anything about fixin' the car window yet. Maybe I should go back and get it...oh, wait a minute." Billy pulled out his smartphone. "Just remembered, I took some pictures of it on my phone." He pulled them up. Three different angles showed the window, and two more the crease along the side of the car. "This be any help?"

Cam studied them. "Well, it supports what you've said...but it doesn't prove anything. For one thing, these were taken on a snowy day somewhere else, not here on Frog Hollow Road before the snow fell. In court, a defense attorney would dismiss this as hearsay. The problem is, you don't have any witnesses to back up your story."

That was a sobering thought. Billy had never encountered anything like this first hand. "So, what they did was criminal, but you can't do anything about it because you don't have any proof, right?"

"Let's not go too fast. I don't have any proof *yet*...not to scare you, but I expect you haven't heard the last from them. You said Beanpole probably could've hit you if he'd wanted. I think you're right. He's a lifelong hunter. I think they just wanted to scare you, so I'm gonna give 'em a warning."

"Won't that just make them angrier?"

"Can't tell with that crowd, but what I know for sure is they're hot heads and they don't always think things through. A warning will get their attention. It could cool 'em off a bit.

"That makes sense. After I get settled here I'd like to find a way to meet those guys...talk to them. If you talk to them it might help."

Cam looked doubtful. "That sounds like preacher talk to me. Don't get me wrong, I ain't against religion, but I don't think you're gonna "bring 'em to Jesus," as the sayin' goes. But that's your business. Like I said, I expect they'll make sure you meet up with 'em again."

Billy didn't respond. He had sort of expected that reaction. "I'll keep in touch and let you know if I think I'm in any danger."

Cam thanked him for the coffee and shook his hand. "Sounds like a plan."

◆ ◆ ◆

As Cam stepped out the door three women walked up. He tipped his hat. "Good mornin' ladies."

They exchanged greetings and Billy welcomed the women into the house as Cam drove off. Carrie introduced herself. She was of medium height with salt and pepper hair in a tight perm that he imagined never changed much. Dressed in jeans and a sweat shirt, she wore no lipstick. Behind wire rim glasses were two hard, penetrating dark blue eyes. He helped her and the others with their coats.

"This is Earlene Josef, the lay leader at Frog Hollow," said Carrie, indicating a woman of similar height who was dressed more for an event than work. He guessed she was a couple of years younger than Carrie. Her face was accented by short gray hair, earrings that matched the color of her cable knit mauve sweater. She had a hawkish nose, light complexion, and wrinkles that gave her a harsh appearance until she smiled with unexpected warmth. As he shook her hand Billy couldn't help thinking what a contrast she made to the three Frog Hollow men he'd already encountered.

"And this is Holly Jinks," said Carrie with a sweeping gesture in her direction. "Holly's our organist and music director at Main Street Church...but she lives in Frog

Hollow. You'll get to know her and her husband, Bernie. They live in a beautiful log house." Billy could see Holly was probably twenty years younger than the other two—a petite woman with auburn hair rolled up in a bun. He noticed a light-hearted twinkle in her light blue eyes. "Holly used to be a school teacher before she moved here. Now she teaches music at church. Oh, and her husband is a writer."

"That's fascinating," said Billy as he shook Holly's hand. "I look forward to getting to know all of you better. Thanks for coming over today." He looked at Holly and Earlene. "It's interesting you two are both from Frog Hollow. I was just talking to the sheriff about that area."

"I'm sure he told you we're kind of in a world of our own. That's one thing Bernie and I like about living there."

The women donned aprons as they talked, then Carrie gave Billy a hard look. "I know you said you'll explain where you went and all once you get settled, but I think you owe us an explanation now."

Billy was taken aback by her sudden change of tone. He was about to speak when Earlene charged in. "I heard some talk about some kind of incident over by the creek Thursday...more of that pipeline stuff. The good Lord knows there are out-of-town folks runnin' around surveyin', buyin' up property, markin' out trees to be cut down. Tell me that don't have anything to do with you."

"I don't know whether it does or not," said Billy. He asked them to sit down, then told the whole scenario, including his trip to Clint and Lottie's, and his decision to come back and get on with his ministry. "God called me to be a pastor, to serve Christ, to minister to people in all sorts of situations. It's becoming clear to me this whole situation needs the touch of God's grace, and he's called me to be part of that." He paused to take in their confused expressions.

Earlene leaned forward. "So, *do you* have any connection with that pipeline? If you do, it probably won't be possible for you to stay here as a pastor."

"Not directly..." Billy started to say.

"What does that mean, *not directly*," said Carrie. "You either do or you don't."

"I hear you, but there is a middle ground. Yes, I worked for EverMore, but only as a clerk in the main office downtown. I wasn't involved in any way with decisions or actions the company made. Being called to the ministry had nothing to do with any of that. I'm as surprised as you at what happened. It caught me totally off guard."

"My husband, Bernie, heard some talk around Coop's sayin' you was sent here as a spy," said Holly, studying his face. "I told him that couldn't be true because you were sent by the Wesleyan Brethren Church, and they have nothin' to do with politics." She paused. "So, you really are a pastor?"

"Oh, yes," said Billy, feeling a little amused at the 'spy' idea, and relieved to have things coming out into the open. "While y'all are cleanin' up around here, I'll be in the study unpacking my personal stuff. I have a framed certificate I'll be puttin' on the wall authorizing me to serve here as a student pastor."

Earlene huffed, "Certificates don't mean nothin'. Anybody can fake a certificate."

"No, but God's Spirit is genuine," said Holly. "In my spirit I know you are who you say you are, and all of this is a sad tale about how scared and suspicious folks can be." She looked at the others, "I think we need to stop all this and have a prayer right now. Whatever happened is behind us, and we need faith to go forward with our new pastor." She breathed a deep sigh.

Her words had a healing effect for however long it would last. They prayed together, then shared a group hug before everyone divided up chores and settled into cleaning the house. Billy felt relieved to have broken the ground and thanked them all for their faith and courage to speak out. Within two hours the house had been dusted, the floors cleaned, and carpets vacuumed, the bathroom and kitchen cleaned and organized, and Billy had made progress organizing his office.

♦ ♦ ♦

After the women left he went into the living room, leaned back in the recliner, closed his eyes and gave thanks to God that things were becoming manageable. His smartphone rang again. This time it was Fletch Waverley.

"William, how are things going? I'm glad to see you got back from West Virginia."

"Hello Dr. Fletcher. I got in last night. Had a chance to talk to the sheriff about that incident I told you about, and I'm ready to deal with it now. A group of ladies just left after helping to clean up the house. I'm ready to get started with my ministry."

Fletch mumbled while Billy spoke. "Mm...yeah...good. Well, we can talk about all of that when we meet. How does Wednesday look for you?"

"That's good...what time?"

"Make it eleven-thirty here at my office. After we finish our meeting I'll treat you to lunch."

"I'll see you then."

"Okay. In the meantime, tread lightly with those folks. They were quite upset Sunday and some of them have short fuses. We don't want any more incidents."

ELEVEN

Standing behind the oak pulpit on a raised platform, Billy looked out across the pews of Main Street Church's sanctuary. The burgundy carpet and pew cushions added warmth to the otherwise cold room. Tall windows graced the side walls with plantation shutters opened just enough to admit diffused light through clear glass panes. A double door in the back exited to the street. Billy tried to imagine himself talking to a room full of people as their pastor. He shuddered. *Sunday is just five days away. Lord, what am I going to say to these people?"*

"Well, you must be the new preacher." The voice came from behind him. Billy wheeled around to see a tall man with sandy hair and glasses who appeared to be in his mid-forties. He extended his right hand toward Billy. "I'm Grant Mackabee, lay leader here at Main Street Church."

They shook hands. "Billy Upshur. Glad to meet you, Grant. I just stopped by to look over the church and get a feel for things."

Grant studied him for a moment. "Folks were a mite upset when you didn't show up Sunday. I guess it's understandable with the weather and all."

Billy tensed up. "Yeah, I apologize for that. Did you have many people?"

"A few diehards, I guess you could say—includin' me. I'm sure you had a good reason for not bein' here. We probably need to talk about that." His manor was more matter-of-fact than judgmental.

Billy relaxed a bit. "I just met Carrie Glossner and some other ladies who came to clean up the house this morning...which I really appreciated."

Grant smiled. "Carrie pretty much keeps things on track. Who was with her?"

"Holly Jinks, who said she's the music director here, and another woman...Earlene something from Frog Hollow."

"Josef. Earlene Josef. She's a widow, comes from a prominent family in the area. Glad you met Holly. You'll probably run into her teaching music lessons at church. I expect both of them can help you find your way up in the hollow."

"Yeah, that's what they said."

"So, let me show you around the building." They toured the kitchen, social hall and classrooms, ending up back behind the sanctuary at the church office. It was a modest room with a large desk, bookshelves, two wingback chairs, and two four-drawer file cabinets next to a narrow occasional table. Billy was impressed.

"You're free to use this office, or the study at the rental house—or both, whatever suits you," said Grant. "Pastor Pete set this up because he lived too far away to work from home."

"Thanks," said Billy, nodding as he settled into the chair behind the desk. "I'll probably work from right here." He motioned for Grant to sit in one of the wingbacks. "Do you have a few minutes?"

"Sure." Grant sat down, crossed his legs and leaned to the right with his elbow on the chair arm. "What's on your mind?"

"I don't want to keep you if you need to get back to work."

"No problem. I work in Peakview...manage a warehouse, so I'm kinda my own boss. Took some time off today for a dental check-up." He chuckled, "Since my wife's the receptionist there I can't get around it. Her name is Elaine, by the way, and we have two teenagers, Brad and Margie, who keep us pretty busy. I just happened to see you coming into the church, so I decided to get acquainted."

Billy nodded. "I look forward to meeting your family. I'm glad you dropped in. Let me tell you what was behind my absence Sunday." He told about his experience with Zeke Thursday morning, and the attack on Frog Hollow Road.

"That's shocking, so say the least," said Grant. "Now Zeke, he's really not a problem to anybody, but he does have some rough edges. He makes his living doing handyman work around the area, you know, cuttin' grass or trees, trash removal, house maintenance. We have quite a few older widows nowadays, and he sort of looks after their needs. As you know, he does maintenance for Oscar. You can trust him, but you need to lay out the boundaries."

"Yeah, he just took me by surprise that morning. Sheriff Bordain thinks the guys who ambushed me belong to some sort of group called the Frog Hollow Boys. Do you know anything about them?"

"Not much, really. I mean, they pretty much stay to themselves up in the hollow. Only time I've heard of 'em hangin' out around town is when there's some big issue goin' on...like this pipeline thing. Whenever that gets stirred up you can count on them bein' present and vocal." Grant nodded emphatically. "I don't know what they might have against you, except you worked for EverMore Energy, which is probably enough to make you an enemy in their way of thinkin'."

Billy told him about his talk with Clint and his resolve to be positive, and to get to know these men if possible. Grant wasn't any more optimistic than Cam had been about that working out. He looked at his watch.

"Guess I'd better get goin'. Told Elaine I'd pick up some groceries. See you in church Sunday, and feel free to call me if you need anything. Oh, by the way, we don't have a church secretary, so you'll have to do the worship bulletins yourself. Carrie's a great list person and she said she'd leave you some instructions in the main desk drawer."

Billy pulled the drawer open to find a yellow folder marked, "Office Procedures." He pulled it out and dropped it on the desk. "Looks like this is it."

"Okay," said Grant as they shook hands and he left. Billy opened the folder. It was highly organized. He heaved a sigh, *here we go. Looks like I've gotta get settled in fast.*

♦ ♦ ♦

Wednesday afternoon Billy kept his appointment with Dr. Waverley. He had worked late getting his personal belongings moved into the office, then reading through Carrie's folder in detail. It was mostly about Main Street Church, but there was also a worship design for the Frog Hollow church, along with the budget, officers, and other administrative details for both churches. He felt good as he left for his meeting.

Rising temperatures made travel much easier, so he arrived a few minutes early and rang the doorbell. He began to wonder if he had the wrong place or time when the door suddenly opened.

"Well, William, you're very prompt." Fletch took his coat as he stepped inside. "Excuse me for a few minutes while I finish a phone call in my office. Make yourself comfortable."

The atmosphere reminded Billy of a doctor's waiting room with a couch, several chairs, lamps and assorted magazines. The walls contained pictures of various churches on the Alleghany District. There was no indication that Fletch had an administrative assistant. Billy had hardly opened the cover of a theological periodical when Fletch emerged from his office. "Come in, William. Did you have any trouble on the roads?"

"No, things are clearing up. By the way, you can just call me Billy."

"Glad to hear that about the roads," said Fletch, ignoring the name issue. He was a tall man with heavy eyebrows, steely eyes, and thinning gray hair combed straight back. He wore a dark suit with a white shirt and conservative tie. Taking his place behind a large desk he motioned for Billy to take a chair opposite him. Fletch leaned forward with his elbows on the desk and his hands folded. "So, what's the status of things at Strong's Creek today?"

Billy felt intimidated but resolved not to show it. "I've met a few people now and I'm impressed with the prospects for going forward. The people I've talked to so far have accepted my apologies for last weekend. They want stability and leadership, and I'll do my best to provide it. From what I've been told, the guys who attacked me are known for disruptive behavior. They even have a nickname...the Frog Hollow Boys. It's like they've isolated themselves from the mainstream of life, and the gas pipeline has riled them up."

"Who told you that?"

"That's what I hear from Carrie Glossner and Grant Mackabee...and from Sheriff Bordain."

Fletch raised his eyebrows and leaned back in his chair. "Well, you're talking to some good people, so I think you can trust that as far as it goes. But what about Frog Hollow itself? Who have you talked to up there? Seems to me that's where you need to put your attention."

"I agree that I need to prioritize that church. From the files I've seen so far it seems they have only a few people attending services. I've met Earlene Josef, who seems pretty closed up, so I imagine that's how most people up there will be, at least at first."

Yes, yes, of course. You'll have to earn their trust, which won't happen if you stir up more trouble. On the phone you said you wanted to get to know those men who attacked you. Seems to me that's asking for more trouble. Best to leave them alone and concentrate on building up that congregation."

Billy felt like a fish looking at a fisherman's bait. He wanted to engage Fletch with a deeper discussion, but sensed it was a hook that could undo his ministry before he even got started. *Best to play along with the boss.* "You bring to mind something from sociology back in college, about informal groups and the role they play under the surface. I want to get to know the people and how they interact. I want them to trust me, so I need to be open with them. I believe they'll show me the steps I need to take."

"You do, huh?" Fletch leaned forward. "Sociology. That's college talk. You're dealing with real people in an explosive situation. I would suggest you keep the sociology in your old textbooks and apply yourself to praying, pastoring and preaching."

Looks like I touched a nerve. "Yes, sir. I understand what you're saying."

Fletch broke off his intense glare, pushed his chair back and stood with outstretched hand. "Okay. I want a report from you by mid-April, right after Easter. That gives you a few weeks to get your feet on the ground. Because of what happened last week, you're on probation as far as I'm concerned. If you can normalize things in the next three months, I'll keep you on at Strong's Creek. If not, we might not be able to use you until after you finish seminary."

Billy shook his hand. "I'll keep in touch."

As he turned to leave Fletch said, "Just a minute. I said I'd take you to lunch, remember? I'm a man of my word." He smiled and reached for a topcoat and hat on a coat tree. "There's a nice restaurant over near the old railroad depot where I often go for lunch. If you want to follow me, you can just head back to Strong's Creek from there after we eat."

"Sounds good," said Billy as he followed him out the door. "I appreciate the invitation."

TWELVE

Thursday morning Billy noticed grassy patches in his yard among the receding snow drifts. The sun's promise of continued melting was compromised by a chilly northwesterly breeze. After breakfast he decided this was the day to get organized for Sunday's services, starting with Frog Hollow. He located Earlene's phone number in the papers Carrie had prepared for him.

"Josef's residence," said a voice that seemed almost mechanical.

"Uh, this is Pastor Upshur." Billy hesitated, trying to adjust to using that title. "Could I speak with Earlene, please?"

"This is Earlene."

"Good morning. I want to thank you for helping clean this house the other day. Since the weather's improving I'd like to visit Frog Hollow Church today, and I could use some help with planning Sunday's service. Would it be possible for you to drop by there today?"

"That depends on what time. I have a commitment in Peakview this morning."

"Well, how about after lunch, say at two o'clock?"

Earlene paused. "Yes...I can do that. Is there anything I need to bring with me?"

"No, all I need is your knowledge about how things get done. I'll see you then."

That being settled, Billy drove to Main Street Church. He'd just gotten settled at his desk with a cup of coffee when a voice interrupted him.

"Good morning, pastor."

He looked up. "Ah, Holly. You're just the person I need to talk to."

She laughed. "I'll bet you want to talk about Sunday's service."

"You're right. Please, come in...have a seat."

Billy shuffled aside his papers, picking up the worship notes Carrie had left him. He was familiar with church services from the perspective of the pew, but not too sure about actually leading one. If his uncertainties were visible, Holly didn't show it.

"Guess I'm kinda new at leading a service. Would you mind going into the sanctuary and walking me through how these different things are done?"

"Sure. You probably feel the way I did when I gave my first concert."

Billy heaved a sigh of relief. "Probably." When they entered the chancel area he noticed an electronic keyboard set up behind the choir screen. He raised his eyebrows, "You don't have a piano or organ in here?"

"Our organ breathed its last chord two years ago," said Holly with a twinkle in her eye. "Seriously, some of the older folks still miss it...and I do too, really...but we decided this was more practical." She turned the instrument on and demonstrated its various features. They spent the next hour going through all the motions, sort of like a rehearsal. When everything was together Billy thanked her and she left.

As he entered his office Billy's smartphone rang. It was Cam Bordain.

"Preacher, I'm goin' up on Frog Hollow Road after lunch. Sorry for such short notice, but I'd like you to go with me."

"I'm just finishing some things here at Main Street Church, then I'm going to lunch. I have to meet someone at Frog Hollow Church at two o'clock. I can go with you as long as I make that appointment."

"Why don't you meet me, say where the gravel road turns off Strong's Creek Road. That way you can just go on up to the church after we finish. Okay"

"Sure. One o'clock?"

"That's fine."

Billy stopped by the house for a sandwich, then made it to the rendezvous on time. As Cam followed him up the gravel road he wondered if he'd recognize the exact location. The road was slushy in places, but mostly clear of ice and snow. Suddenly he rounded a curve and knew this was where the van had blocked the road. He stopped and walked back to Cam's Interceptor.

"This is it. The van was parked right where I stopped. Look over there," he pointed. "Those ruts are where my wheels dug in when I hightailed it outa here." Cam turned on his emergency lights in case someone came up the road, then got out and walked with Billy. "Those guys jumped out of the bushes right up here." He pointed to a brushy area that was still snow packed.

"Hmmm," muttered Cam. "Did Beanpole fire at you from behind the bushes, or had he stepped out onto the road."

"Oh, they were all on the road."

"You know what a shell casing looks like, don't you?"

"Yeah."

Cam walked to his car and came back with two dark green pads. He handed one to Billy. "We'll probably have to get on our hands and knees and dig around a bit. It'll help to kneel on this."

After nearly thirty minutes Cam said, "Hey, here it is." He dug up a small shell casing with his pen knife and showed it to Billy. "There's probably another one around here, but this will be enough." He put it in a small plastic bag. "This looks like a 22-caliber round. My guess is those guys were just playin' with you. If they'd have meant you harm, they'd have used somethin' bigger."

Billy shuddered at the thought. He looked around at the terrain. "So, where's this pipeline? If they're tearing down houses and trees, it should be visible."

"This is just the road up to the church and the little community around it. The actual hollow is down in a ravine about a half-mile up from here. You turn right and follow a narrow road. Down there's where the pipeline's goin' in...and where the Frog Hollow Boys live. The pipeline installation hasn't started yet. They've acquired property and marked trees for removal. Haven't torn down any houses yet."

Billy got the picture. "So, how much farther to the church?"

"'Bout a mile. You say you're meetin' with Earlene Josef? She'll probably be comin' along most any time now. This is the only way to get there."

"She said she lives up above the church," said Billy. "I guess she comes up through here all the time. Makes me wonder why those guys felt it was safe to ambush me here."

"Well, she wouldn't come this way to get to her house. It's on the paved road."

"Paved road? You mean there's a paved road to the church?"

"No, not to the church. The ravine runs between it and her place, which is also on a higher elevation. Earlene's husband owned a small chain of local grocery stores, so he had to get in and out of the hollow no matter what the weather. He pulled some strings someplace and got the state to pave a road right up to his house."

"Ah, so, where's that road from here?"

"You gotta go back to Strong's Creek Road and continue about three quarters of a mile past this gravel road to find it."

Billy nodded. "Well, I can see I've got a lot to learn about the area. Guess right now I'd better get on up to the church." As he spoke a silver Buick Lucerne pulled up behind them, and Earlene got out.

"What's going on?" she said with a concerned expression. "Has there been an accident."

"No, ma'am," said Cam. "I just turned the flashers on so nobody would run into us stopped along here."

Earlene looked puzzled. "Oh...well, I'm glad nobody's hurt or anything. I'm on my way up to the church." She looked at Billy. "Do you still want to meet with me?"

"Oh, yes, this has nothing to do with our meeting. I'll see you up there in a couple of minutes."

Everybody got back in their vehicles. Billy noticed in his rear-view mirror that Cam turned off on the narrow road down into the ravine. When he got to the church he and Earlene parked in front of a small white weathered frame structure with a red metal roof that had obviously been there for a long time. It was nestled among some cedar trees and a rather large cemetery extended out from it on one side.

As they walked up to the door Earlene said in a concerned tone, "I hope the sheriff didn't give you a ticket for speeding or something."

Billy realized how it must have looked to her. "Oh, no, nothing like that. You remember I told y'all the other morning about a rough experience I had on Frog Hollow Road?"

She nodded.

"Well I was showing him where it happened."

"Oh." That seemed to settle the subject for her.

Stepping inside Billy noticed a musty odor. The pine floor boards creaked with each step. Old pews with hard seats and straight backs caught his attention. He asked the obvious question, "How old is this building?"

"It's one of the oldest buildings in Limestone County. It was built in 1830. Two years ago we got it registered as an official historical landmark."

It was cold inside, and Earlene went over to a rustic looking oil stove and turned it on. "Originally this was a log stove. We had someone down in the village convert it to oil. It'll warm up sooner than you think."

While the stove made popping sounds from expanding metal, Billy went over details about the service for Sunday, how many people to expect, and various other details. Earlene was helpful and, like Holly, seemed sensitive to Billy's newness as a pastor. The room did warm up more than Billy had expected during the forty-five minutes they were there.

As they went to their cars Earlene pointed up to a ridge behind the church. "That's my house up there.

Because of the ravine I can't get to it directly from here...have to go around to the paved road. Do you know about that?"

"Yes, the sheriff told me about it."

"When you get ready to visit the folks up here, I hope you'll give me a call. I can fill you in on everyone and how to find them."

"Thanks. I appreciate that. See you Sunday."

Heading back down Frog Hollow Road he noticed the road leading down into the ravine, and the Frog Hollow Boys came to mind. *One thing I need to do next week is go down there and explore things. I've gotta see where that pipeline's going in and get to know these folks.*

THIRTEEN

In contrast to the weekend before, spring-like conditions greeted church goers on Sunday morning. Billy's spirits were high as he arrived at Frog Hollow Church in bright sunshine serenaded by warbling birds. After investing much of Friday and Saturday in study and preparation he felt good about his pastoral role. Notably absent when he entered the building was the musty odor he'd noticed a few days earlier. The room felt warm and welcoming.

Earlene was seated at the piano. Next to her was a man holding a guitar, who wore wire glasses, and had long brown hair pulled back into a pony tail. He appeared to be in his mid to late thirties. "This is my son, Ralphie," said Earlene. "He's gonna favor us with one of his gospel songs today."

"Good to meet you Ralphie," said Billy. "I look forward to your music."

As they shook hands a slight smile curled the corners of Ralphie's mouth. "You're younger than the last preacher we had. Mama says this here's your first time to lead a church service. The Lord bless you."

"Well, thank you, Ralphie. With God's help I'm sure we'll have a great time together."

Three older couples entered the church somewhat tentatively, as though they weren't sure what to expect. Earlene called their names as she waved them inside. "This here's our new preacher, Pastor Upshur."

The women smiled meekly while the men mumbled a greeting. They quickly found seats in scattered sections of the small room where Billy imagined they'd been sitting for decades. After an awkward few moments during which no one else arrived, he stepped up to the rustic pulpit. "It's a pleasure to be with you. I look forward to serving as your pastor. Let's...."

One of the mumbling men seemed to suddenly find his voice. "Where was you last week if you're so glad to be here?"

Billy felt like the wind had been knocked out of his gut. *Okay, so this is how it's gonna be. Easy does it.* "We had a pretty bad storm last week, didn't we? I'm afraid I was stuck over in West Virginia with my family."

The man was not to be put off. "Ya wouldn't have been over there if ya hadn't run off from here on Thursday. Word gets around, y'know."

A voice seemed to rise within Billy's spirit, *'Love him, don't fight him.'*

"I'm glad you mentioned that. Let's talk about it after the service, okay?"

"Humph," said the man, turning sideways in his pew and staring at the opposite wall.

Billy went on to introduce himself, explaining he was new in the ministry and welcomed their help as he got started. His words were met with blank expressions throughout the opening prayer and scripture lesson. Billy sat down while Ralphie sang a bluegrass folk hymn that obviously resonated with the small congregation.

He stepped back to the pulpit, thanked Ralphie and proceeded with his message. It was 10:30 when he pronounced the benediction and he knew he had to leave quickly to be at Main Street Church on time.

As he opened the door his adversarial congregant shouted, "Thought you was gonna tell us about last weekend?"

"I did say that, didn't I." He closed the door and faced back into the room. "I guess it'll take me a while to learn how to manage my time better. How about if I come back this afternoon and we can talk about it? Would that work for everybody?"

"I've got a better idea," said Earlene. "We all gotta eat lunch someplace. Pastor, after you finish at Main Street Church come on up to my house. I've got a big pot o' chili I made yesterday—plenty for everyone. All of y'all come, we can talk things out while we eat. Does that suit everybody?"

The people looked at each other and shrugged. The man who had challenged Billy said, "Yeah, we'll make it suit. This here's more important than anythin' we gotta do." He looked at the others who quickly nodded assent, then turned back to Billy. "You let us down this time and there won't be no reason for ya to come back here."

Billy turned to Earlene. "That's a wonderful offer. Thank you. I can assure all of you I'll be here, and we can talk as long as you want."

♦ ♦ ♦

He arrived at Main Street Church a few minutes before the service was to begin. "We was gettin' worried, Preacher," said Grant as he entered the building. "Thought you might've gotten lost up there in the hollow."

Billy smiled. "No, I just haven't learned how to time myself. I'll be here in plenty of time next week."

Grant slapped him on the back, "Sure, I understand. Anything you need from me before we start?"

"If you'll make whatever announcements are needed, I'd appreciate it. Then introduce me and I'll make a few comments about last week,"

"Great," said Grant. "I think that'll clear the air. By now most folks have heard what happened on Frog Hollow Road. I think we're all ready to just move ahead."

When Billy told what had happened he sensed both curiosity and concern. After he finished Grant mentioned his and Billy's talk during the week. "We've all had things throw us off balance sometimes, and I know we'll give the preacher our prayers and support. I believe God sent him here, so let's make him feel welcome."

A spontaneous swell of applause broke out. Several people called out to him.

"Welcome, preacher."

"Don't worry about last week."

"We're glad to have you with us."

It was obvious Grant had been talking to some people in the background to prepare the way. Billy heard him whisper, "Amen."

He did experience a few awkward moments leading the service, but no one seemed to react. Peoples' comments were positive as they left the church. When everyone had gone he heaved a sigh of relief. *I made it. Thank you, Lord.*

♦ ♦ ♦

Thirty minutes later he found the paved road to Earlene's house marked by a sign that read, *Josef Lane*, and another beneath it, *No Outlet*. The road wound its way through beautiful wooded terrain with several houses of various sizes set back in the trees. It ended in a cul-de-sac where he turned up her driveway. The house was a large frame colonial with a Queen Anne roof, and Williamsburg Green shutters. Smoke curled from a large chimney and the fragrance of wood smoke floated through the air. Several cars were already there. It was 1:15 when he rang the doorbell.

A dog barked, followed by Earlene opening the door. "Come in, Pastor." She took his coat and hat, then he leaned down to rub under the chin of a very friendly Airedale Terrier whose tail wagged energetically.

"How did the service go in the village?" said Earlene as she reached for the dog. "Lie down, Poochie." The dog gave a whine and obediently curled up on a braided rug.

Billy smiled. "Things went well. We had good attendance and I didn't stumble too much."

Earlene led him to a great room at the back of the house that looked out through multi-paned windows across the ravine. He could see the church clearly. Beyond it, ridges and valleys rolled out toward distant mountains. The room was abuzz with conversation. Everyone he'd seen in church was there. Crackers and drinks were set up on a side bar and a roaring blaze in a large fireplace created warmth. The aroma of chili wafted in from the adjacent kitchen.

Earlene raised her voice, "Okay, y'all, the preacher's here." Instantly the mood in the room shifted from relaxed to tense. She was undaunted. "Y'all come on into the kitchen now and get y'selves some chili. Preacher, why don't you pray over this?"

Billy obliged. The people insisted he be served first, so he sat down at the table before the others. Earlene sat across from him, and the man who had challenged him during the worship service sat next to him. Once people were settled and began eating Billy sensed a degree of intimacy, as though they were all related, like one large family.

"Tell me your name again," he asked the man beside him.

"Barney Giles." The man spoke without looking up from his plate.

"I guess you've been in Frog Hollow all your life, right?"

Barney stopped eating and looked at Billy. "How long I've lived here ain't got nothin' to do with why we gettin' together today. A better question might be why you're here?"

Billy almost choked at this unexpected brashness. *So much for a friendly discussion.* "I'm here to be your pastor." Everyone stopped eating and looked at him. *What's going on?*

The tension was broken by Poochie barking and the sound of someone entering through the front door. Earlene left the table.

"Why don't we finish eatin' and then talk about this?" said one of the women.

"Ain't nothin' to be gained by waitin'," said Barney.

Earlene returned with a younger woman everybody seemed to know. One of the women called out, "Hey, Cindy! Where ya been? Ain't seen you for a while."

Billy looked up. Cindy appeared to be in her early thirties, about his height, dressed in a light blue knit turtleneck sweater, designer jeans and stylish casual boots. She wore her auburn hair in a shaggy cut, framing a face with bright blue eyes, and a smile that would light up any room. Silver loop earrings completed the contrast she presented in the group. *Who's this? She doesn't seem to fit this crowd*, thought Billy.

As if in answer, Earlene introduced her. "Pastor, this is my niece, Cindy Barker. She lives down the road a piece and *sometimes*"—she rolled her eyes— "comes to church. I invited her for chili today before I knew we were gonna have this meetin'."

Cindy smiled and shook Billy's hand. "Don't pay attention to Aunt Earlene. I come to church when I can, but I work a lot of Sundays."

"Oh, what do you do?"

"I'm a nurse at the Vital Care Center in the village...and I do some volunteer things that take a lot of time. Sometimes I work Sundays, sometimes I'm away."

"Enough of the small talk, y'all two can get acquainted later," said Barney. "I know all about what you're up to, and preacherin' ain't the half of it."

Cindy gave Billy a puzzled look as he turned to Barney. "You said something like that earlier, so I'd like to know what you're talking about."

"What you're up to."

"I'm sorry...I don't think I know what you mean."

"He's talkin' about what ya done to them Frog Hollow Boys t'other week. It's all over town," said one of the other men. "We might as well call a spade a spade here. How can you do somethin' like that and call y'self a preacher?"

Billy was puzzled for a moment, then he caught on. "Why don't you tell me what you've been hearing?"

"I been tellin' him he should ask you first before passin' gossip along," said the man's wife.

"It ain't gossip," snapped the man.

"Okay, please, let's calm down. I've heard it said that I'm a spy for EverMore Energy, if that's what you mean. I'm sure you know what a huge company that is. They're involved with a lot more than the gas pipeline. I did work in their office but had nothing to do with whatever has gone on between them and y'all." He went on to tell about his call to the ministry and assignment to Strong's Creek. He told about the incident on Frog Hollow Road, and his trip home, and his return. I think this is a good time to work through this whole thing."

"Well, the way you tell it ain't the way I heard it. I heard you set up a road block and stopped them boys from gittin' home. Then you told 'em you was sent here to make sure they stop interferrin' with the pipeline workers or they'd answer to you. That's when they fired a shot in the air and you run off scared. They been laughin' at you all over the hollow."

Billy couldn't believe his ears. "That's the most preposterous thing I ever heard. Look, I was sent here to be the pastor at these two churches, and that's what I aim to do. I have no personal connection with the pipeline."

He studied the faces around the table. Everybody except Earlene and Cindy were studying their chili bowls. Earlene got up, walked around the table and put her hand on his shoulder. "I believe Pastor Upshur," she said. "The Frog Hollow Boys have been a wild bunch for as long as I can remember. I think it's time we all take a deep breath and meditate—get ourselves back on track."

Shocked at the outbursts, Cindy got up and stepped back from the table with her hands on her hips. "I can't believe this just happened. What's gotten into y'all? I've known most of y'all since I was a kid. I may not be in church every Sunday, but I pray, and I believe in the Lord, and try to follow his ways. I don't know why I'm sayin' this, but Pastor Upshur, I apologize for all this garbage that's being dumped on you. I wouldn't blame you for walkin' outa here and never comin' back."

Cindy turned to Earlene. "The chili was great. Sorry, but I don't think I can stand the company in this room right now."

Earlene was nearly speechless and obviously embarrassed. "Well...if you...wait a minute. You can leave if you want to, but I'd like you to stay. We need to pray together."

Ralphie had been silent through the whole thing. "Mama's right," he said suddenly. "I've seen people get off on the wrong track and make a big mess sometimes—I've done it myself—but I thought we got together here in the name of Jesus. So why aren't we askin' him what he wants us to do?"

Billy stood up from the table. "I apologize for getting riled up myself, and I think Ralphie's right...we need to pray. I promise you, I didn't come here just to be your pastor when things are sunny and bright. God sent me to be with you through the storms, too, and we've got a real storm brewing here. Maybe it was brewing long before I arrived. As I've said, I have no active connection with the pipeline project. I've been hearing arguments for and against it for years. To y'all this is very personal, and I want to learn from you. I want to thank you for telling me what's going on so we're all on the same page."

The tension eased, and Billy asked everyone to join hands and go around the table speaking whatever they needed to say to God. "Sometimes we have to ventilate everything, so we can be quiet and hear God. He has a word for us today. Let's join in prayer and listen for his Spirit."

After the prayer people hugged each other. Several came to Billy and asked his forgiveness for all the turmoil after he preached such a nice sermon that morning.

Barney shook his hand and looked him in the eye. "Guess I owe you an apology...I shoulda spoke *to* you before I spoke *about* you. I probably woulda done the same thing you did if I'd run into a situation like that."

"It's okay, Barney. I understand where you were coming from. This week I plan to go down into the hollow and get to know these folks. God willing, I hope to meet the guys I let run me away. Maybe God will do some healing for all of us."

Barney looked at him wide-eyed. "You serious? You might be takin' your life in your hands doin' that."

For a moment his words were like an electric shock. *Guess I hadn't thought about it that way.* A sense of assurance filtered into his spirit. He surprised himself with his words. "I know it's dangerous, but I believe the Lord will be with me."

Barney put his hand on Billy's shoulder. "Preacher don't go there by yourself. Let me go with ya. I know them folks."

Billy was surprised, beginning to understand his plan might not be so easy to carry out. He looked at Barney's wife. "How do you feel about this?"

"Me and Barney's been married a long time. I've learned if he sets out to do somethin', he's gonna do it. He's a man of his word and he does know lotsa folks there."

Cindy had been standing near Billy throughout the whole situation. "Pastor, I know a lot of people there, too. I think this is a good idea and I'd like to go with you and Barney."

Billy felt overwhelmed. "Thanks. I'll accept anybody who wants to go. I do think we need to do it right away. When would suit y'all?"

"I'm usually off on Tuesdays," said Cindy.

"I'm pretty flexible," said Barney.

"Okay, let's do it Tuesday morning. Why don't we meet at the church at ten o'clock?"

Barney and Cindy agreed. They all joined hands and prayed for God's Spirit to go before them and bring healing in the community. Billy felt good that evening as he relaxed with a movie before going to bed.

FOURTEEN

Visiting in the hollow suddenly took a back seat for Billy on Monday morning. He was at his desk when Cindy called from the clinic. "I thought you ought to know one of your church folks just went into the hospital in Peakview."

He sat up sharply. "Oh? Who is it? What's going on?"

"I expect you haven't met her yet...Teachie Smiley. She's 97, a retired school teacher...suffers from congestive heart failure. Lives with her daughter."

Billy flipped through the folder Carrie had prepared. "Ah, here's a Smiley on Village Lane. So, what happened?"

"Her daughter brought her in with swollen ankles and she could hardly get her breath. She'd had a rough night and all her vitals were down. We sent her to the hospital for evaluation. It doesn't look good."

"Peakview," Billy muttered as he shuffled through the folder. "Ah, here's the address.""

"Wait, there's more. The receptionist just handed me a note. She's in the emergency room...it looks like she had a stroke in the ambulance on the way."

Billy swallowed hard. "Okay, thanks for the call. I'm on my way there now."

"Oh, before you hang up, I just found out I have to work tomorrow, so I can't go with you and Barney. One of our nurses has the flu."

"Oh, I'm sorry, but that's okay...don't worry about it. I'll talk to you later."

He hung up, grabbed his coat and rushed out to the car. The weather had turned sharply colder overnight. As he started the Wrangler and let the engine warm up he said a brief prayer. *Lord, I don't know what to do with this. I'm leaning on you.* It occurred to him that he should let somebody in the church know about the situation. He called Carrie Glossner.

"I was just about to call you about the same thing," she said. "I'm heading to the hospital now...do you know the way? You could ride with me if you wish."

"Thanks, but I'm actually on my way right now."

"Then I'll see you there in a little while."

Carrie arrived minutes behind him, which relieved some tension at the ER desk. The receptionist was going through a digital file on her computer screen. "We don't have her listed, sir. Could she go by a different name?"

Billy tried to remember the full name he'd seen at church, but he wasn't sure. *I should have written it down.*

"Her name is actually Judith Renee Smiley, said Carrie as she walked up. The receptionist found the entry and gave them temporary passes and directions to the cubicle where Teachie was being evaluated.

"Are you family?" asked a nurse as they approached.

"I'm her pastor."

"Just a moment." The nurse consulted with the doctor then came back to him. "You can see her now." As she spoke Teachie's daughter, June, walked up. Carrie motioned to Billy that she would go with her to the waiting area.

Billy took in the cubicle scene. Teachie's complexion was pale, her brow furrowed as though in pain, and her mouth was drawn on the left side. An IV rack with several plastic bottles fed her body through lines attached to her arm. The small space was crowded with two nurses and a doctor responding to digital graphics on a monitor above her head. The staff stepped aside as he drew closer to her. He touched her cold hand lightly. She didn't respond.

He leaned in closer. "This is Pastor Upshur from Main Street Church. I came to pray with you. I know God loves you and is with you this very moment. He took her hand again. "Lord, touch Judith's spirit with your loving presence. Take away her anxieties so she can trust your healing grace. Be with her family and give them strength and assurance."

As he finished the technicians rolled in electrocardiogram equipment and began attaching leads to Teachie's body. The nurse ushered him outside the cubicle, closing the curtain. "She will be admitted to the Cardiac Intensive Care Unit as soon as arrangements are completed." Billy thanked her and went to the waiting area where he sat down with Carrie and June.

Searching June's eyes, he said consolingly, "I know this must be very hard for you."

June stared blankly for a moment before speaking. "It is. You think you're ready, but you actually aren't." She looked directly at him, "We've had a few trips over here in the last year, so I know one day it will be too much for her. At her age she's blessed to have lived this long. Thank you for your prayer. I'm sure she appreciated it."

Billy stayed with June and Carrie until after Teachie was admitted to the CICU unit, then he left, feeling a warm inner glow of satisfaction as he drove back to Strong's Creek. God was with him in this ministry. He heaved a deep sigh of gratitude, glad he'd gotten a grip on his fear and returned.

Tuesday morning Carrie called to tell him Teachie had suffered a massive heart attack in the early morning hours and died. Billy's heart sank. He knew she was at peace, but it was his first journey on the precipice between life and death where pastors often travel with people. He called June and arranged to meet with her, then called Barney to cancel the Frog Hollow trip.

The next three days involved an often-confusing shuffle, digging through the worship book for funeral resources while keeping up with questions from parishioners, and staying in touch with June. He quickly learned that Teachie got her nickname from years of teaching at the old one-room schoolhouse. She had lived in the hollow most of her life until recent years.

Friday was cold and blustery for the graveside service on the Frog Hollow Church grounds. Billy felt nervous as he looked out across a sea of faces. Here and there he recognized people from both of his congregations...Barney and Myrtle Giles, Grant, Carrie, Holly and Ernie. "In my father's house are many mansions..." he intoned from the John 14 passage, feeling more confident. All eyes were fixed on him as he finished the committal and pronounced the benediction. He paused to speak to each family member before stepping out of the tent.

The funeral director handed him a small envelope. "From the family."

Billy nodded, "Thanks." He put it in his coat pocket.

Just then someone jostled against him. He turned to find himself looking squarely into the face of the oldest of the three men who had ambushed him on Frog Hollow Road. Cold, steely eyes bore right through him. A shiver ran down Billy's spine. Without a word the man turned abruptly and disappeared into the crowd. Momentarily unnerved, Billy remembered Clint's words, *ya gotta get to know them guys.* A moment of fear flashed through his mind and he self-consciously checked his coat pocket...the envelope was still there. *What was that all about?*

"That was a wonderful service, Pastor Upshur."

Billy recognized the voice—Cindy Barker. "You can call me Billy...and thanks for the compliment. This was my first attempt at a funeral...but I guess you knew that."

She smiled. "I know, and you did a great job. It looks like God had other plans this week instead of visiting down in the hollow. I should be off next Tuesday for sure, if you want to reschedule."

"Sounds good, God...and Barney...willin'."

"Oh, I just talked to Barney. He said one of the Frog Hollow Boys is here...Gus Wheeler. Mrs. Smiley was probably his teacher back in the day."

"I'll bet she was. Actually, he just bumped into me a few minutes ago, but he disappeared before I could talk to him."

"I expect the other two guys are here as well, but I haven't seen them. Funerals and weddings are about the only times they ever set foot in or around the church."

Billy thanked her again for calling him about Teachie. "You were a big help."

"Any time." She waved as she turned and walked away.

♦ ♦ ♦

Sunday morning Billy was surprised to find the Frog Hollow sanctuary over half full. People called out to him and offered handshakes as he walked down the aisle. Both Earlene and Ralphie greeted him with open arms. He was overwhelmed.

Earlene stepped up to the pulpit as people settled down. "I wear a lot of hats around here, and as lay leader I want give our new pastor a proper welcome. Thanks to all of y'all for comin' out this morning." She motioned for Billy to step up to the pulpit, then continued. "Pastor, we all want to thank you for the wonderful funeral you did for Teachie Smiley this week. As you found out, she had a place in all our hearts. We appreciate you takin' time to learn who she was so we could give her a fittin' send off."

Billy looked across the pews as she spoke. Barney and the others who had been there last Sunday were smiling. He counted 23 people, mostly older, but a few he judged to be in their forties, plus a couple with two children.

Cindy was seated near the front with two women who seemed to be her friends. Several large floral sprays from the graveside service were placed around the altar. Their fragrance melded with the enthusiasm of the people, creating a sense of familial unity.

With a week of pastoral work behind him, Billy felt more confident leading worship and preaching. At the end of the forty-five-minute service people flocked around him. Cindy introduced her two friends who worked with her at the clinic.

She said playfully, "Surprised to see me today?"

He laughed. "Should I be?"

"I mean, after I told you I only got here occasionally."

"Well, pleased, but not surprised. I'm glad you came...all of you."

"I grew up in the hollow and went to school in the village, but for my folks and so many others, Teachie was the only teacher they knew, and they loved her. You captured that so well."

"The credit goes to y'all, really. I listened to the stories people told me about her and God gave me a picture of her life. It was my privilege to do her service."

"So, are things still on for Tuesday?"

The two women with Cindy gave her a wide-eyed look and an expression that said, "Oh, what's this?"

She noticed. "No, it's not what you're thinking. Some of us from the church are gonna help Pastor Upshur find where people live so he can get acquainted."

She turned to Billy. "Excuse them."

Billy nodded. "As far as I'm concerned, yes. If anything changes I'll let you know." He gestured inclusively, "Maybe I'll see y'all again next week?"

"Maybe," said Cindy. She pointed to her watch. "You'd better get movin' or you'll be late at Main Street."

Billy laughed. "You're right. See ya,"

When he reached the Wrangler and looked back Cindy and her friends were just coming out the door. They waved as he drove away.

Under his breath he whispered, "Thank you, Lord." He felt elated.

FIFTEEN

The morning sun promised to warm the chilly air on Tuesday when Barney arrived first at Frog Hollow Church. "Guess we coulda jest met down to my house," he said as Billy arrived and got out of the Wrangler. "But then, you don't know where I live yet."

They shook hands. "Maybe we can fix that today."

"'Spect we can." Barney seemed ill at ease. "Maybe we oughta talk about this pipeline."

"Okay."

Barney seemed to be searching for words. "That thing's kinda like a dose of poison here in the hollow. Some folks are losin' property that's been in their family for generations...and for what? To make some rich guys a lot more money than they already have." He kicked his foot in the gravel as he talked.

"I hear you," said Billy, wondering where this conversation was headed. "So, are you losing property?"

"No, unlike some of my neighbors, my place ain't settin' right in its path. *Eminent domain.*" He spat out the words. "That's jest some fancy law them lawyers cooked up to push folks around."

Billy could feel his pain and anger. "Yeah...tell me, how does that work?"

Barney looked at him questioningly. "You tellin' me you worked for EverMore and you don't know how it works?" he scoffed. "Get outa here."

Billy sensed he could lose some ground if he wasn't careful. "Like I've said, I was just a clerk in the office. I only know how it works in theory. The company shows cause why it's in the public interest to do their project. They get approval to have the land they need condemned and then offer a fair market price. At least I always heard it was fair. I guess they assume money will heal the loss...if they even think that deeply about it."

"Well, it don't. It don't heal nothin'."

Barney's expression tightened, and he clenched his fists as he spoke. Just then Cindy drove up in her bright blue Chevy Colorado. She tapped the horn as she opened the door and stepped out. "Sorry I'm late. Thought y'all might have gone on without me."

"We wouldn't go without ya," said Barney in a brighter mood. He gave her a friendly hug.

She looked at Billy. "So, where are we goin' first."

"I guess all this started because I want to get to know the Frog Hollow Boys, see if we can get past the stuff that happened when I first got here. Plus, bein' the new pastor in the hollow, I'm sure some of these folks are church members I need to meet."

Cindy pulled back with a concerned expression. "Now, let me get this straight. You're not talkin' about visiting Gus and his buddies *today* are you?"

Billy recoiled. "Well, maybe not...."

"Good, because that'll never work. I grew up here and still live up on Josef Lane." She looked both men in their eyes. "My idea would be to take a soft approach. Let's visit a few of the older folks today, let them start spreadin' the word that you're not such a bad guy after all." She smiled toward Billy. "A few people have already figured that out."

"That's why we need you with us," said Billy. "I didn't mean I want to visit the Frog Hollow Boys today. I know it takes time to build up trust." He glanced toward each of them, satisfied that the issue was settled. "I'm relyin' on y'all to tell me where we should we go first. One of y'all drive and I'll sit in the back seat and take some notes."

They piled into Barney's four-door Silverado, Cindy in the front passenger seat. "Let's go see Miz Plunket first, and we can decide who else after that."

Barney nodded in agreement.

Cindy turned to Billy. "She's a widow who lives on what's left of her family farm. She's got a lotta pride but can't afford to keep the place up anymore. Things are falling apart."

Billy nodded. "How old is she?"

Cindy and Barney shared a glance. "Don't reckon' anybody knows," said Barney. "She was born in the same house she lives in now. They didn't keep no records back then. If you ask her she'll say she's 'older'n spit.'" He chuckled. "I believe it."

They had turned down the unpaved, rutty road into the ravine. Barney eased across a dry creek bed. "When it rains this creek floods and folks up this way don't get out."

"I can understand that...and nobody gets in, I expect," said Billy. They passed several houses nestled in groves of trees, then came to a fork in the road where Barney turned left. Billy's attention was caught by a split rail fence.

"Well look at that...I'll bet that fence has been here forever."

Barney nodded. "Long as I can remember. 'Course, it's kinda fallin' apart now. Nobody left to split new rails when the old ones rot out."

The road bordered a stand of woods on the left with an open field to their right. He could see an aging frame house a quarter-of-a-mile ahead with several sheds leading out from it. When they pulled up to the house he took in a scene that seemed frozen in time. Electric wires strung on poles told him the house had electricity, but it needed some roof repair and a paint job.

"I'll bet this was quite a place in its day."

"Sure was," said Barney.

An old rusty car with broken tail lights and no tires was up on cinder blocks with weeds grown up around it next to a shed near the house. Barney saw him looking at it.

"That's a 1958 Ford Fairlane. Ain't got no motor...and probably not much of anything else. Miz Plunket's oldest boy, Catfish, started workin' on it when he was a teenager, but he got drafted during the Vietnam War. He never come back."

"You mean he was killed?" asked Billy.

"Afraid so. Her youngest boy wasn't interested in the car. He went off to Richmond lookin' for work. He jest stayed there. Came home sometimes fer a while, but not so much nowadays."

"She had a daughter who got married and moved to California," said Cindy.

"Yeah... got herself killed out there in an accident on the freeway. Lots of sadness at this house."

Billy felt overwhelmed and he hadn't even met Mrs. Plunket yet. They all got out of the truck and started toward the front porch. "So, this lady lives here alone?" He just couldn't imagine how she managed.

Putting his weight onto the first creaking step, Barney said, "She's got a niece livin' with 'er. Woman's retarded or somethin', but she cooks and keeps the place up."

The porch floorboards creaked even louder than the steps as they stepped to the door. "Everybody calls her Miz Plunket but her name's Mazzie," said Cindy. "Barney's talking about Flo, who lives with her. I'll fill you in on her later."

Barney knocked on the door which was partially open. "Miz Plunket? You okay today?"

There was no immediate reply. He pushed the door open and motioned for Billy and Cindy to step in with him.

"Who's that?" Mrs. Plunket's voice was stronger than Billy had expected. He took in the modest sized room with worn draperies, well-worn stuffed sofa and chairs, and a nearly threadbare oriental rug. The room was clean yet held a musty odor. The old woman was sitting in a goose neck rocker in the center of the room. She sat erect with a shotgun aimed right at them.

"It's jest Barney, Miz Plunket...I got Cindy with me, and the new preacher."

Mrs. Plunket started at the word preacher. She squinted then her right eye popped into a hard stare. She tossed her head and lowered the gun. "Can't be too careful these days. Too many strangers walkin' around." She nodded toward Cindy then gave Billy a long stare. "So, you be the new preacher, eh. Heared 'bout ya...heared ya done a good job on Teachie's fun'ral." A tear moistened the corner of her eye. "Guess she was 'bout the oldest person still here in the hollow, 'cept for Mama Jean...an' me."

Cindy stepped over and offered Mazzie a tissue, then rubbed her back while her emotions subsided. "We all miss Teachie," she said.

Billy extended his hand to Mazzie who reached to accept it. "Heared ya come from Richmond." She looked him up and down while muttering, "Never did see much o' that last preacher."

Billy guessed he had passed inspection as the old woman turned toward the kitchen, slapped her knee and bellowed, "Flo, git y'self in here."

A shy middle-aged woman with unkempt hair wearing a nondescript housedress and dirty apron that had once been white stepped through the door from the kitchen. She quickly took in the mood of the room and squeaked, "Y'all need somethin' Mazzie?"

"This here's the new preacher...the one who done Teachie's fun'ral."

Flo nodded with downcast eyes. "Pleased t' meet'cha."

Billy decided she was an emotionally fragile woman, so he smiled politely without stepping toward her. "Glad to meet you."

Mazzie looked toward Cindy. "Y'all want somethin' to drink? And, please, find yourselves a seat. I didn't mean to be impolite."

Cindy looked at Billy and Barney with a glance that said, "I've got this." She turned to Mazzie. "You always have the best apple cider, Miz Plunket. If you happen to have some handy, we'd be pleased to have a glass."

The semblance of formality seemed to please Mazzie. "Flo, go get our guests some of that apple cider we made last fall."

"Yes Ma'am." Flo disappeared into the kitchen.

One of the arm chairs had clothing piled on it. "Excuse us," said Mazzie. "Flo was fixin' to do some ironin' today."

"That's okay," said Barney as he sat in the other arm chair. The couch was more of a love seat than a full sofa, and Billy felt self-conscious when he and Cindy sat on it together. Flo brought out the cider and then disappeared again.

Billy took a sip of the bittersweet liquid. "This is very good. You and Flo made this yourselves?"

Mazzie smiled. "With a little help from some neighbors. Got an old fruit press out in one of the sheds but can't do it all that by myself nowadays."

"I expect you've lived here a long time," said Billy, not acknowledging that he already knew the answer.

"I was born right through that door over there," said Mazzie, pointing toward what was obviously a bedroom. She talked about growing up in the house, then cut herself short. "That's 'nuff about me. I heared some more things about you," she said, looking at Billy. "Heared somethin' 'bout you ambushin' some of our men here a few weeks back."

Billy shifted his weight, feeling apprehensive at the direction the conversation was suddenly taking. "Well, that's not exactly what happened...."

Mazzie interrupted. "Lookin' at ya I can tell what I heared ain't true. People's real upset about that pipeline comin' through here, and they like to say most anythin' when they feel afraid."

Barney said to Billy, "This here's one o' them houses they takin'." He glanced at Mazzie, whose expression indicated it was okay to talk about it. "Y'see the way it's laid out, they comin' down through them woods up behind the house, then right through this very room where we're settin'."

Billy was shocked. "Have they settled with you for the house?"

Mazzie's face turned pale and drawn. "It ain't 'bout money. It's 'bout invadin' the only place I've ever lived."

Billy wanted to console her but wasn't sure how. "Are they paying enough to build you another house...right here on your property? Surely once the pipeline's in and buried underground you'll still have room for that." He glanced around the room, feeling extremely uncomfortable.

"Problem is, they gotta have a seventy-five-foot wide right-of-way, plus another fifty feet for their equipment 'n stuff durin' construction. Can't build nothin' on it. It's goin' right down the field ya saw when we was drivin' in, goin' under that ole dry creek bed, and through another woods. Ya might say Mazzie's losin' everthin' she has."

Shocked, Billy stumbled for words. "Wow. I've heard lots of stuff about the pipeline being built to provide energy for people over a wide area, but this is the first time I've seen it from this perspective. I can understand why y'all feel like you're being assaulted."

Cindy put her hand on Billy's knee as though to comfort him, then pulled it away self-consciously. She looked into his eyes. "You're just finding out how things that sound so great can sometimes have a costly effect on people."

She looked back at Mazzie. "I've been prayin' for you, Miz Plunket, and so has my aunt and other folks in the hollow."

Mazzie looked away. "Prayer's okay, but it don't fix nothin'."

Cindy got up and knelt next to Mazzie's chair, putting her arm around her shoulder. "I know God hears our prayers. You can't see it now, but I know he's got an answer for you."

Mazzie leaned forward. "Get me my jacket and cane. I need to walk around."

Flo had apparently been listening to the conversation and suddenly appeared with the requested items. Mazzie put on the jacket and stood up, wobbly at first, then moved toward the front door tapping the floor with her cane. "Y'all come along."

She took them onto the porch where she pointed off toward the field Billy had seen driving in. "I told 'em I wouldn't object if they run their pipes back behind the sheds and through that empty pastureland. We ain't got no cows grazin' there no more. But they said thar's a lotta limestone back there and it'd cost 'em too much money and be too much trouble to do that. I'm jest sick o' the whole mess. I'm an old woman and I've prayed that God would take me home before all this gets tore down."

Mazzie sat down on a wooden chair. Barney was enraged. "Y'see, that's what we're all mad about here in the hollow. They got no respect for nobody but themselves." He paused a moment, studying Billy, then went on. "Preacher, I done some checkin' on this here pipeline. You know how long that thing's gonna actually be used once they git it built?" He didn't wait for an answer. "Probably less than ten years. That's right. Them suits from Richmond think we too dumb to know what's going on. Well, we ain't. They's beatin' that gas outa rocks up someplace in Pennsylvania. How long ya think that'll go on? Some people sayin' it ain't worth all this trouble. They's jest after the money they can make in the short-term. Don't care a whit 'bout who they hurtin'."

Having spoken his mind, Barney left the porch and walked out toward the shed where they'd seen the old car. Cindy sensed how hard this was for Billy to suddenly run into so much emotion. She walked over and touched his arm. "Are you okay?"

Billy swallowed his shock with an inner prayer. *Lord, forgive us for the way we treat your creation. Heal these people. Show me how to be here for you.* Billy closed his eyes a moment, breathed deeply, then put his hand on Cindy's. "Thanks."

She squeezed his arm and stepped aside. Billy turned to Mazzie. "We probably need to go, but I want you to know I'll be back. It sounds shallow to say "trust God" in the midst of all this, but that is the answer. I know God is greater than even this burden." He looked up at Cindy, and then Flo, who had been standing in the background. "You're all in my prayers."

Turning to Mazzie he said, "Can I help you go back into the house?"

She had been staring blankly out across the landscape. When she turned to look at him her gaze softened. "I know you speak the truth. Trusting God is the way we've gotten this far. We ain't gonna stop now. The

Good Book says today's trouble is enough for today...to cast our burdens on the Lord."

Billy was moved. He saw into her soul where, instead of a beaten down old woman, he saw a strong person who found her help in her Lord. He offered a prayer, then asked her again if she needed help getting back inside.

"No," she said with a smile. "I'm just gonna sit out here for a while...just me 'n God."

Barney came back to the house, then the three of them got back into his truck and drove away. As they crossed the dry creek Billy said, "I want to thank y'all for bringing me here. I'd love to visit some more, but this is about all I can handle for one day. Just take me back up to the church and we can visit some more another time."

Back at the church Barney excused himself and drove off to run an errand in town. Before Cindy left she stood beside her truck with Billy for a few minutes. "I'm so glad we did this," she said. "We probably can't change the pipeline now, but I think God sent you here to help heal the wounds...and I believe you're up to it. Please, include me when you want to visit some more, okay?"

Billy felt an inner warmth. He and Cindy were connecting at a spiritual level he hadn't anticipated. He smiled, "Sure, wouldn't want it any other way."

They embraced briefly, then Cindy popped back into her blue truck and waved as she drove away. Billy went into the church and knelt at the altar. He felt God's presence as he put his face into his hands and throbbed with sobs of grief. Clearing his eyes and blowing his nose, he looked up at the bronze cross on the altar. "Lord Jesus, you died for the Mazzie's and Flo's of this world...and for the pipeline exploiters, too. Show me how to be your servant here."

Closing his eyes, he remained at the altar for a time, then got up, walked out of the church and drove home. He felt like a new person.

SIXTEEN

The Frog Hollow visits receded into the back of Billy's mind as he became engrossed in pastoral duties for the next few days. A week later it all came back into focus. Earlene Josef asked him to stop by her house on Friday afternoon. Poochie was in the yard when he arrived with her tail wagging, begging for attention. He leaned down and rubbed her neck as Earlene opened the door.

"That's enough, Pooch." As if it were an invitation, the dog scurried past her into the house. "Excuse her, she does this with everyone. You'd think nobody ever came around here. Come on in."

The day was cool and cloudy, forty-nine degrees with a chance of rain. Earlene had a fire going, and some papers laid out on the coffee table in the great room. "Do you mind if we talk in by the fire?"

Oh, that's great." Earlene took his coat and Billy stepped over to warm his hands at the fireplace.

Can I get you something? I made some coffee...or I have...."

"Coffee will be fine."

Cream and sugar?"

"Just a little cream."

He sat down in a chair placed diagonally to the couch as Earlene brought his coffee, then picked up a large paper from the coffee table and unfolded a map of Frog Hollow. Billy cocked his head to study it.

"I thought this might help you see where folks live...and how this pipeline project is affecting us." She paused. "I think I can explain this better if I put the map over on the table. Okay?"

Sure." Billy picked up his coffee cup and followed her. When she reopened the map, he was immediately fascinated by the work she had put into it, showing the contours of the ridges and ravine. She had drawn small numbered squares at various places indicating where people lived. Pointing to one of them she said, "Cindy told me y'all went to see Mazzie Plunket last week. This is her house."

"Really. It helps to see it on the map." He nodded as she pointed out several more places where church members lived. Her demeanor seemed to change from what he'd experienced previously. She was suddenly all business. Where she had sometimes slipped into the slang that was common to the area, she now used nearly perfect diction. Obviously, this was an educated woman with a variety of skills. A line drawn with a red marker began up on the same ridge where the church was located, then angled down through the woods to the Plunket farm. From the house it went down through the field, crossed the dry creek bed, then went through more trees to another house.

Earlene paused, "Now this is Mama Jean's place." The line continued through more wooded areas, skirted very close to several other homes, then off the edge of the paper. "I thought this might help you to see why the pipeline is such a threat to folks in the hollow."

Another green line began at the same point but stayed on the ridge crossing right through the church and cemetery. "This is where they were going to go at first. It was a much better route for them and us, except for one thing...it took out the church and we'd have to move the cemetery. That got everybody fired up."

Running parallel to the red and green lines on each side, a penciled area showed the width of the right-of-way and how it affected properties. "You see, Mazzie loses most all of her cleared land. Same thing with Mama Jean's house."

They had been leaning over the map, now she stepped back. "As you saw the other day, these people are too old to deal with stuff like this, and we just don't have the young people around to do it for them. Besides, how would an old woman like Miz Mazzie handle the stress of leaving everything she's ever known and settling into a strange new place...and then there's Flo. If I know Mazzie, what she'd do with that money from the property is get Flo into some kind of facility that can take care of her." She slapped the pencil she'd been holding onto the map. "It's an absolute mess."

Billy sensed the depth of her anger. "I see what you're saying. By the way, I noticed you referring to Mazzie Plunket as 'Miz Mazzie.' Is that another way of saying 'Mrs'?"

I think it started that way, but I don't know for sure. 'Miz' is like a nickname that just got tacked on over time."

"How old is she? I asked Barney and Cindy, but they said nobody seems to know."

"Cindy knows...she has helped me work with Mazzie's bookkeeping and taxes. She'll be 101 this July...she just doesn't like to broadcast her age." Earlene winked, "She doesn't like people 'fussin' over her,' as she says."

"Wow. I've never known anyone that old. Can't imagine the stress all of this puts on her."

"Well, it gets even more complicated with Mama Jean."

"So I've gathered. I've heard about her role in the community and how people consider her property to be a sacred place."

Earlene walked over to the large picture window overlooking the ridge. It had started to rain, casting a gloomy pall over the landscape. She turned around and faced Billy, throwing up her hands, palms open. She heaved a huge sigh. "I never thought I'd say this, but what hope is there? Soon they'll be moving heavy equipment in here, cutting trees and tearing down houses."

Her whole body shook as if to discard her dismal mood. "Sorry. This is not what I meant to do today. I just wanted you to know where we all are. We're invisible. We've protested. We've marched. We've presented facts, listened to what EverMore had to say, and argued for our own situation. It's all dragged out for so long, and for what? They got their approval. Why does God let this happen to good people?"

Silence filled the space for a long moment. Billy knew she wasn't asking to discuss the problem of evil. He gave her the space she needed.

Squinting her eyes, Earlene balled her hands into fists and squeezed them tightly, arms stiff at her side. *This is more than just her grief,* Billy realized. *She's carrying the load for everybody in the hollow...my people, the one's you gave me to serve, Lord.* He knew their burden was becoming his as well.

Earlene released her anxiety in a huge sigh, then they moved to the couch and sat down facing each other, hands joined. *How can I be a pastor to her? To this whole community?* He found words swelling from somewhere in his spirit. "I feel your pain, but I don't know the answer any more than you or anybody else. I do know God is greater than this problem, and *he* has an answer. Sometimes his answers seem to increase the pain of injustice, but in the long run, if we keep faith, God's answers prevail."

Earlene exhaled deeply again. "I know," she whispered, nodding her head and wiping her eyes. They prayed together, then Billy got up to leave. "May I take this map with me?"

"Yes. I made several of them for the protests. If it helps you, take it." She smiled. "Thanks for letting me vent a little."

Billy gave her a hug, took the map and left.

♦ ♦ ♦

Saturday morning he got up early and settled into his sermon preparation. After an hour he remembered he hadn't eaten breakfast. He went into the kitchen, fixed a bowl of cereal and some toast, then closed his eyes meditatively. Images from his conversation with Earlene floated before him. When he came home after visiting her he had left the map folded on a table in the study. He went back and fastened it onto a bulletin board where he kept a growing assortment of notes and reminders. That done, he settled back into the sermon. An hour later the phone rang.

Half absent-mindedly, he picked up the receiver. "Hello, this is Pastor Upshur."

"Billy...how are ya doin', Sonny? Your ma and me been wonderin' why we ain't heard nothin' from ya."

"Pop." Billy sat up straight. "I've been meanin' to call y'all, but every time I think about it, somethin' new comes up. So, are y'all doin' okay?"

"We squeakin' around about like a coupla rusty old folks oughta. Sounds like ya got yer hands full. Tell me what's goin' on."

Billy went through the whole scenario about getting past the congregation's reactivity from the weekend when he went missing, Teachie's funeral, and his visit with Mazzie Plunket. "I haven't met up with those guys who ambushed me, but I will. Cindy says its best to lay some groundwork...get myself accepted...and they'll likely come to me."

"Who's Cindy?"

"Oh, she's a member at Frog Hollow Church. Sorry, I didn't mean to mention names. She's a nurse in town who lives on Josef Lane. She and a guy name Barney Giles have been introducing me to people."

"Hmm. Sounds like a smart woman. You say she's a nurse?"

"Yeah, at the clinic in town, and she grew up in the hollow. Knows all about everybody, and Barney's a retired guy who's kinda rough in his ways, but he does a lot for people."

"Sounds like a good guy. Hang on a minute, yer ma wants to say a word or two." Billy heard Clint fill Lottie in on the conversation, then she came on the phone. "Hi, honey, how are you doin' over there. Gettin' enough to eat?"

Billy laughed. "Probably not, but I'm surviving. Sometimes I go to the diner for supper. I'm okay. It's good to hear your voice."

They talked a few minutes then Lottie handed the phone back to Clint. "Sonny, are you gettin' along okay with that Wrangler?"

"Oh, yeah. Hey, I'd like to hang onto it for a while. It's much better suited around here than the Honda."

"Thought it would be. Like I told ya, it's okay with me if we jest swap. When you comin' back to visit? We can do the paperwork then. Lottie loves that little Civic."

"Pray for us, Pop...you and the folks in your church. This is a really hot situation with the pipeline. Before I came here I thought it was probably a good idea, you know, making clean fuel available to more people, but now I see the cost to people when their property is taken over. It's not just them, but their whole heritage that gets blown away. I'm trying to visit as many of them as possible as quickly as I can."

"So, tell me more about this woman y'all visited t'other week."

Billy described Mazzie and her history—and Flo—the whole story. Clint took it all in, then offered a thought. "It ain't up to me to say nothin', but I jest had a thought. What ya need to do is get some publicity out, tell the 'people stories' from there in the hollow, help people to feel what you're feelin' now. Do ya follow me?"

"You mean like gettin' on the news or something? Thanks for the idea...I don't know if that would mean anything at this point, but I'll share the idea with some of the folks."

"Sounds like them boys that attacked you was feelin' desperate, like they's all madder 'n a nest o' hornets. Trouble is, that don't cause nothin' but more trouble and resentment. Y'all need to get past that hurdle."

Billy scribbled down some ideas as Clint talked. "Yeah, I gotcha."

"Sounds like that woman who's workin' with ya...what's her name again...."

"Oh...Cindy."

"Yeah. Sounds like she'd understand exactly what I'm talkin' about and probably knows who to talk to t' git it done. You say she's lived there a long time?"

"Yes, all her life as far as I know...but she's a younger woman, about my age actually. There are some others who are older that I believe might take to this idea." Billy paused. "Say, why don't you and ma come on over here and spend a few days. I've got room for you right here at the house...and tell ma I sure could stand some of her good cookin'."

"Ya mean Cindy ain't cooked nothin' fer ya yet?"

"Cindy? Why should she? Oh, you think she might be interested in me more than just being her pastor."

Clint didn't answer the question. "Good idea about visitin'. We could use a getaway trip. I'll git back to ya about that. Meanwhile, ya jest keep on prayin' and pastorin' them folks. God'll show ya the way."

When he hung up Billy got lost for a few minutes thinking about Cindy and how he felt about her. *She's different than anybody I ever knew...and pretty, too. We do seem to hit it off fairly well. Lord don't let me go chasin' a rabbit here. I want to keep focused on what's important.*

Checking the clock, he realized he'd better get back on task if he was going to be ready for Sunday. He tried to clear his mind as he settled into his sermon preparation. Sometimes, though, Cindy's voice floated into his consciousness. He finished the sermon and prayed before going to sleep...*Lord, are you tellin' me Cindy is part of what's important?*

SEVENTEEN

Monday morning Billy was eager to get back into Frog Hollow. His Sunday services had gone well. Attendance was good, and people were generally upbeat. This concerned him a little...with all the tension in the background it would be easy for them to expect too much from him. *Suppose they start relying on me to fight the pipeline, just like they have with the Frog Hollow Boys?* He shivered at the thought.

Cindy came to mind and he called her cell. *Maybe I should talk to her before we go there tomorrow.* He left a message. "Good morning, Cindy, this is Billy. I've been thinking about our plan to visit in the hollow tomorrow. Would you have a few minutes to talk about that sometime today? Please, give me a call."

Remembering that the Wrangler was due for an oil change, he decided this was a good time to take care of it. *Everybody says Coop's Pit Stop is the place to go. Guess I'll give 'em a try...wonder if I have to make an appointment? Nah, that's big city stuff.* He decided to just go in and take his chances.

The old cottage style station and general store looked busy as he drove up. He filled his gas tank, paid for it at the pump, then went inside and looked around. To his left was a self-service snack area where several people were standing in line to pay for their purchases. A teenage clerk manned the register. To his right was an expanded retail area with an old-time stove surrounded by several unoccupied chairs. In a corner among merchandise display racks two men were engaged in an animated conversation. Their voices were audible, but he couldn't make out the words.

He stepped up to the main checkout counter in front of a wall filled with racks of cigarettes, chewing tobacco, and e-cigarettes. There was an array of lottery ticket dispensers next to the cash register. A middle-aged female clerk wearing a bored expression said, "Can I help you?"

"Yes, I need an oil change. How much is it?"

"$46.98."

"Can you do it while I wait?"

"Let me check." She went to a side door and hollered to the mechanic, "You got time to do another one?" She returned. "Mike's finishin' one now, so you're next. What kind of car is it?"

"A 2010 Jeep Wrangler."

"Synthetic or conventional oil?"

"Conventional." He handed her his keys as she scribbled a note for the mechanic. "Be ready in about 25 minutes."

Billy went back to the snack area, bought a cup of coffee, then wandered around getting the feel of the place. The two men he'd seen talking broke up their conversation with a guffaw of laughter. The man who'd been facing away from him slapped the other on the back. "That'll be the day!" he said loudly. Billy recognized him as the owner, Bunk Cooper. Cam Bordain had introduced him to Bunk a few weeks ago.

"Bunk probably knows more about this whole area than anybody in town," he had said. "You need somethin', you see Bunk."

Recognizing Billy, Bunk introduced him to the other man. "This is our new preacher in town, Pastor Billy Upshur."

"Clay Grainger," said the man. "So, how long ya been in Strong's Creek?"

Before Billy could answer Bunk said, "Clay's the guy who built that new development outside of town, toward the creek. A lot of farm land's just sittin' idle nowadays since the big feed and seed companies took over farming. At the same time lots of folks up in Northern Virginia are retirin' and lookin' for places to resettle. Clay's tryin' to help 'em out, but this danged pipeline's causin' problems."

Bunk caught himself. "Oh, I forgot you worked for EverMore Energy...."

Clay gave him a strange look and seemed to retreat from his open friendliness. "Used to work there," said Billy, explaining that he hadn't had anything to do with the pipeline. He wasn't sure Clay believed him.

"Well, they sure are messin' me up," said Clay with a touch of anger. "I got this nice two-hundred-acre plot I'm developing over across the creek with exclusive five-acre plats...and that danged thing's gonna cut out nearly a third of my land with its hundred-twenty-five-foot right-of-way."

"How far along are you?"

"We're well into it... got streets laid out, done with most of the clearing and grading, got sewer, water and power service in—and we're almost finished with the first five houses." He clicked off each item with his fingers as he spoke. "Probably gonna have to scale everything back, maybe put in some townhomes."

The three men talked a little longer, then Clay left. "Didn't mean to hold you up," said Bunk.

"Oh, no problem. I'm just waitin' around while your guy changes my oil."

Bunk smiled and motioned toward a door. "Well, in that case, why don't you come back to my office and talk a bit."

Billy accepted the invitation. Bunk sat behind an aging gray metal desk and motioned for him to sit in one of two rustic arm chairs that had seen better days. He had a desktop computer, a phone and a stack of papers in disarray on the desk. His chair squeaked as he leaned back, folded his hands under his chin and looked at Billy.

"Heard you met Miz Mazzie up in the hollow."

Billy nodded, surprised. "How'd you hear about that?"

"Oh, people come in here talkin' about all kinds of stuff. What did you think of her?

"I think she's a remarkable woman. I wonder how she'll manage if she has to move out of her house. The folks up at Frog Hollow Church are doing a good job keeping in touch with her and I'm sure they'll help."

"They likely will but there's a little more to the story. Comin' outa Richmond and havin' worked for EverMore, I'm sure you know this pipeline's a done deal. They ain't gonna do no more negotiatin'—and they don't really care about what happens to folks like Miz Mazzie."

What's goin' on here? Billy studied the floor a moment, then said, "Buck, I appreciate what I think you're trying to tell me—I've walked into a volatile situation I may not be ready for. And you're right up to a point. Until I was sent here I'd sort of ignored the pipeline fray. It just seemed like a political power game."

He paused, gauging Bunk's response, then went on. "What I saw in Miz Mazzie...and the Frog Hollow Boys when they ambushed me...is the resilience of people in a small community who just want to live their lives. They're down to earth folks. Natural gas, global warming...that all belongs to another world. They just want to be left alone, but that other world's moving in on them, like an invasion. People are mad, and they're not finished fighting the system. Don't tell them there's no more negotiating."

Bunk grinned. "Okay. You're pretty astute. I didn't mean to butt in where I ain't needed or wanted." He stood up and extended his hand. "You're a young guy, and I just didn't want to see you get blind-sided up there."

Billy stood and shook his hand. "Already happened...but I appreciate your thoughts. Guess I'd better check on my car."

Bunk walked him out to the counter. "Has Mike finished the preacher's oil change yet?"

"Yes, sir. Car's out front," said the clerk as she handed Billy the bill.

Bunk reached over and took it from him. "First time here, it's on me. No charge...now next time's another story." He laughed.

Billy was caught off guard but recovered quickly. Clint's words came to mind, *Don't try to play humble and refuse a gift when it's offered...lessen they's strings attached, of course. It can be just as important to receive as it is to give.*

"Well, thanks! I'll return the favor sometime. I enjoyed our conversation."

He went out and got into his car with a warm feeling inside. *God is good. Thank you, Lord.*

◆ ◆ ◆

Back at the house he checked the mailbox and found a letter from Fletch Waverley. *Oh, yeah, he wanted me to send him reports and I forgot all about that.* He fixed a sandwich, then sat down at the table and opened the envelope. The letter was on stationary that proclaimed, "Alleghany District, The Wesleyan Brethren Church." Fletch wasted no time. "William, I'm expecting a report from you as you move into your second month at Strong's Creek Circuit." He listed the things he wanted to know...how many people were attending, what the mood of the people was and how he'd handled their anger at his missed Sunday. Billy read through several more items, then put the letter down and closed his eyes.

The tone was brusque, as was Fletch, but not threatening. *I hadn't thought about keeping all those numbers. I'll bet Earlene and Carrie can help me pull that together. Easter is just a couple of weeks away, so that should at least make the numbers look better.* He took the letter into his office and put it on the desk as the phone rang. He recognized the pleasant voice on the other end.

"Hi, Billy. I got your message. Hope you haven't been waiting around to hear from me."

"Cindy, glad you called. I've been over at Coop's getting my oil changed. Just came in for lunch."

He heard voices in the background. "Look, we're really busy here today. I've just got a minute...what did you want to talk about?"

"Listen, it's nothing that can't wait. Just wanted to think ahead with you before our visit to the hollow tomorrow."

"I think that's a good idea. Look, I've got to go. Would you have time to talk when I get off...hey, maybe we could meet at the Valley Farmer's Kitchen for supper. It's just around the corner from the clinic. Have you been there yet?"

"No, I haven't, but I know where it is. What time?"

"I get off at seven, is that too late for you?"

"Seven it is. See you then...and thanks for calling back."

The Valley Farmer's Kitchen was a popular restaurant that billed itself as offering the county's best down-home meals. It was a large room with pictures of farm scenes on the wall interspersed with nostalgic farming paraphernalia. Billy arrived a little early and was seated by a hostess who handed him a menu. "I'm expecting a friend in a few minutes. Could I have another menu."

She handed it to him and walked away. Billy gazed around the room deciding he liked the ambience. *If the food's as good as the atmosphere, I'll have to come here again. Could get to be a habit.* He began looking through the menu when Cindy arrived.

"Hi! Hope you haven't been waiting too long."

He got up and helped her with the jacket she'd worn against the evening chill. She looked fresh despite having worked a long day. A waitress arrived to take their drink orders. They both laughed after responding at the same time, "Water, please."

"So, tell me about your day. I've always wondered what it was like to work in an urgent care clinic. I imagine it's a lot like an emergency room."

She smiled. "There's nothing glamorous about it, and it can be exhausting—a constant flow of patients and their needs." She opened her purse and pulled out a small mirror. "I'll bet I look like a wreck."

"Not to me. I think you look great."

"Thanks." She put on some fresh lipstick, then closed her purse, flashing him a smile. "Now, tell me about *your* day...I've always wondered what preacher's do between Sundays."

He laughed. "Oh, you can't pull that one on me. You already went with me on one of those days *between Sundays.*" They both laughed. He told her about the conversation with Bunk Cooper, and Dr. Waverley's letter. He was so taken with her that he forgot about the conversation with Clint. "I started out this morning thinking about tomorrow, then stuff just happened, and I never got back to it."

The waitress brought their drinks and took their orders. "So, tell me more about yourself," said Billy. "I know you're from the hollow—and you're a nurse—and people think the world of you."

She looked aside as if to wave the comment away, then became more serious. "Well, I left Strong's Creek for a few years after high school. I got married and moved to Fayetteville, North Carolina." Raising her eyes to engage Billy, she went on. "It only took a few weeks to realize what a huge mistake I'd made. We had almost nothing in common, and he was demanding, sometimes abusive. Within a year we separated, and then got divorced. For a long time I blamed myself for not sticking it out."

"I know how that is," said Billy. Cindy cocked her head to the side with an inquisitive expression in her eyes. He went on, "There was this really attractive single girl in the office where I worked who was playful with everybody. She and I seemed to hit it off and dated a few times. Things got serious very quickly and after a few months we got married. Almost from the start it was clear to each of us that we had no idea who the other person really was. We were not well matched."

Billy paused. He saw compassionate interest in her eyes. He told about the religious retreat he'd attended and his call to the ministry. "I hoped she could understand, but she got vindictive. After a few more months, as I continued my preparations for the ministry, we decided we might be married on a piece of paper, but we certainly weren't in spirit. So, we split up. The divorce was final last year."

Their food arrived and as they ate they continued to talk. "I have felt there was something incomplete or mysterious about you from the first moment I met you at Aunt Earlene's. Thanks for telling me what that was about."

Cindy did not seem judgmental as he'd feared. He wanted to know more about her. "Okay, I've told you my story, now it's your turn to fill me in a little more. Why did you choose to become a nurse?"

"That was Aunt Earlene's doing. When my marriage failed I came back to the hollow. Uncle Ernie was beginning to have heart failure then...he died of a heart attack five years ago. He had some other issues, too, and sometimes I helped her care for him. She encouraged me to look into nursing, so I did...studied at VCU in Richmond, and got my RN. A few years ago this job opened up in Strong's Creek and I moved back. With Earlene's help I bought the house on Josef Lane." She shot him a perky smile. "So, here I am."

"And I'm glad."

"Tell me, what did Bunk have to say?"

Billy went over the conversation. "I think what we're doing, visiting the people whose lives are threatened by this pipeline, is essential. I'm forming my own opinion about the pipeline, but my purpose is not to take sides. The pipeline has rattled peoples' sense of well-being and I feel God sent me here to help people through whatever comes next. I think my ministry is to go through this with them—to bond with them."

Cindy had been watching him intently as he talked. They were both thoughtful for a few minutes while they ate. Billy went on, "I see the stress affecting people. There's so much hatred that's been built up by some people, like the Frog Hollow Boys."

Cindy shuddered. "It's gotten to be all about fighting, instead of building each other up. I know they're gonna keep on protesting. What bothers me is, what can be gained by that now? I sometimes feel like we're right on the edge of some kind of disaster."

Billy nodded. "I've only been here a few weeks, and I see that same thing." He chuckled, remembering the ambush on Frog Hollow Road. "In fact, I got hit square between the eyes with own 'disaster' my first day here...but I got over it. In fact, I've grown through the experience."

Cindy reached across the table and touched his hand. "I'm so sorry that happened to you. I have prayed for you, and I admire how you're handling things."

She pulled her hand back. The emotion in her words embraced Billy's spirit. "Well, tomorrow you can help me take the next step. Who should we visit?"

They spent the rest of supper talking about different people in the hollow and their circumstances. When the waitress brought the check, Billy reached for his wallet.

"No, I'm paying for this," said Cindy. "It was my idea to come here." For the second time in a single day he recalled Clint's words about accepting unexpected gifts.

"I know you did, but I don't mind paying for both of us...just from friendship." He looked at her appealingly.

"Well, let's each pay for our own meal this time...maybe we'll do this again and we can do it differently...okay?"

"Okay...but I'll leave the tip."

"Touché."

The air was chilly as they walked to their cars. "See you at church at ten," said Billy. "Thanks for your time." They embraced, then backed away. Billy drove home with a light-hearted sense of joy he hadn't known for a long time.

EIGHTEEN

Billy arrived at Frog Hollow Church early the next morning, got out of the jeep and began strolling through the cemetery, studying family names and dates on tombstones. He wanted to get a sense of the people who had settled in this remote place. Soon he came across the Josef family plot where a headstone bore the dates of Ernest's birth and death. Earlene's name was inscribed next to his with her birth date only. The stone was newer than most of those around it, featuring a carved cross and open Bible encircled by an olive wreath. Beneath it was an inscription, *"Blessed are the peacemakers, for they will be called children of God."* Billy mumbled to himself, "I'd sure like to know more about this family."

Nearby he found the Plunket plot with headstones dating to the late nineteenth century, many of them weather worn and nearly illegible. *Wow, I know that old house doesn't go back that far...I wonder if it was built around the first log cabin? What a history.* A gravestone bore the name of Mazzie, and her husband. In front of the plot were stones commemorating the son and daughter she had lost. Billy's heart felt heavy with the burdens this woman had borne, yet he felt lifted by the strength she exhibited. He noticed an inscription under her name, which bore no date of death yet. It read, *"They shall mount up with wings like eagles, they shall run and not be weary."*

Billy knew the quote came from Isaiah 40:31. It seemed to express what he'd already sensed when he'd visited Miz Mazzie. There were many more grave sites he hadn't seen. He closed his eyes to take in the energy he felt was present. A gust of wind rustled leaves in the trees, and he sensed a reassuring whisper of God's Spirit. This was a sanctuary that existed above and beyond the throes and woes of life at any given time. He felt strength and peace.

"Hey, whatcha doin'?" Billy snapped into reality at the sound of Cindy's voice. "Didn't think I'd find you in the cemetery."

Billy turned to see her walking toward him. She had on a medium weight jacket, black slacks, and wore a colorful scarf around her neck. Her bright blue eyes captured his full attention as she brushed away some strands of hair the wind had swept into her face. Her appearance complemented the late March sun as it chased away morning clouds, promising a pleasant warming trend.

"Just talking to the saints. It seemed like a good thing to do since I'm new around here."

"I didn't know anybody else did that."

Her reply surprised him. "Really—you do that?"

"I have, a couple of times."

"Well, this is my first time...I never even thought about doing it before." He gestured toward the cemetery. "I'll never remember all those names, but I saw a few I recognized...including the Plunkets."

Cindy nodded that she understood as they walked toward the cars. "Did Barney call you?" she asked.

"No. Is he not coming?"

"He said he tried to reach you...he'd forgotten Myrtle had an allergist appointment today. She suffers from asthma, especially at this time of year. He apologized."

"Do you know when they'll be back home? I'd like to look in on them."

"I'm not sure...you might want to call him later. I'll show you where he lives."

"Thanks." A moment of caution flashed through his mind. "Maybe we should call this off until Barney can join us."

Cindy stopped in her tracks and looked at him quizzically, reading his thoughts. "Are you uncomfortable with just the two of us doing this today."

"I wouldn't say I'm uncomfortable, but I've already been the subject of gossip. I don't want to stir up any more."

She nodded. "Small towns...and hollows...*are* known for that."

"So are big cities." He winked, "I think we can trust each other to behave."

She laughed. "Enough said."

"Let's take my jeep. If I drive, I'll remember the way better. Oh, and your aunt gave me a map that shows where people live and where the pipeline is coming through."

"That's Aunt Earlene. As you've found out, she's very organized." She climbed into the front seat, buckled in and produced a small notepad. "I jotted down a few notes from our conversation last night. I know you mentioned Mama Jean—so, let's visit her first."

Billy reached into the back seat and pulled the folded map from a backpack. "Here's her house," he said, unfolding it and pointing to a note Earlene had made. "Is she still living in this house?"

"She stays with some of her tribe at night, but she's been at her house during the day. There might be some people there...if we see cars we'll just leave and come back another time. Okay?"

"Whatever you say. I'm following your lead."

They drove down into the ravine and headed up between the ridges where Cindy pointed out a few landmarks. It was heavily forested for about half-a-mile, then they entered a cleared space with rolling hills and limestone outcroppings. He noticed a purple house with a yellow roof ahead and to the right. Pointing toward it he said, "Never seen anything like that before. Who lives there?"

Cindy laughed, "That's where we're going. That's Mama Jean's house...and there aren't any cars so she's probably alone."

Billy turned onto a rough, overgrown path that led right up to the house. He could see tracks where vehicles had recently been there. He turned off the ignition. "Tell me about this place...why the purple and yellow paint?"

"Mama Jean says the colors are for royalty and spirituality. She started using this color scheme when she became a Christian several years ago. Her faith is kind of rolled in with her native chants, stories and practices. I don't know where she got the idea, but she says when you put these two colors together, all of God's Light is present. That's all I know, except Waya and some of the other Cherokee guys keep the place up."

Billy was taken aback by the whole scene before him. The house had a back porch that he guessed opened out from the kitchen. A small table and a single green rocking chair sat there. Cindy gestured toward it, "She'll be setting out potted plants and tending her roses and lilies this spring. She often sits out there during the summer days."

"What strikes me is there's none of the usual stuff, like old boards, buckets or boxes sitting around in the yard and on the porches."

Cindy pointed to two unpainted utility buildings set in among some cedars behind the house. "Mama Jean teaches that cleanliness is next to godliness, and she makes sure the guys who help her keep everything neat."

He saw that one of the buildings looked like an outhouse. "I guess she doesn't have indoor plumbing."

"Actually, she does. The outhouse is for the boys to use when they're working here. As far as I know, she doesn't have any monetary income. The Frog Hollow folks keep her supplied with everything she needs. In return, she is their nurse, counselor, soothsayer, and so forth. That's why losing this particular house is so personal to people."

They got out of the Wrangler and walked toward the building. "Which door?" asked Billy."

"Front. Back door's only for family, which is everybody in the hollow. I could go to the back door, but you're a stranger, so we'll go this way."

Billy gave the porch an uncertain look. The roof lacked several support columns and sagged in the center. The floor wasn't much better, and the whole front of the structure seemed to be supported by two heavy plywood panels wedged up against it. There was a set of steps that looked fairly new, but no railings. Billy hesitated.

"It's safe," said Cindy. "The boys have been rebuilding the porch."

She led the way. Billy noticed the floor boards creaked when he stepped on them, but then he remembered so had Miz Mazzie's. *Situation normal,* he thought. To the right of the door hung a wooden hoop about a foot in diameter with webbing that narrowed to a hole in the center. Caught in the webbing he noticed a small stone. On each side of the hoop and at the bottom feathers were attached. Cindy said it was called a dream catcher.

She knocked on the door. "Mama Jean, it's Cindy Barker."

"Come on in," said a strong but thin voice from inside. Cindy opened the door and announced, "Mama Jean, I brought somebody for you to meet."

Stepping inside Billy discovered a room with tapestries hanging on the walls, rustic furnishings, and rugs both braided and bear skin stretched across the floor. A fireplace glowed with embers from its morning warming task. The hearth was flag stone, and there were two dream catchers hanging, one on each side of the mantle with its array of candles. Overhead a rustic chandelier provided light for the room. Mama Jean sat in a rocking chair similar to the one on the back porch with a quilt over her lap and legs. Her white hair was brushed straight back into a pony tail anchored by a piece of leather with a dowel through it. Wire rim glasses sat on her nose. Several books, including a Bible, were gathered on an end table. She had a prominent nose and chin, and her dark eyes seemed to penetrate Billy's very soul.

"This is our new preacher up at the church, Mama Jean. I'm helpin' him get acquainted with folks."

Cindy sat down on a chair while Billy remained standing. Mama Jean said something he couldn't understand, then closed her eyes and chanted with a clear, lilting voice. Although he couldn't decipher her words, he felt the power of her spiritual presence. Billy closed his eyes as tears welled up from somewhere deep inside. He felt himself tremble.

Suddenly Mama Jean chanted in English. "We lift our hearts to you, O Creator God of our ancestors. Great are you in the sun, moon and stars. The rain brings your tears and the sun your power. Humble us before you, Living God, align our spirits with yours and sow good seeds in our hearts. Thank you for the stranger you have sent. May his spirit please you."

Billy dropped to his knees and lifted his arms. "Thank you, Lord, for your love that calls us into your Spirit. In the name of Christ, I praise you. Bless this house and she who serves you within it. Amen."

He opened his eyes and looked into Mama Jean's still firm, but softer, countenance. She reached her hand toward him. "Welcome to my house. I sense strength and goodness in your soul."

Billy moved to a chair. "I've heard good things about you, Mama Jean, and now I see they are true."

"You have come with concern for me. I want to give you concern for those who would harm us and others in their worship of money and power."

"I've been meeting some wonderful people here in the hollow. My heart is saddened that so much pain and loss is falling on you all. God has sent me to share this journey with you. I have no idea where we're all headed, but I know God is in it." He asked to read from her Bible and she handed it to him. He thumbed through to Jeremiah 29 where he read several verses, ending with verse seven. *'But seek the welfare of the city where I have sent you into exile, and pray to the Lord on its behalf, for in its welfare you will find your own welfare.'* Mama Jean, I believe these words are sent from God for just such a time as we are facing now. We may suffer, but God's plan is good, and he will never forsake us."

Billy offered a prayer, then noticed Mama Jean seemed weary. "Are you okay?"

She said softly, "I tire quickly. Thank you for your visit. When you come back please use the back door."

"Can I get something for you," asked Cindy.

"I am fine. My friend Twila will be here soon. God will take care of me. Go and be blessed."

She lifted her voice in a Cherokee chant as they left the house. Driving away Billy said, "That is one of the most spiritual experiences I've ever had. I can see why the Frog Hollow Boys are so stirred up. This pipeline isn't about money or property nearly as much as it is about casting aside the rich heritage people in this hollow share. I've heard all about the endangered wildlife and water contamination that people are concerned about. I never heard anyone really talk about the people."

He looked at Cindy, who had a pensive expression. "I almost forgot...my dad called the other day and he had an idea that now makes a lot of sense to me"

She looked at him. "What kind of an idea?"

Billy told her briefly about Clint's publicity suggestion. "I don't know how anything can make a difference now with the pipeline approved and work starting. Still, Mama Jean and Miz Mazzie both made me want to explore this."

They arrived back at church and Billy turned off the engine, then turned to face Cindy. "I'd really like to talk to you about this some more...are you game?"

"Absolutely. When did you have in mind?"

"Oh, I just thought...Easter's a couple of weeks away. Maybe I'll be too busy to deal with that for a while. That's something else I wanted to ask you about—the traditions here at Frog Hollow for Palm Sunday, Holy Week and Easter."

"I can't help you there. Aunt Earlene can...and so can Holly Jinks. Sometimes the two churches do some stuff together for special occasions."

They got out of the Wrangler and he walked with her to the truck where they paused. Billy felt self-conscious. He found himself liking Cindy more all the time. He liked who he was when they were together, a sort of completeness he'd never really known before. It certainly hadn't been that way in his brief marriage.

They faced each other and joined hands. Billy stumbled for words. "I, uh, I don't want to come on too strong, but I really like being with you, Cindy." The look in her eyes expressed her feelings before she said a word.

"Me, too...I mean that. I want to spend more time with you. Do you ever eat at Panera Bread? They have one in Peakview and, well, I go in to work late tomorrow so I have some morning errands to run. Would you like to meet there for breakfast...do you have time?"

They spontaneously embraced. "Absolutely...when?"

"Nine o'clock too early?"

"I'll be there."

Suddenly they kissed. As they pulled apart Cindy put her hand to her mouth and laughed. "I'll bet Aunt Earlene's standing up there looking down here and laughing her head off at us." She got into her truck and threw him a kiss, then drove away.

NINETEEN

Billy and Cindy's visit to Mama Jean did not go unnoticed. Waya had been on his way to check on her when he saw Billy's Wrangler parked at the house. He continued up the road around a curve, then parked and walked back through the woods. His uncanny ability to move undetected allowed him to slip in through the back door and stand inside a broom closet, listening. Out of respect for Mama Jean, he didn't want to step into the room unless he sensed she was in danger. Seething anger quickly morphed into confusion as he overheard the prayers and conversation. He was baffled. Not only did Upshur seem to be making a routine pastoral visit, but it sounded like he was against the pipeline. It had to be a scheme.

When he heard Billy drive off, Waya went into the room, startling Mama Jean. "What you doin' here? You move so quiet, I didn't know you was in the house."

"Been here, Mama Jean. Been listenin' to them two. Don't you trust that man. He's one of them EverMore people plannin' to knock down this house."

"Oh, nonsense," said Mama Jean dismissively. "I sensed a genuine spirit in him. He says God called him to be here. He ain't like that other preacher who didn't want to talk about what he called *worldly* things...like the pipeline. I know y'all are tryin' to protect all of us here in the hollow, but we don't need to be protected from him."

"So, he didn't tell you he worked for them EverMore scoundrels?"

"Didn't have to...I already knew that—and don't you call 'em scoundrels. I've heard all them rumors about him, but the Spirit of the Lord says they ain't true. If God wants a pipeline right where this house is sittin', then he's gonna git a pipeline. I don't think pipelines are God's main business anyhow. Be better for all of us if you'n your buddies would jest stop all this protestin' and set y'selves to makin' the best of whatever is."

Waya decided to give up with her. "Anything I can do fer ya before I leave?"

"Come over here and let me pray over ya. Twila's comin' round in a bit and she'll take care of anything I need." Twila was a neighbor woman who had made it her business to check on the old woman and help her with housework, or whatever else she needed.

Waya feared Mama Jean's spiritual power. He'd seen her turn out to be right when everybody around her was off on something that turned out to be wrong. He'd seen her pray over sick people, and they got well. She'd prayed for hopeless things to change, and they did. Sometimes she'd also prayed for her own people to step aside or get a different attitude...and they had done it. He liked who he was and how he lived, and he tried not to have her pray over him too much for fear he'd lose control. At the same time, she was the best thing Frog Hollow had going for it.

He thought back a few years to the tribal ceremonial event he'd attended in North Carolina. Small clans like theirs in Frog Hollow didn't hold such elaborate ceremonies. He pictured the pit fire that was tended so it burned all day and into the night. He could still feel the energy created by the Stomp Dance with shell shakers dancing, creating rhythm with leg rattles made from turtle shells filled with pebbles. Whenever Mama Jean spoke he remembered the sermons the elders and Medicine Men preached all day and into the night calling them to a love that embraced the earth and all its creatures, and all mankind. He had gone to the water for cleansing and smoked the pipe. It had all been done in the Cherokee language and when Mama Jean sang her chants he felt that power return. He also knew with shame how far short of his people's values and beliefs he fell in his own life.

Waya got on his knees, which was something he never did for anybody, and Mama Jean chanted a song of grief over him. When she was finished he walked silently away.

◆ ◆ ◆

On Thursday evening Billy met several key leaders from both congregations at Main Street Church to plan the Palm Sunday and Easter services, and to go over the statistical reports Fletch Waverley had requested. Carrie Glossner said she would have the figures for Main Street on the Monday after Easter. Earlene offered to do the same for Frog Hollow. Billy went over his thoughts for the services and the group helped structure the music and other details. As they finished, Grant brought up another topic. "I heard you've been visitin' some folks up in the hollow, preacher. I wonder if you could share some of your thoughts or impressions while we're all together?"

Billy noticed the question seemed to take everyone by surprise. He paused a moment before responding. "I'm glad you brought that up, Grant. I guess the answer is that I see the situation up there in a more personal sense, if you follow me. Visiting Miz Mazzie and Mama Jean, getting to know Barney & Cindy, seeing the people and property involved has been helpful. I can see the injustice of this. For those who are affected, it's as if a living, breathing monster is closing in on them."

He paused to see how people were taking his words, but facial expressions revealed nothing. He went on, "I see a lot of strength, physically and spiritually, among the people we've visited. I believe God has put me here to help people find a way through something none of us can fully grasp or ultimately control."

Grant rubbed his chin thoughtfully. "There are some who aren't taking it in stride...fighting to the last breath, so to speak."

"Yes, there are. As you know, I ran smack into that bunch when I first arrived. But, that will change, if we don't play into it. Frog Hollow Church can be instrumental in finding a healthy outcome for everyone."

Earlene spoke up. "Some of us have been trying not to, as you say, play into it. The biggest problem is the Frog Hollow Boys. They think they're doin' the right thing, but I think they're really making things worse."

"Well, I have a different concern," said Carrie as everyone shifted their attention to her. "I hear what you're sayin', and it sounds good, but I'm afraid it could be divisive in our churches. I mean, it sounds like a major part of your time's gonna be spent in the hollow, while we've got a large congregation at Main Street that needs pastoral attention, too. How are you gonna balance all of this?"

"Honestly, I don't know, but I'm working on that." Carrie looked shocked. Billy went on, "What I do know is I've been praying for God's guidance, and I'd like y'all to do that, too."

"Well, sure, we'll do that," said Carrie while glancing toward the others, who nodded agreement.

"Since the two churches are linked together as one pastoral charge, I'm sure things will balance out...." A thought suddenly struck Billy. "I just had an idea. You said neither church does a sunrise service at Easter..."

"That's right," interrupted Earlene. "As we said earlier, everybody goes to the community service at the high school."

"Well, I have an idea. Why don't we break that habit this year and hold a Strong's Creek Circuit Sunrise Service up at the Frog Hollow Cemetery?"

Carrie waved dismissively. "Oh, we tried that a few years ago, but the only ones who came were the Frog Hollow people."

"Wait," said Holly. "I kinda like this idea. We've been working on a medley of Easter songs with our Main Street choir...I can rearrange things a bit and have the choir sing for that service as well...and I can bring the keyboard up there. This way we'd be involving people from both congregations...."

"But that takes electricity, which y'all don't have at the cemetery, right?" said Carrie.

"Oh, that's no problem...we've got some long extension cords. We'll get power from the church," said Earlene. "And, we can fix a big breakfast afterward." She looked pleased with herself for the idea. "What do y'all think?"

"Well, I like it," said Grant. "Instead of focusing on the bad news up in the hollow, we can focus on the Good News of Christ right here in the heart of the issue."

The group came alive with enthusiasm, then Carrie expressed another concern. "What if it rains? We'd have to go inside, and you can't fit our choir and a lot of extra people in that little church."

Without hesitation Grant said, "If it rains we'll just hold it here at Main Street."

"Since we don't have a full kitchen," said Earlene, "We'll fix breakfast dishes at home and bring them in. We can just change to Main Street. I think this is a great, fresh idea."

Carrie sighed. "I guess you're right—that doesn't need to be a problem. I guess we should do it."

With the issue settled, the meeting adjourned. Billy went back to the house feeling good. *Thank you, Lord. I pray that this will be a time of faith revival.*

♦ ♦ ♦

The phone was ringing when he stepped in the door back at the house. It was Clint. "Is that invitation to visit you still good, Sonny?"

"It sure is!" Billy was excited. "Y'all fixin' to take me up on it?"

Lottie answered, "We sure are. We haven't been on a trip anyplace for quite a spell. Now I want ya to tell me if this is too much for ya...we'd like to come for Easter. I know you'll have a lot to do that day, but we'll come Saturday mornin' an I'll do some cookin' and maybe help ya out around the house so's you can get yer work done."

"Well, that's fantastic. It will be a busy time. We're planning a sunrise service up at Frog Hollow Church."

"No problem. We're used to that."

"I know you are. Gosh, this is great. What time do you think you'll get here on Saturday?"

Clint came back on the phone. "I'd say we'll be there by ten o'clock. That okay with you?"

"Perfect."

He called Cindy when she got home from work. "I've got some exciting news."

"Don't tell me...they called off the pipeline project."

Billy laughed. "I wish. No...you remember that meeting I told you I had tonight? Well, they decided to do an Easter Sunrise Service on the cemetery grounds at Frog Hollow."

"You're kidding. That is good news, if you can get the Main Street folks there."

"Got that covered." He went on to explain the details, then told her about Clint and Lottie's visit. "I want you to be part of this, to be at the house with me on Saturday. Can you do that?"

"Yes, I'd love to, but won't you be busy getting ready for Sunday?"

"That's true, but I'm talking about you coming for supper."

"Aw," she sighed, sounding disappointed. "You mean it's not okay for me to meet your folks when you're not there?"

He could tell she was being playful. "So, that's a yes. You just come on whenever it suits you, but be prepared, Lottie'll put you to work."

"Good. Maybe I can learn some things from her. I'm looking forward to it."

TWENTY

As was their custom, Gus, Burly and Beanpole planned a get-together at Gus's place after work on Friday to talk about the pipeline and play a little poker. Gus grilled some burgers, then went out on the porch to await his buddies. It was past seven o'clock and night sounds began to shroud the wooded area with a comforting serenade. He sensed a growing chill in the air, glanced at his watch, then picked up a piece of hardwood he'd been whittling and ran his thumbs along the grain. He looked up to see Burly get out of his truck and saunter up to the house. An old Adirondack chair complained as he sank himself into it.

"Hey, Gus, you still tryin' to figger out what to carve outa that old wood chip?"

"Jest listenin'...waitin' fer it to tell me what it wants to be." He raised an eyebrow as he looked at Burly. "You look plumb beat, man. Where's Beanpole?"

"Rough day at work...Beanpole said he'd be a little late. So, what's goin' on?"

"I got holt of somethin' we might could use. They's a protest comin' down up at Bear Trail Pass in the mornin'."

Burly perked up, "No kiddin'...tomorrow? Man...that's short notice. Who's behind this?"

"SOM...them same ones that come in here and helped us save the graveyard a couple years ago."

Burly knew SOM stood for "Save Our Mountains." The organization's slogan was, "Mountaineers Against Pipeline Pollution." He scratched his head. "They been active down in the Southwestern part of the state. I'm surprised Beanpole didn't know they was back up this-a-way."

"I hear somebody mention my name?"

Beanpole was leaning against a tree just off from the porch. "Danged if you ain't the quietest man I ever done seen," said Gus. "Can't never tell when yer walkin' around."

Beanpole stepped toward them, laughing. "Jest comes natural. Hey, I heard that preacher's been goin' around talkin' to folks. What'cha make 'o that?"

Gus got up from the porch step where he'd been sitting. Ignoring the comment, he said, "Time to eat, guys. Them burgers been waitin' fer ya." They went inside, and he stoked the fire he'd started in the wood stove. Burly and Beanpole sat down at the table and Gus served up a platter with burgers, buns and condiments. "Git y'self another'n when yer ready." He got drinks from the refrigerator then sat down at the table.

"Preacher movin' 'round ain't nothin' new...I done heard about that a coupl'a weeks ago," said Gus, referring to Beanpole's comment.

"Yeah, but ya ain't heard this. He's done been to visit Mama Jean, and she like's 'im."

"So, what's wrong with that? Figgers he'd git t' her house sometime," said Burly. "Mama Jean likes ever'body she meets, which is why we gotta protect her interests."

Gus could tell Beanpole was agitated and wanted to talk more, but he wanted to get back on track. Swallowing a bite of hamburger, he made eye contact. "You been up to Bear Trail Pass lately?"

Puzzled, Beanpole replied, "Not lately...why...should I?"

Gus gestured with a wave of his hand. "They's a protest goin' on up there this weekend."

"You mean tomorrow?"

"That's what I heard. I checked it out on SOM's website. They lookin' fer a coupla' guys to set up in them tall trees so EverMore can't cut 'em down."

Beanpole rolled his eyes. "So, what's that s'posed to do?"

"Slow 'em down, I reckon."

Beanpole leaned back in his chair and stared at the ceiling. "Maybe we oughta go up there an' help 'em out."

Gus and Burly exchanged glances. "Speak fer y'self," said Burly. "Me an' Gus is gettin' a little old fer that stuff."

"I'm sure they's a whole lot more to it than that. Whoever sits up there's gonna need food and water. Somebody's gotta provide it."

Burly seemed to warm up to the idea. "Gonna need lotsa folks fer support, ya know. That's inside the National Forest, so they prob'ly gonna be some po-lice there, includin' the feds."

Gus raised his eyebrows. "Yeah, if we join 'em, we be breakin' the law."

"Won't be the first time," said Burly.

"Okay," said Beanpole, "so it's got some risk to it. They's even more risk if we don't help 'em out, 'cause then we givin' up. I ain't gonna do that."

"We all with ya there," said Gus. "The big question is, what can we really hope to git outa this, I mean, like the whole danged project's been approved. We ain't gonna change that...are we?"

"You got a point, but we sure can slow 'em down and cost 'em money," said Burly.

Beanpole snapped his fingers. "Yeah, and they's another thing might could be in our favor."

They looked at him with curiosity. He went on, "Ya'll know what a fuss them environment people made about protectin' endangered animals, and soil erosion. They's cuttin' down a lotta trees that hold the ground in place. Them barriers they buildin' is 'sposed to make up for that...but who knows if it'll work? Nobody. So, we could see that whole issue comin' back up if we git us a hard rain that washes stuff away and pollutes the creek."

Gus turned that over in his mind. "We done talked 'bout that before. It could happen but can't count on it."

"Still, it *could* happen," said Beanpole. "A big spring rain could make 'em re-think their route. Might even save Mama Jean's house if that happened."

"Yeah, but they already paid her fer that prop'ty."

"She ain't spent a penny of it," said Beanpole. "She'd jest as soon give it all back."

Gus sensed they'd bantered the issue around long enough. "We can sit here an' jaw 'bout this thing all night, but it won't git us noplace. So, I say let's go on up to Bear Trail Pass tomorrow and check things out. Y'all game to do that?"

"Yeah, you're right," said Burly. Beanpole pitched in his okay as well, and they cleaned up from supper and called it a night.

♦ ♦ ♦

Billy was busy with Palm Sunday sermon preparations in his study Friday afternoon. He finished at supper time and tuned in to the Peakview TV station's news report while he worked in the kitchen. Nothing much caught his attention until he heard the words *EverMore Pipeline*, and *Strong's Creek*. He stopped what he was doing and went into the living room to see what was afoot.

The news anchor announced that reporter Ray Brinkle was live outside Coop's Pit Stop in Strong's Creek. The video showed cars coming and going with people either entering or leaving the store. Some gathered in small groups outside. "Exactly where are you, Ray? Tell us what's going on."

"I'm standing outside a local convenience store where I'm told a group called *Save Our Mountains—SOM* as they're known—is trying to recruit participants for a pipeline protest starting tomorrow."

"That's interesting, because I thought the pipeline was a done deal now."

"Well, it never has really been settled. EverMore did get FERC approval, true, and they are into the initial stages of clearing and grading a swath about as wide as a super highway with five lanes running each direction. So, nobody expected to see protest rallies again."

"Something must have happened to renew this kind of activity. Do you know what's behind it?"

"I've heard about two things. A group of environmentalists have produced evidence that some additional endangered species in the National Forest are being threatened. Then there have been reports that EverMore's engineering does not adequately protect the area from erosion and water pollution as the trees are removed and grading begins. They have gotten a court order to stop the project while this is investigated further, but a company spokesman told me that just means they can't proceed with soil stripping and trenching. They plan to keep moving with clearing and grading. As I understand it, that's what the protest is about."

"Didn't the community there gain some changes in the route of the pipeline last year?"

"Yes. That was when a local group acted to protect a historic church and cemetery on a ridge in an area called Frog Hollow. That was the company's preferred route, enabling them to cross Strong's Creek at a more favorable spot farther upstream. Now the pipeline has been rerouted through an area where it will displace several homes."

"I take it the protestors want EverMore to reroute again, is that right?"

"That's what I understand."

"I wonder what's really going on, with SOM involved. I mean, they're not even from that area, so what brought them in all of a sudden?"

"I can't really answer that. The local people I've talked to aren't all opposed to the pipeline. Some told me they believe it will save electricity costs down the road, and they talk about bringing jobs to the area. To the locals who are opposed the issues seem to be about property rights and the disruptiveness to life in a small, isolated community."

"So, will the protest take place at Frog Hollow?"

"No, the project hasn't reached them yet. My understanding is they plan tree-sitting protests farther upline in a place called Bear Trail Pass. Clearing and grading that area will open the way for the company to proceed through Frog Hollow."

The video display shifted to a drone view of the terrain in question as the anchor said, "We've seen them use tree sitting tactics before, but eventually the people who do that are arrested. Bear Trail Pass *is* part of the National Forest, isn't it?"

"Yes, it is."

"That means the feds will get involved, along with state and local law enforcement. Thanks for your report, Ray. We'll look forward to updates from you tomorrow."

"Yes, we'll be on site at the pass. Talk to you then."

Billy switched off the TV and went back into the kitchen. He was shocked. There had been no mention of the Frog Hollow Boys, but he wondered if they were involved. Curiosity surged through his mind as he ate supper. He decided to call Earlene.

"This is Billy Upshur," he said when she answered the phone. "I just heard on the news about some kind of pipeline protest that's getting fired up, and I wondered if you know anything about it?"

"Actually, I don't. I've probably been listening to the same reports you have, and it's all new to me. I understand SOM is involved. I'm concerned that this could get out of hand, especially if Gus and his guys get into it."

"I was wondering about that. I didn't hear them mentioned."

"Well, you probably won't. In the past they have shown up at protest rallies, but they do their own thing most of the time. I've been thinking about going up there myself, out of curiosity...and to be supportive. Would you like to go along?"

"Thanks for the invite. I was thinking about asking Barney to go with me—but I'm not sure his health will allow that."

"Barney'd go in a heartbeat, but you're right about his health. I was about to call Cindy. She knows the best way to reach the pass, if she's not working tomorrow."

"Okay, I'd like to go with you, and we can use my Wrangler if you'd like."

They agreed to leave early the next morning. When he hung up, Billy sat back in his chair and smiled thinking about Cindy. *I hope she can go.* He picked up the phone and called her.

"Hi, Cindy...you got a minute?"

"Sure. What' up?"

"You're about to get a call from your aunt."

Cindy's tone changed from playful to serious. "Is she okay?"

"She was a few minutes ago. She's going to call to see if you'd like to go up to Bear Trail Pass with us tomorrow."

"Bear Trail Pass? I can think of a lot of great places to go, but that's not one of them. What's going on there?"

"I take it you haven't heard the news lately." He told her about the situation and Cindy sounded cautiously interested.

"I'm glad you're not going there by yourself. That could be dangerous. Sure, I'd like to go. Not only am I dying with curiosity about this, but mostly I'll enjoy being with you."

Billy was taken aback by this unexpected statement. *Wow! It sounds like Cindy and I are thinking alike.* "Well, I'm flattered. Is six-thirty okay at the diner for breakfast, and we'll go from there?"

"Perfect. I'll pick up Aunt Earlene and see you then."

TWENTY-ONE

Rain fell Friday night then tapered into heavy clouds hanging in the sky Saturday morning, with blustery wind gusts. The thermometer hovered in the mid-fifties, casting a sour note of uncertainty over the planned visit to Bear Trail Pass. Stepping into the diner, Billy saw Earlene and Cindy sitting in a booth opposite each other. As always, Cindy looked stylish in a maroon sweatshirt with a plaid scarf around her neck, her glasses pushed up into her hair. She looked up at him with a teasing grin, "Hey, Preacher, I thought you were gonna bring some sunshine with you. What happened?"

Earlene looked in his direction and Billy laughed. "Oh, I left that out in the car...thought we might need it later on." The two women rolled their eyes and Cindy motioned for him to sit next to her. He slid into the booth just as Evie walked up.

"Good mornin', y'all. How 'bout some coffee?"

"Good idea," said Billy as they each extended empty cups toward her.

Evie deposited menus with them and turned to wait on another table. "Breakfast is on me," said Billy. "Think I'll have a short stack with bacon. Y'all get whatever you want."

Earlene protested, "Order what you want, but this is on me."

Billy glanced toward Cindy. "Why don't we just put it all on one bill and everybody pitch in to pay it when we finish."

"Good out," said Cindy with a wink. "Not many people can get around my aunt when she sets out to do something."

"Y'all are gangin' up on me." Earlene feigned an insulted look, then they all laughed again as Billy and Cindy nodded, saying in unison, "Yes."

After they gave Evie their order, Billy said, "Exactly where is this pass we're going to? I put it in my phone and came up with nothing."

"It's about thirty miles from where we're sitting," said Earlene. "Bear Trail Pass got its name from being a popular hunting area decades ago...mind you, that was before my time. I know it's heavily forested, and rocky. There's a creek that's fed by a waterfall farther upstream. Cindy is probably most familiar with it—it's been years since I was there."

"Well, it's been a while, but I believe the pipeline skirts around the waterfall, running down through a flat area known for its tall hardwoods. EverMore has cleared the trees and begun grading part way through the flat. That's probably why SOM chose it for a tree sitting protest. We'll go west for a few miles, then branch off on a narrow road that twists up around one of the ridges and drops down into the flat. We probably need to leave as soon as possible."

Their food was delivered and as they ate Billy noticed Earlene's glances toward Cindy and him. A glance at Cindy told him she'd noticed, too. "Oh, if you're noticing that Cindy and I are friends, it's true." He looked at her and she smiled approvingly.

"We've had a few dates," said Cindy.

Earlene smiled. "Gee, glad you told me. I never would have guessed."

They all laughed, divided up the bill and tip when they finished eating, then stepped out to the parking lot. "Cindy, I told Earlene I'd like to drive us up there, so I get the feel of the area...plus I have four-wheel drive if we need it. Do you want to leave your truck here or at, say, Main Street Church?"

Looking around, Cindy said, "There are a lot more vehicles out here than people in the diner...so, maybe some others had the same idea. I'd prefer the church."

They dropped off her truck and headed west, then cut off on the side road. When they got to the unpaved part, Billy found himself dealing with a lot of mud and pooled water. "I can see we're not the first ones up here today," he said, maneuvering over ruts that sometimes caused his Wrangler to slide sideways. He shifted into four-wheel drive. The most difficult part was the series of narrow horseshoe turns up the ridge. "It wouldn't take much to slip over the edge."

Periodically there were places wide enough to accommodate two vehicles side-by-side. He assumed this was how drivers coming up the road handled the problem of meeting vehicles coming down. He said a prayer that they wouldn't have to do that maneuver. They didn't.

Emerging into the level area just beyond the ridge they saw a wide swath where trees had been cut. Beyond the clearing a ridge rose up similar to the one they'd come across, with dense trees and vegetation, and rock outcroppings. Tree stumps and branches were piled near them waiting to be hauled away, and stacks of tree trunks awaited removal. Several bulldozers were parked, waiting for the next section of tree cutting to be completed. The ground was muddy from the earlier rainfall.

"My hat's off to the guys who can handle this work," said Billy. "Especially the guys that maneuver log trucks on that road we just came over."

"There's another way out," said Cindy.

Billy glanced at her. "And we came *this* way?"

"I don't mean a public road, but the company has an access easement that intersects with a paved highway. You'd have to go a long way around to get to it, plus it's only for company use."

"Oh. Makes sense."

"I'm surprised how many people are here," said Earlene. Cars and trucks were parked along the roadway and wherever the terrain permitted. "Must be a lot of sightseers from the news coverage. Look, there's a rescue squad ambulance from town, and it looks like Sheriff Bordain and his deputy are here...and there's a state police cruiser."

"Yeah, and it looks like Ray Brinkle and his TV crew found their way up here," said Cindy, pointing to some nearby news vehicles.

Billy found a place to park the Wrangler, then they walked toward a wall of tall trees staked out for cutting. The tree sitters were located on two platforms about thirty feet high, built between trees with tall ladders for access. The platforms were sheltered with tarpaulins, and each had a variety of plastic buckets and bundles of things necessary to support them. Ropes and pulleys were used to raise and lower supplies.

"Looks like those guys are ready to sit up there for quite a while," Billy observed.

"Makes me shudder to think of it," said Cindy. "I can't help thinking how vulnerable they are to storms...both natural and man-made."

A dozen or so people, obviously supporters who were communicating with the sitters, gathered around the trees. Several people were busy getting a gas-powered generator running and setting up a microphone. Banners broadcast the theme, "Save Our Mountains." Some people were handing out signs that read, "Never More to EverMore." Fanning out from this scene were dozens more people who didn't seem directly involved with the protest itself.

The sheriff had strung red tape to funnel people walking in from their vehicles through a check point. As Billy, Cindy and Earlene stepped up, Cam Bordain said, "Well, preacher. Surprised to see you here."

"Curiosity, Sheriff. All of this has some impact in the hollow, you know, so a couple of us decided to see what's going on."

Cam nodded. "You had any more trouble with them Frog Hollow Boys?"

"I saw one of them at a funeral a few weeks ago, but that's it. I have visited with Mama Jean."

Cam raised his eyebrows. "Sounds like you're doin' okay."

"So, what's with the checkpoint?"

"Security. Especially since the TV folks got into it, we have to be alert. Don't want one of them shootin' incidents like we've heard about in other places.

Speakin' of which, I need for y'all to step over there," he pointed to several people checking for possible weapons or other indications of foul intent. "I know y'all ain't armed, but we gotta check ever'body."

Once through the check-in procedure, they walked up to the crowd around the trees. Earlene knew some of the people and got into conversations with them. Cindy went over to the ambulance and spoke to the emergency techs. Billy decided to seek out the SOM leader, a woman whose name he remembered from the TV story, Abi Durango. She was busy with the group setting up the sound system and handing out protest signs and banners.

Billy introduced himself. "I'm pastor at the Frog Hollow Wesleyan Brethren Church. We have a lot of folks in the ravine whose property is threatened by the pipeline, so I came to see for myself what's going on."

Abi was a rugged looking woman dressed in boots, jeans, a sweatshirt and windbreaker. Her dark hair was pulled back into a pony tail that fed through the opening in the back of a baseball cap with SOM embroidered on it.

"I'd like to be up front with you, Ms. Durango," said Billy. "I used to work for EverMore in their Richmond office, so being sent as pastor to people in the path of the pipeline has been a new experience."

"Look, Reverend, if you're here to argue with me about this, get in line. I'll have a few words to say and then I'll be glad to hear from anybody who agrees or disagrees. Our whole purpose is to save our mountains and the heritage of people who have lived in them for generations."

She turned aside brusquely after barking out her pronouncement. Billy was stunned. He'd never been involved with anything like this. He felt like he'd just stepped on a land mine. *Lord, what have I gotten into now.* He took a deep breath and felt assured, so he spoke again.

"Ma'am, I'm not..."

She twirled to face him. "Don't call me ma'am...name's Abi."

"Excuse me...Abi...I'm not here to take sides, but I do know some people who are being impacted personally by the pipeline. This new court order, along with your protest today, has given them some hope that maybe it's not all a done deal after all. I understand the arguments for and against the pipeline, but I also feel the pain it's causing."

She looked up from what she was doing, her eyes snapping. "So, where are you going with this. I'm very busy."

Billy surprised himself with his answer. "Where I'm going is to offer my services. I'd like to offer a prayer before you start whatever proceedings you've planned...unless you already have someone to do that."

She looked him up and down and her expression softened. "No, we hadn't thought of that. Hadn't thought this was quite so formal...but maybe it's a good idea." She looked at her watch. "It's ten o'clock now so we're about ready to get started. I'll call on you."

Cindy walked up as Billy stepped back. "What's going on?"

"I was just getting acquainted with the lady who organized this...I'm gonna offer a little prayer before she speaks."

Cindy looked at him with puzzlement. "I thought you just wanted to observe. Didn't know you planned to get involved."

Billy wasn't sure how to read her comment. "I don't, really, but I sense a lot of tension here and it might help to seek God's presence...don't ya think?"

Cindy smiled. "Yeah, I think. You know, I'm coming to like you more and more each time we're together."

♦ ♦ ♦

Zeke Stoner, dressed in military camouflage and carrying a backpack and an AR-15 rifle made his way carefully through rocks, scrubby brush and dense trees along a ridge adjacent to the cleared protest location at the pass. The wet ground increased the danger of slipping, so he had to move carefully. The last thing he wanted was to call attention to himself. He focused on the crowd that was gathering two hundred yards away. There were more people than he'd expected, but he had a clear view of the tree sitters and the protest leaders setting up their equipment.

Crouching behind a large flat boulder with scrubby cedars, wild geraniums and tall grasses butting up against it, he went over his plan. The rock made a perfect shooting platform. He slipped off his backpack, squinting as a swatch of sunlight emerged from dissipating clouds to flood the terrain before him. A flock of birds suddenly took flight a few yards away, perhaps startled by a small animal. No one seemed to notice.

He pulled out a cartridge clip and inserted it into the rifle, then affixed the scope and adjusted the weapon's sites for the distance to the target. This was precision work...no mass shooting—one shot. When all was ready he leaned back against the rock, closed his eyes...listening, relaxing. He practiced controlled breathing to reduce his pulse rate. Calmness meant everything in this business.

The presence of the TV people was a surprise. He'd not been told they would be there. In fact, all he'd been given was a picture of the target, and he'd memorized that. The reporters wouldn't matter, in fact, they'd make his hit more effective. The plan was for pro-pipeline agitators in the crowd to launch a tirade of panicky accusations toward the protest leaders for having stirred up dangerous and useless anger. It would play well.

He went over his escape route. Fifty feet behind him, up through a screen of oaks and red cedars, was a thicket masking a sharp drop-off he would use to disappear quickly. He breathed in deeply and controlled his exhale, then checked his pulse: 62. Good. He'd been trained as an assassin in the army and had served effectively in Afghanistan where he was good at creating havoc and confusion, maximizing the enemy's vulnerability to his unit's mission. He imagined himself back in a combat setting. The thing about Zeke Stoner was that nobody in Limestone County knew his military record, or that he occasionally still took on assignments if the price was right. He was the perfect choice for this job.

Zeke waited. Listened. He'd know when it was time to strike.

TWENTY-TWO

Billy observed, "There are more people here than I would have expected from what Abi said. She thought there might be some opposition from pipeline advocates. It sounds like somebody wants to manipulate this situation."

Cindy touched his hand. "I've been thinkin' the same thing. I know an awful lot of people, both in the village and around the county, and I don't see many familiar faces. It also struck me as odd that SOM was recruiting protestors at Coop's, as the news reported. They usually have more subtle ways of tapping into local protestors."

"My thoughts, too," said Billy as he offered her one of the bottles of water he'd brought.

A generator started up and the speakers crackled as one of the SOM people did a test. The clouds lifted to allow a sudden flood of brightness about the same time. Billy looked into Cindy's eyes. "You're beautiful in this sunlight, do you know that?

"It's just the power of the moment," she said dismissively. "Go on over there and pray, preacher." She smiled. "I'm going back with the EMT crew."

Abi stepped up to the microphone with some papers in her hand. "Save our mountains," she shouted. The crowd of protestors lifted signs and waved banners, chanting in return, "Never More to EverMore...Never More to Evermore...."

"That's why we're here," Abi shouted. "EverMore has been halted by a court order, but they refuse to obey." She made a sweeping gesture. "They're ready to turn these majestic old trees into a stumpy field they'll bulldoze and grade to plant a gas pipeline nobody but their accountants and chief exec's want."

The crowd roared, and the TV cameras rolled.

"We're glad you came out to support our call for sanity and common sense. I have someone here who will speak to the issues that brought about that court order. But first, I want us to take a minute for..."

A strong gust of wind caught her off guard, ripping the papers from her hand. Instinctively she lunged to retrieve them, but suddenly grabbed her shoulder and crumpled to the ground. At the same time the report from Zeke's rifle pierced the air.

For a moment everyone was stunned, then panic broke out. Billy never got to speak his words of prayer. Instead he reflexively plunged toward Abi shouting, "Noooo." All around him people were screaming, grasping for loved ones, falling to the ground, looking for cover, or running toward the trees. It didn't seem to matter whether they were protestors or agitators, confusion reigned.

Cam Bordain and the other police officers jumped into action. Rafe produced a bullhorn from his cruiser, handing it to Cam who bellowed to the crowd, "Stay down. Don't run, stay in place." A few people heeded his instructions, but most were so unnerved the words just bounced off their consciousness.

"Sheriff...over there," shouted one of the tree sitters, pointing toward the ridge. "I saw somebody up in those rocks, near that cedar grove."

Cam stopped and tried to see where he was pointing but couldn't be sure. "I'm comin' up there...show me."

He turned to Rafe, "Call this in. We need help up here pronto." Grabbing the bullhorn, Cam ran to the tree and climbed up the ladder without a thought for how dangerous it might be. When he reached the platform the tree sitter helped him onto it.

Breathing heavily, Cam said, "Where? What did you see?" The man pointed out the location. "When I heard the shot, I looked where it seemed to come from and I saw movement...like somebody ducking out of sight."

It seemed plausible. "I don't think he's still there," said Cam. "If he was he'd of shot some more people."

At the same time this was happening, Cindy and the EMT's rushed to Abi who was still down, bleeding and in pain, but conscious. They jumped into action, assessed the wound, then moved her onto a stretcher. The ambulance was equipped with digital equipment and direct communication with the Peakview hospital ER. The EMT's moved Abi into the ambulance and Cindy helped treat the wound. "It's a good thing she moved when she did, or this would have hit her heart. As it is, the humerus bone in her upper arm is severely broken, maybe some cracked ribs. Not sure about internal injuries. We need to get her to the hospital as fast as possible."

Billy offered a prayer for healing and an end to the violence, then spoke to Cindy as she got into the ambulance to ride with Abi. Suddenly she said in a startled voice, "Aunt Earlene...where is she?" Her eyes revealed that she felt pulled in several directions at once.

Billy squeezed her hand. "She's pretty resourceful. I imagine she took shelter. I'll find her and take her home. After that I'm going to the hospital. I want to follow through with Abi...and I can bring you back to your car when you're ready."

Cindy gave him a quick hug. "Thanks. Keep the prayers going. I'll see you later."

As Billy turned away he noticed Cam up in the tree stand and suddenly realized there hadn't been any more shots. Cam bellowed through the bullhorn, "Okay, folks, let's keep calm and stay in place. We think we know where the shot came from and we've sent for help to flush the shooter out, if he's still there. We hope there won't be any more shooting, but let's play it safe just in case. The ambulance is taking Ms. Durango to the hospital, and there are two more EMT's here if you need assistance."

Billy could feel the tension ease somewhat although a number of people ignored Cam's instructions and headed for their vehicles. Cam responded by asking them to stop. One of the troopers moved a cruiser up to block the road. "Don't try to drive out of here yet," Cam shouted to the crowd. "That road's narrow and dangerous. We need to keep it open for incoming help." A few guys tried to run their trucks around the cruiser, but they quickly bogged down in mud.

Cam called down to Billy, "Preacher, we need a prayer right about now. Is that mic down there live?"

They had turned off the generator when the shooting occurred, but it was intact, so the crew started it up and Billy took the mic. "Let me have your attention. We're in good hands here. Please follow Sheriff Bordain's instructions. I want to encourage you to trust God's presence as well and keep calm. Let's pray for Abi, and for everyone's safety." Silence fell over the crowd and Billy offered a prayer seeking God's healing presence.

Two deputies who had come with Cam and Rafe worked their way toward the rocky area where Cam had directed them. They called back, "It looks like someone was here, but must have left right after he fired. We're looking for a shell casing."

Cam told them to keep searching the immediate area and use caution. He came down from the tree and called people together. "Y'all have been through hell today, and we're thankful nobody else was shot. As soon as we get more help in here we'll ask you to line up and drive out of the area carefully. We'll catch whoever did this and get to the bottom of it. Let's all keep cool."

Not long after his announcement a SWAT team, two more ambulances, a fire truck and several county officials arrived. It looked like over-response, but Cam was thankful. A state police supervisor introduced himself, "I'm Major Max Short, and the governor has instructed me to coordinate the response here, sheriff. Tell me what occurred."

Cam described everything up through the shooting, then pointed to the ridge and said, "One of the tree sitters saw a man leave about two hundred yards out there. I went up on the stand with him and it looked like he could be right, so I sent two deputies up to check out the location."

"Yes, I know about that, the SWAT team is getting ready to go up there with dogs and see if we can pick up a trail." He gave Cam a hard look. "So, you went up on the tree stand?" He pointed in that direction. "Since I see someone up there now, I take it you did not arrest the man."

Cam sensed where this was going. "My first concern was to assess the situation and take appropriate action for the safety of everyone who is here. He offered helpful information and I followed up. I told him he has to come down, and so far he has resisted, but in my judgement, this is not the time to deal with that."

"Well, I question your judgement. He's responsible for everything that happened here...he and everybody involved with him. They fanned the flames of a volatile issue and it backfired. If they hadn't set this up, that lady who was shot would still be okay."

"Excuse me," Cam interrupted. "The lady who was shot was the organizer of the protest. She had a valid permit. I think we need cool heads dealing with this."

The major gave him a beady-eyed look. "Well, I intend to arrest the sitters and everyone who's helping them. This is National Forest property and federal authorities will be arriving soon. Until then, the governor has put me in charge, and we'll do this my way. We will interview people. I want you and your men to help process that, and as soon as we're able, I want you to evacuate this area. I want you to be responsible for setting up a road block and securing the site until things are cleared up."

Cam stood his ground. "I expected you would do that, and we're prepared. Major, I've been in this area for many years and know a lot of the people and their situations. I will cooperate with you in any way I can."

Billy and Earlene overheard the exchange. "Cam's about the best sheriff we've ever had in Limestone

County," she said. Billy nodded as they walked toward his jeep. "I've experienced a lot of adversity in my life, but this thing today scares the daylights out of me."

"Yeah, I can't figure out what this was about. Obviously, the shooter had only one target...but why? What did he or she accomplish?"

Earlene shook her head. Major Short called out, "Reverend...uh, Upshur, is it?"

Billy spun around. "Yes?"

The officer stepped up to him. "I understand you were standing right next to Ms. Durango when she was shot, is that right."

"That's right. I'd offered to give a prayer and she was just about to introduce me when it happened. We were all in a state of shock." He told about kneeling to comfort her and the quick response of the EMT's. "This is Earlene Josef. She and her daughter, who is a nurse, had come with me to see what this protest was all about. I serve a church at Frog Hollow, and many of my parishioners have been impacted by the pipeline."

"How close were you to her when she was shot"

"Oh, maybe a foot or so."

"And what did you see and hear?"

"I heard her gasp, grab her shoulder and fall to the ground. About that same time, I heard what sounded like a rifle shot. It did not sound like the shooter was very near."

The major made some notes, then asked Billy for a number where they could reach him if necessary. Billy explained that Cindy had assessed the situation and accompanied Abi in the ambulance. "If you're finished with me, I need to take Mrs. Josef home now."

The major looked up. "Yes, of course, thank you for your help. You're certainly free to leave."

Another state trooper stepped up and the major handed him his notes, instructing him to finish interviewing people, then conferred with some other individuals who had come to the scene with him, and they walked toward the tree sitters.

Billy and Earlene talked the whole thing over on the way to her house. He could tell she was deeply shaken by it all. "Do you think someone local did this? Has anything like this happened with protests before?"

"No, to both questions. I mean there are strong feelings about the pipeline all over town, but I've not seen violence...until now. What sense was there to this? I've seen Abi Durango and the SOM organization handle rallies before, but this...." She looked at Billy. "She could be dead right now."

When they reached her house, they sat in the jeep a few minutes. "I'd hate to think EverMore had anything to do with this."

Earlene put her hand to her mouth. "Oh, I hadn't considered that"

They prayed for Abi and the medical staff tending to her, the protestors, the police...and the shooter. When they'd finished, Billy walked her to the door. Poochie was barking inside the house. "I hope you can get some rest tonight. I'll go check on Abi and bring Cindy back. Hopefully tomorrow will bring some fresh hope."

◆ ◆ ◆

At the hospital he was told that Abi was in stable condition. Just as he asked about Cindy, she showed up. "Am I glad to see you. This has been a day...did Aunt Earlene get hone okay? I worry about her...maybe I should go there tonight. I'll call her when I get back to town."

They were walking toward the parking deck and Billy put his arm around Cindy's shoulder. "It all hit her hard, but she's tough. I believe God will see her through this. How about you?"

She glanced at him. "I'm okay. I'm really glad we went today...although I really don't know how to take it all in."

"I wanted to visit Abi tonight, but they asked me to come back in the morning, which I will."

"One of the hospital chaplains was there." They reached the Wrangler and as Billy started the engine Cindy said, "You were great comforting her while we assessed the situation and got things moving."

"I guess I just did what seemed natural at the time. Do you think she will have complications from her wound?"

"That will depend on what the tests show. I think it's possible...I also believe she will recover. She's a strong woman."

They talked some more as they drove. At Main Street Church he walked with her to her truck, and they stood a moment in an embrace. He saw warmth in her eyes. "Thanks for being who you are," she said.

"I can say the same to you." They kissed, then pulled apart and she drove away. Billy watched her leave, then went home with feelings of deep anxiety mingled with an inner satisfaction he'd never known before.

TWENTY-THREE

When he'd squeezed off his round, Zeke saw Abi fall, so he knew he'd hit her. He'd been told it didn't matter whether he killed her, just so he took her down. He turned quickly from the rock, picked up his shell casing and left the scene. His escape route would take him some distance up a stream to confuse any dogs used in searching for him. Hearing the commotion his shot had stirred behind him, he slipped through a maze of cedars, oaks and pines, then down a steep grassy slope. The wet ground caused him to slide uncontrollably, landing up against some rough junipers, just short of an outcropping of rocks bordering the creek.

Shaking off his tumble, he plunged into the raging rush of water that seemed intent on washing him away. His heavy socks and wet boots made each step require maximum effort as he sucked in his breath and bent into the flow. With his backpack and the rifle slung across his shoulders, his hands were free to tackle each relentless challenge. Once when he ducked behind a large boulder to catch his breath, he was nearly washed away by a large tree limb plummeting over him, barely missing his head. He stuck with it for over a mile, emerging at the foot of the waterfall that cascaded over a ledge thirty feet above him. That ledge was where he needed to go.

Holding onto the trunk of a fallen tree, he leveraged himself out of the water and ducked into a brushy den of cottonwoods, red maples and shortleaf pines. Panting, he sat down on the damp ground that smelled of fetid leaves compounded by blooming skunk cabbage. Zeke put his head between his knees and wrapped his arms around them, practicing controlled breathing exercises. As calmness settled in he raised his head, listening intently, like an animal ready for fight or flight. He heard nothing but the insatiable sound of the rushing water, punctuated by bird calls. An insect flew into his face and he swatted at it, then heaved a sigh. "I made it," he whispered, opening the backpack and pulling out a waterproof bag containing a dry towel and a change of clothes.

Even with the sun warming the air, Zeke shivered as he changed into the dry clothing and stuffed his wet things back into the waterproof bag, then replaced it in the backpack. His body ached, agitated by bruises and scratches he'd suffered during the creek ordeal. He pulled his weapon into his lap and disassembled it, packing the pieces into a canvas bag. He checked the time: 12:15. It had taken him an hour-and-a-quarter to get this far.

"I've gotta do better," he muttered to himself. Gathering his things, he used a leafy twig to rough up the area where he'd been resting, then set off climbing up the steep terrain that consisted of hardy oaks and pines, heavy brush, and frequent rocky outcroppings. Twenty minutes later he arrived at a less severe terrain and walked through the woods to an area where he'd left a Harley-Davidson motorcycle camouflaged among the debris of numerous fallen trees. He strapped his gear behind the seat, donned a helmet, then walked it toward a rutted dirt road where he fired up the engine and took off.

Thirty minutes later he turned onto a narrow, paved road that took him to an old abandoned barn set in a grove of cedars. It was a weathered structure with rusted metal roof and splintered siding. He unlocked the padlock on a garage door that wasn't visible from the road, then pushed the cycle inside next to his old battered 2003 Nissan Frontier. The building smelled of mildew and old hay—dozens of bales were piled up in a corner.

The first thing he looked for was a leather pouch that was supposed to be hidden under the bales. He found it. "Whew," he breathed aloud, opened it to make sure the money was there, then put it under the seat of the pickup. He lost no time moving the hay around enough to conceal the motorcycle. Next, he pulled a worn suitcase from behind the seat in the truck cab, changed from his motorcycle clothes, bundled everything into a plastic trash bag which he took twenty feet behind the barn and dropped down into an old well shaft along with the backpack, helmet and weapon. Hearing the debris hit the bottom, he threw in a bundle of branches and leaves, then went back inside the barn.

The persona of a derelict moonshine addict he displayed at Strong's Creek to protect his real identity had worked for over a decade. Nobody really took him seriously. He pulled an old tarp off some bottles of moonshine, pulled one out, took a swig and splashed some on his jacket, then put it back. If he was stopped, he wanted to look and smell like his cover story...that he had been delivering his product to some guys he knew who wouldn't want their names revealed.

"Five hours," he said to himself as he checked his watch. "Time to move out."

He backed the truck out of the barn, closed the door but didn't lock it, tossed the padlock into his glove box, then pulled out onto the road. So far, he hadn't seen another vehicle or person. He'd been on back roads all the way, but that was about to change. Feeling satisfied that all was well, he lit up one of his trademark cigars and headed for Strong's Creek, singing along with some bluegrass music from a local radio station.

♦ ♦ ♦

On the evening news the Peakview TV station played a tape from the protest site earlier in the day. Scenes of confusion ran in the background as reporter Ray Brinkle spoke. "What began this morning as a curious, unexpected pipeline protest at Bear Trail Pass, quickly turned into a crime scene. Abi Durango, organizer of the SOM protest, had just begun addressing the crowd when a shot was fired, and she fell to the ground. As you can see, that triggered massive confusion and panic."

"So, how many shots were fired?" asked the news anchor. "Were other people hit?"

"Actually, there were no other shots or injuries. It's almost like she was specifically targeted by some person or group. I know she's controversial, but to my knowledge she's never before been physically attacked."

He explained that she'd been evacuated to the Peakview hospital with non-life-threatening injuries. The Limestone County Sheriff and members of the state police were shown moving quickly to restore order and help people leave the area.

"So, what about the tree sitters? Are you saying nobody targeted them?"

"That's right. Actually, they helped the sheriff locate where the shot came from, but whoever fired it was gone by the time the authorities got there. It all seems to have been planned ahead of time, as these incidents often are."

"Do they have a suspect?"

"Not yet. They've brought in a K-9 unit, hoping to follow the perpetrator's scent, so maybe that will produce something."

"You say the tree sitters helped the sheriff? Does that mean they came down from their trees and gave up the protest?"

"Actually, just the opposite. They have said they intend to stay so EverMore can't continue clearing the land. I have state police Major Max Short with me. Major Short, what's the latest on tracking down the suspect? Do you have any ideas yet about who did this and what might be a motive?"

"Whoever it was, the shooter left very little evidence behind. We can only speculate about motive at this time. Our dogs tracked the suspect's scent to a creek that is filled with rapids, spawned by a waterfall a mile or so upstream. We have teams going in both directions along the creek, hoping to find an exit point. It would surprise me if the perpetrator actually stayed in the water for very long."

"In a strange twist," said Ray, "it seems like someone who wants the pipeline to proceed attacked the protest by trying to take out the leader of the movement behind it. Would that be a fair assumption?"

"At this point any assumption is fair. No group or organization has contacted us to take responsibility or deliver a message. The governor is aware of the situation and has asked me to continue with the investigation. Since this happened in the National Forest, we also have some assistance from federal authorities."

"There you have it up to this point," said Ray as the major stepped away.

The news anchor thanked Ray. "This pipeline issue has been contentious from the start," she said. "Even though the utility has proceeded legally in every sense, and made concessions whenever challenged, it seems there are people who continue to seek ways to stop the project. Some protests are centered around property issues, which often occurs when eminent domain is invoked. In this case, however, much of the protest is rooted in ecological concerns. With me in the studio is one of the people who has made a study of this side of the issue."

She introduced the man. "What, specifically, is the harm in taking out a small portion of a huge forest for utilitarian purposes?"

"I'm glad you asked that question, because the concerns we represent are not always visible. For instance, we have concern about storm water runoff when a heavy rain occurs. The company has taken steps to address this, but we question whether they are adequate. When you remove a large quantity of trees and growth that have held the soil in place, you could find uncontrollable landslides occurring, which ultimately impacts water quality in streams and wells."

"But, isn't it true that we have engineering advances to address these concerns?"

"Theoretically, yes, but we're dealing with a particular region that may not fit textbook solutions. If the pipeline goes through as anticipated, the only way we'll answer those questions is through experience."

"What other concerns do you have?"

"We're also concerned with preserving certain species of wildlife that have occupied these forests longer than humans have been around. They could become extinct."

"I hate to cut you off, but we're running out of time. Thank you for talking with us."

With that the news report ended.

♦ ♦ ♦

Back in Strong's Creek people anxiously awaited each new development. Bunk Cooper had the news on at Coop's Pit Stop. His customers were vocal as they paid for gas and other purchases or paused for a break at the snack area.

"I wondered about them people in here yesterday tryin' to sign up protesters," said one man as he watched the news report. "Didn't seem right to me. Y'all wanna know what I think, them danged protesters jest wanted to look good so's they could pull off somethin' like this."

"That don't make no sense," said another man standing near him. "The gunman only shot one person, and she was the one what was in here tryin' to organize folks. Ya notice didn't none o' them tree sitters git shot. This was somebody with some other gripe...like maybe somebody up in them ridges that was losin' his property to th' pipeline."

"Yeah, maybe," said a third person. "It sounds like organized crime to me. That weren't no local guy shootin' somebody. What did they say...he was 200 yards away? Sounds to me like a professional assassin."

The first guy laughed, "Oh, you think so? How come he didn't kill 'er then? I think this was somebody who wasn't used to shootin' folks."

So it was the speculations mounted during the afternoon and evening. About seven o'clock Zeke Stoner pulled up and filled his junky old rattletrap of a truck with gas. Bunk happened to notice him and when he came into the store and said, "Well, if it ain't Zeke. Where ya been keepin' y'self? Bet ya been up there firin' up that old still, eh?" Bunk laughed and slapped him on the back, then said to the cashier, "I'll pay for Zeke here...he don't do much drivin' anyway."

"Now, Mistah Cooper, y'all don't need to do that."

"Sure I do. It's my good deed fer the day."

Zeke studied the floor, thanked him shyly, and left.

Bunk picked up the receipt and did a double take at the amount as he watched Zeke pull away. "Whoa, I thought he was jest toppin' off his tank. Looks like he's been travelin' someplace." He mused over it for a moment, then put the receipt in his pocket and went to his office.

♦ ♦ ♦

Billy found several phone messages from Fletch Waverley when he got home. He called him back. "Dr. *Waverley*, this is Billy Upshur. I'm sorry to call so late, but I just got in."

"Upshur, I've been trying reach you all day. What's going on over there? I've seen television reports about a shooting at a protest rally. They interviewed a state policeman who said a preacher was involved in some way...was that you?"

"Well, that could be a bit misleading. I was there along with two of my church members from Frog Hollow. I wasn't part of putting it on or anything, but I was going to offer an opening prayer. That's when the shooting occurred."

"Do you mean they shot at you, too?"

Billy explained that there was only one shot and he never got to offer his prayer before everything fell apart.

"So, you were there as part of your pastoral duties. I'm glad to know that...the trouble is, this is the second time a shooting has happened since I sent you there. Maybe I need to send in somebody with more experience."

Billy did a double take. "I hear what you're saying, sir, but I disagree. I've been visiting people in the hollow, and I feel their grief and anger over the disruption the pipeline is causing. I think we're all on the same page. Frankly, I have done nothing to cause these shootings, and I believe the effectiveness of my work would be lost if you bring in somebody new."

"You do, huh? So, tell me one positive thing you've actually accomplished."

Billy told him about the sunrise service they were holding at Frog Hollow on Easter morning. "Holly Jinks is bringing the Main Street choir up for this, and we'll serve breakfast afterward."

Fletch was silent a moment. "Well, I'll have to say, if you've gotten those two churches to agree to have a service together you must be doing something right. Maybe I'll come to your sunrise service and see for myself."

"That would be great. I hope you will."

Billy hung up after Fletch agreed there was more to the situation than he could see on the surface. Leaning back in his chair he closed his eyes and touched his fingers to his temples. *Lord, it's so easy to get sidetracked by all the fringe issues here. I need a larger perspective...to see your hand at work.* As he relaxed, his mind took him back to his visit with Mama Jean. He remembered opening her Bible and reading from Jeremiah 29. Suddenly it was like the flash of a light bulb illuminating something he already knew was there.

"That's it," he shouted, jumping up and getting his Bible. He re-read the passage—the prophet's words to the Israelite leaders as they entered Babylonian captivity. Verse seven seemed the most powerful, *"But seek the welfare of the city where I have sent you into exile, and pray to the Lord on its behalf, for in its welfare you will find your welfare."*

He re-read verses 1-14. "Yes," he said aloud, "that's what my ministry here is about. Thank you, Lord, for showing me your answer. We don't have to protest. The pros and cons of the pipeline don't really matter. The impact on people is what matters. What happened today matters because it was the result of desperate people trying to manage the unmanageable. How we live with whatever happens next matters. Trusting you matters. Help me lead these people in what matters, Lord."

TWENTY-FOUR

The Palm Sunday services at both churches were well attended. At Frog Hollow Billy was surprised to see Gus Wheeler and Burly Bransone walk in the door, which caused a stir. People shifted in their seats and whispered to one another. Billy imagined this was one of very few times they ever came into the church, and he wasn't sure why they did it now.

Gus and Burly smiled, nodding greetings to those near them, then sat down on the back row. It was a cool morning and they wore clean shirts, slacks and jackets...not at all their usual attire. Billy gave them a welcoming nod as he continued with the service. People quickly disengaged their attention from the Frog Hollow Boys.

"When I think about the crowds who waved palm branches and cheered Jesus on," Billy said, "my mind goes to the protest rally yesterday at Bear Trail Pass." This brought an audible reaction. He smiled, "No, we didn't go there to praise God. Far from it, we went to push back against something we saw as evil. We went out of fear and anger, the same emotions that led people to change from cheering Jesus to demanding he be crucified.

"In a real sense, I believe the message of Palm Sunday and Easter for us this year involves some essential questions: *'Where is God?', 'Which side is God on?'*" He paused while people shuffled in their seats, whispering, thrown off guard.

"I'll tell you where God is...God is here, with us this moment. God is with the tree sitters up in the pass. God is with the pipeline construction workers. God is with Abi Durango in the hospital, and I believe God is very much present with the shooter, whether that person knows it or not.

"This whole issue of the pipeline has been imposed on us from outside. In visiting with some of you I've found out how hard it has hit you. Most of us in this room just want it to go somewhere else."

There were mutterings of approval. Billy continued. "That would be good for us in Frog Hollow, but it would mean somebody else along a different route would have to face the same challenges we face." He told about God directing him to Jeremiah 29.

"I wonder if God is asking us to simply trust *him*...whichever way this goes...trust God to bring good results, heal hurts and wounds, and create new blessings. I'm like you...I don't like change. I don't like to let go, but if I don't, then I stand to put myself in competition with God. The next step is to find myself suddenly crying out to crucify Jesus, rather than praising and worshipping him."

Part way through Billy's message there was some commotion at the door as two men in sport coats bearing the TV station's monogram came inside. They were expressionless, attentive, alert for trouble. Billy felt the tension rise as Gus and Burly stiffened but kept their peace. He went on as though none of this was happening, then ended the service with Isaac Watts's hymn, *"Jesus Shall Reign."*

After the benediction he immediately left the church, so he would be on time for the service in Strong's Creek. The two reporters came out right on his heels. "Pastor Upshur, you gave us quite a surprise in there. Where do *you* stand? Whose side are *you* on?"

Briefly Billy thought of Fletch. *Oh, Lord, this is just what he didn't want.* Stopping at his jeep, he turned to the reporters, noticing there was a cameraman recording everything. "I'm sorry, I can't talk to you now. I have to be at another church."

By now the congregation was flooding out of the building, shouting and rushing toward him. Billy gave a shrill whistle and the frenzy abated. "Let's remember who we are," he shouted. "We're God's people. God is in charge. God is greater than this issue. Let God guide you."

The crowd hushed as he spoke. People looked at each other, then someone shouted, "Amen. Let the preacher go...he's gotta git to Main Street."

Billy turned to the reporters. "If y'all want to come down to Main Street Church in the village, I'll be glad to talk to you after that service."

As he opened the door to the Wrangler, Cindy came up. "Do you mind if I ride with you?"

Surprised, he said, "Sure. Climb in." People moved aside as they drove out with the TV crew loading up and following.

"You made a lot of sense back there," said Cindy. "I just wanted to ride with you to give you a little encouragement. Are you going to say the same things in town?"

Billy looked at her. "Yes." He smiled. "Thanks for coming along. When I got home last night God told me what really matters." He told her about Fletch's call. "Something good's going to come out of all of this, by God's grace."

She touched his shoulder and smiled. "I know. Isn't it exciting?"

◆ ◆ ◆

The sanctuary at Main Street was filled, and people responded supportively to Billy's sermon. He realized he was just scratching the surface of what God wanted to reveal. It would take time for people to grow, but most sounded at least curious about letting go and letting God lead the way. After the service he greeted worshipers at the door, then as the sanctuary emptied, he allowed the TV camera crew into the chancel as he sat down with the two reporters for a talk.

"Pastor Upshur, we've heard your message twice today, and it's intriguing. We understand you worked for EverMore Energy before you came here. So, are you in favor of the pipeline?"

Billy explained about his previous job as a clerk in the Richmond office. "As to your other question, I already answered it in my sermon. I'm neither for it nor against it. I do understand where people are coming from on both sides of the issue."

He noticed one of the reporters puff himself up, ready to spring at him with another question or comment, so he kept on talking. "It troubles me deeply that someone turned to violence yesterday. I have no idea what that shooting was about. I believe God will show us how to get past the stress of the moment—if we *trust* him."

It was obvious to Billy that the men wanted to hear something different. "Pastor, that's a good *churchy* answer, but we're talking about real life here. It doesn't matter where you came from, you're the leader of people on this small piece of real estate called Frog Hollow, and they don't want this pipeline uprooting their lives. How does waiting for God, or whatever you're talking about, *help* these folks?"

They were sitting on chairs in a circle. Cindy spoke up. "Actually, I'm one of 'these folks' you're talking about. I live in Frog Hollow. I grew up there, and I'll tell you what trusting God is about for us. It's about having a healthy perspective and the strength to endure things we can't control. It's finding spiritual resources to help us accept things we can't change, and the courage to do what we can. Even if things go against what we want, we can find our way through it positively, and usually become stronger in the process."

"So," said the reporter, "why did you two go to the protest rally? Seems like that's the opposite of stepping back and waiting for God to fix things."

"In the first place," said Billy, "you seem to have misunderstood what we're saying. Trusting God is active, not passive. Being active means being present in the moment. I know I speak for Cindy as well as myself saying we went to see first-hand what was going on."

Rather than continue the discussion, the reporters pulled back. "That's the latest word from Limestone County where a natural gas pipeline is seen as a threat to life in the isolated community of Frog Hollow. Protestors continue to sit in trees at Bear Trail Pass, blocking EverMore's land clearing process."

Billy felt exhausted after the TV people left. "I'm tired, but I still need to look in on Abi Durango," he told Cindy. "Do you want to come with me?"

"Yes, absolutely." She smiled, "Tell you what, when we come back I'll fix us supper at my place. Does that work for you?"

Billy laughed. "Sure beats scrounging up something for myself. What's on the menu?"

"I don't know. You'll just have to take pot luck."

"Okay. Count me in."

At the hospital Billy found Abi's husband, pastor and several of her friends in the ICU waiting room. He introduced himself and Cindy, then asked how she was doing.

"I want to thank both of you for your quick action yesterday," said her husband. "What really hurts is I was supposed to be with her but got called in to work unexpectedly. She has a great passion for this cause, and so many close friends that I just felt she would be safe. Now this! His temper flared as he hit his right fist into the palm of his left hand. "I'd like to get my hands on whoever did it."

"I know you love her and I'm sure you feel helpless right now," said Cindy.

He turned toward her, eyes closed, nodding. "Yes," he said under his breath. "I just don't understand what purpose it served." He recovered his composure. "Oh, I understand that it shut down the rally, but the protest is still goin' on, as it should. These are real issues that aren't goin' away. My wife believes in this and I support her."

His pastor and friends surrounded him with hugs and support, then they prayed together. "I'm glad you're here," Billy said to the pastor afterward. "If you don't mind, we'd like to step in and visit with her before we leave."

"I hope you will. Thanks for coming today and for all you both did yesterday."

Billy and Cindy excused themselves, checked with the nurse's station, then made a brief visit with Abi. She was connected to various monitors and IV's. Billy leaned in closer. "Abi, this is Pastor Upshur and Cindy Barker from Strong's Creek. We came to see how you are doing."

She opened her eyes slightly. Billy could see she was in pain and perhaps somewhat disoriented. "Thank you for coming," she said in a strained whisper.

"Your pastor, husband and some friends are here."

"I know."

"I believe God is with you, no matter what." He introduced Cindy as the nurse who had been with her.

Abi looked toward her. "Thank you."

"I'm glad I was there when you needed someone."

"Would you mind if we pray with you?" said Billy.

She blinked her eyes. "Okay."

He offered a brief prayer for God's healing spirit to be at work in Abi's body, mind and spirit, and faith to trust that justice would be done. Then he and Cindy wished her well and left.

◆ ◆ ◆

Back in Frog Hollow, Cindy picked up her truck at the church, then Billy followed to her house, a frame bungalow located back a long driveway on Josef Lane. He noticed a large picture window in three panels that peaked in the center with the pitch of the roof. Billy could see she had a flair for gardening, although he had no idea how she could ever find time for it. A row of colorful pansies bordered the driveway. Azaleas across the front of the building promised an impending splash of spring color. Tulips in assorted colors were also in bloom under several trees.

They parked at the back of the house in front of a garage, then joined hands walking along a flag stone path to a deck that featured a colorful umbrella shading a rectangular wood table and several casual chairs. He noticed a gas grill with a cover over it. Beyond the deck was a small landscaped pond with lily pads. Shrubs and trees complimented the scene.

"Wow, I'm impressed," said Billy as she unlocked the door and invited him to follow her into the kitchen. "Your house is beautiful. How do you find time to keep it all up?"

Cindy smiled dismissively. "Oh, that's easy. Aunt Earlene has her gardener come by here and look after it."

Billy nodded, "Generous of her."

"Yes, it is. Sometimes I think I'm her favorite 'project.'"

The inside of the small house was cozy and as inviting as the gardens had been outside. Cindy motioned for him to have a seat at a round, glass-topped table with a floral centerpiece. She opened the refrigerator, then turned toward him.

"I'll bet you're really hungry."

"Somewhat...how about you?"

"Same. How would you like a tossed salad? I've got some fresh greens, and we could have ham and cheese sandwiches with it. I've even got a bottle of Zinfandel, so we can have a glass of wine with our meal. Okay?"

"Absolutely. That's far beyond what I'd probably fix for myself."

Cindy busied herself preparing the supper, then sat down just around the table from him. They offered a prayer, then settled into eating."

"You know, I came back to the hollow because I love the privacy, quietness, and beauty out here. I appreciated it more once I lived away from here going to school. It was a real blessing to get a job at the clinic."

"I hear what you're saying. I've never lived anywhere like this, so I'm discovering what I've missed." Billy paused a moment. "That's one of the things that has struck me so powerfully...how can people callously come in and just say, 'Okay, folks, you're in our way.'" He spoke in an affected authoritative voice. "Step aside there. Here, we'll give you a few bucks so you can forget about your losses."

Cindy touched his hand. "That's what bothers me, too. I don't know what will come of this pipeline, but I expect in the long run we'll just have to live with it."

They looked at each other and laughed, saying at the same time, "Like I/you said in church today...."

Her hand felt warm and affirming, and Billy placed his other hand over hers. He looked into her eyes. "You're a very special blessing in my life. I'm so glad we have found each other."

She had a blissful expression as she responded. "I feel the same way."

They leaned together and shared a kiss that lingered. "I guess I need to get home. We've only known each other a few weeks...."

She touched his lips. "I know. We have time."

When he drove back to the rental house and stepped inside, the place felt cold and foreign again...kind of like it had that first night in February. He had talked about pursuing what matters in life. As he settled down to sleep he whispered to himself, "Cindy matters."

TWENTY-FIVE

Zeke Stoner slept fitfully Saturday night. Beneath the haphazard handyman persona he projected was a highly disciplined individual with many contradictory layers to his life. He awoke when physical pain overrode his need for sleep, challenging his denial about the impact his fifty-three years had made on his body.

Twenty years earlier he would have easily shaken off the effects of his escape from the pass, but now it took more effort. Never one to risk addiction to pain killing drugs, he had always used self-talk to stay focused on his overall objective—accumulating enough money to ultimately disappear into a world of pleasure and self-indulgence. Coupled with that was an intensive exercise regimen. He sighed with an unspoken awareness that he couldn't keep up this pace much longer. Maybe it was time to retire.

The digital clock said it was two in the morning. Putting on his sweats, he went downstairs to a room he'd built under the cabin for his exercise equipment, weapons, a computer, and clothing he used for his clandestine work. There was also a large safe where he kept records related to his jobs, and cash until he could process it into an offshore account.

He threw himself into a rigorous exercise routine, then showered an hour later. Opening the safe, he pulled out the pouch he'd picked up from its hiding place in the old barn. At the time he had glanced inside to be sure the money was there. Now he counted it, then returned it to the safe. Spinning the dial locked it safely away. His thoughts went back to the night he'd taken the contract for the pipeline hit.

It had been just three weeks ago, a nondescript voice on an incoming call. "We need a specialist with your talents and you were recommended. If you're interested, meet me tomorrow night." The caller named a hotel forty miles away near a truck stop on the interstate. When he went there, a courier who wouldn't identify who he represented, said, "You're the best. This job is made to order for your talents."

Zeke didn't really need to know the source of the hit, but he needed some assurances. "Look," he said to the courier, "if I do this, I'll be takin' a big risk. This is right in my own back yard. This'll take a lot of plannin' and it ain't gonna be cheap."

"We didn't expect it to be cheap. I've got twenty grand right here." He showed him the money. "You get the rest when the job's finished."

"Okay, here's the deal. I want a hundred grand total...in addition to some props—a motorcycle and a place I choose for a hideout."

"I don't know, that's pretty steep," the man had said, then called whoever sent him and they worked it out. Zeke nodded. "Don't hang up yet. It ain't gonna take rocket science to figger out this ain't some local yokel who got a lucky shot. They're gonna think professional hit. So, do you want me to set up some distractions to muddy things up, throw 'em off fer a while?"

The courier had relayed the message then turned toward Zeke. "No fancy stuff. Stay with the plan."

Turning out the light and heading up the spiral staircase wrapped around a pole that came out in a fake closet upstairs, Zeke smiled. The distractions would have made his escape easier, but it had worked out. He was satisfied. Locking the closet door, he felt relaxed and went back to sleep.

At six o'clock he was awakened by someone pounding on his front door. Clicking the safety off a loaded Glock he kept under his pillow, Zeke opened a kitchen cabinet where he had monitors for several surveillance cameras hidden in trees. Standing at his front door was a figure dressed in sweats with a hoody that was pulled over his head. Seeing no weapon, and no evidence of anyone else around, he closed the cabinet, tucked the pistol into his pocket and went to the door. Opening it against a safety chain he said, "Yeah?"

The teenage boy before him shivered in the early morning chill. "I...I'm sorry to bother you, mister, but I need some help."

"What kinda help?"

"Uh...I, uh, ran out of gas." He patted his pants pockets frantically. "I dropped my cell phone the other day and haven't got it fixed yet. I saw a mailbox with a number on it next to this lane, so I walked up here."

"How old are ya, son?"

"Seventeen."

"Uh, huh." Zeke looked him up and down then released the chain, opened the door and invited him inside. Closing the door, he said, "Now s'pose y'all jest tell me why yer really up here on private prop'ty at this hour. Sun ain't hardly up yet. Yer mama know ya be out wanderin' 'round in Rooster Holler?"

"No...." The boy seemed more nervous now. "I ain't supposed to come up here, but a buddy told me this road leads to Crowfoot Knob, and I wanna take my girl up there sometime."

"So, ya jest told mama ya was goin' out early to find this place where yer gonna take yer girlfriend?" Zeke made a move toward the boy as anger and suspicion set in.

The boy backed away. "N...n...no...I told my dad I was going out early to run some laps on the track at school. I have to get back in time for church."

The story rang a little truer. Zeke pulled on an old jacket and his cap, then opened the door. "I'll give ya some gas, but don't ya never show yer butt 'round here again." He led the way out back to a shed where he kept tools, an old tractor, a lawn mower, fishing gear, and a gas tank with a hand pump. He picked up an old gallon can, wiped spider webs off it and handed it to the boy, then showed him how to work the pump.

"Fill that up. I ain't asked yer name yet. Who are ya?"

"I'm Brad...Brad Mackabee...please, don't tell my dad I was up here."

"Well now, that depends on you. See, I live ou'chere 'cause I like t' be alone. I don't want nobody messin' 'round with m'stuff. So, y'all ever come back here agin, fust thing I'm gonna do is tell yer daddy...and the sheriff."

"You don't have to worry about that, sir," Brad stammered.

"Where's your car?"

"Like I said, it's right beside your mailbox out on Rooster Holler Road."

Zeke pulled out one of his cigars and chewed on it while they walked out the quarter-mile lane to an old Volkswagen Beetle parked on the shoulder. Brad poured the gas into it, then handed the can back to Zeke.

"Y'all keep it to remind ya not to come back here." He handed the can back to Brad and pointed to signs posted on trees on either side of the lane. "Ya see them signs: "No Trespassin'." This here's posted property. Y'all was trespassin when ya come up this here lane. I coulda called the sheriff on ya. Now, git yer butt outa here."

Brad started the engine, which took some pumping to get the gas flowing, then drove off with a spray of gravel.

"Danged kids," muttered Zeke as he lit his well-chewed cigar and walked back to his cabin.

♦ ♦ ♦

Up at Bear Trail Pass the hunt continued. Major Short had other responsibilities to tend to so he asked Cam Bordain to work with the searchers. He remembered a waterfall that was the source of the creek. By Sunday some of the raging water had calmed down so the rapids weren't nearly as treacherous as they had been the day before.

He called the three men working with him and his deputy, Rafe, together. "I got an idea. This creek originates from a waterfall on up the way. There's an old forestry road that leads to a clearing up above the falls, maybe a half-mile hike. I'm thinkin' our perp might have walked in this creek right to the falls, then climbed up the cliff and out to the road."

He looked around at the group. One man wasn't sure. "That sounds pretty farfetched to me. In fact, don't the West Virginia state line run up through there? We'd be out of our jurisdiction."

"It does, but not right there. That waterfall stems from a lake where I've gone fishin' a time or two. The more I think about it, the more I'm convinced we might pick up his trail. Shoot, he might've had a boat up there and escaped across the lake."

They all agreed, hiked out, drove up to the place Cam was talking about, and hiked in to the lake where the falls broke across the rocky ledge.

"This is rough territory up here," said one of the men. "I guess if I was runnin' from the law, this might be where I'd try to lose m'self."

Turning to Rafe, Cam said, "Come with me. We're gonna climb down there and have a look around." The two men worked their way down through the rocks and trees, then walked to the waterfall and began backtracking down the creek. The sound of cascading water was energizing. Cam spotted something on the ground in a clump of trees. He called Rafe.

"Over here. There's somethin' in this clump of trees, looks like it might be a muddy piece of cloth or somethin'."

Rafe worked his way over to Cam. "See how that tree limb goes out into the creek? If I'd have walked all this way in that cold water, my feet would be numb. An old tree like that would make it easy to climb out."

"You're right."

They moved in through the cottonwoods and pines and Rafe picked up a damp, muddy utility sock. "I'll bet the guy changed to dry clothes right here."

"Might be. Looks like he was gettin' tired by this point...got a little careless. Let's call in that team with them dogs. Maybe we can get a fresh scent and find out where the perp went next."

"Ya know, I'm thinkin' somethin' else. We've been assumin' this person was young, but maybe not. If he or she was so exhausted from the creek that he got careless, I'd say we're lookin' fer an older person. 'Course, I don't know what difference that makes in things."

"I think ya got somethin' there, Rafe. It could mean a lot of things...maybe he'll slow down or leave some other clues."

Cam and Rafe climbed back up to the top of the ledge and told the others what they'd found. They got on the phone and called back to the staging area at the pass. It took close to an hour for the team to find their way in, but they made it. When the dogs picked up the scent they went wild, pulling the men back to the clearing where Cam and his men had come in. Then the trail stopped.

The dogs sniffed and whined. The men looked at each other. "Whoever this is had a vehicle up here. Who knows where he might be by now."

"Vehicles leave tracks," said Cam. "Start looking for 'em. This place doesn't appear to be used much...I think I remember they started clearing it for somethin', then stopped for some reason. That's why there's so much brush rottin' away."

After a short time someone said, "Hey, I got somethin' over here." Cam and the others went over and saw evidence that someone had spun a wheel in the dirt and left a track toward the gravel road. "That guy's got him a motorcycle."

Cam called in the report. "The West Virginia line's not too far from here. We need to team up with their folks and see if can get out a bulletin about the motorcycle. It's hard to say where this person went from here, but it wouldn't hurt to find out if there are some old abandoned houses or other buildings within, say, a ten-mile radius. We think this might be an older person who has gotten fatigued and might be lookin' for a place to lay low for a while."

Cam congratulated his team and thanked the dog handlers. "Y'all done good," he said.

♦ ♦ ♦

Beanpole wasn't with Gus and Burly when they went to Frog Hollow Church Sunday morning because he was off on a mission of his own. On Saturday, they had all three gone to the protest rally out of curiosity, talked to Abi Durango while people were arriving, then talked to the two tree sitters.

"So, how does this work?" Gus had asked one of the men. "Y'all got a team of folks gonna trade times settin' up there, or what?"

"Can't do no swappin' around. That's all they need is to grab us and shut down the whole thing. No, we up here for however long it takes to either git results or git removed. We ain't doing nothing to hurt nobody...jest takin' a stand for what's rightfully ours."

All three of the Frog Hollow Boys had noticed Billy walk up to Abi and begin talking about something. At first, she brushed him off, but then they seemed to agree about something.

"Wonder what that's all about?" said Burly.

Beanpole had blustered, "He's prob'ly tryin' to talk 'er outa havin' this here rally. I don't trust him fer nothin'."

"It's a little late fer that," said Gus. "Besides, I think he's an okay guy." He turned to Beanpole. "I thought you said Mama Jean likes 'im. You don't fool her much about folks."

"That's what she said...her opinion, not mine."

"Well, I see the preacher came here with two women from the hollow...I think he's got a hankerin' for the young one...Buddy Barker's ex."

"They been hangin' around together," said Beanpole. "She was with 'im at Mama Jean's."

"Well, since she done went off an' got to be a nurse, then moved up there on that ridge, don't seem like she's one o' us no more. Hard to tell what might be goin' through her mind."

"Oh, Burly, she's too young fer the likes o' you anyway," said Beanpole, jostling him.

"Says who?"

Gus had interrupted their banter as Abi and her crew tested the mic. "Okay, looks like she's gonna start things a-rollin' here."

Burly noticed Billy step up beside Abi. "Well, if that don't beat all. That preacher's gonna say somethin'.

Visitin' folks down in the hollow musta made a difference."

"We already found that out...." Gus was interrupted by the shot that took Abi down. They saw Billy plunge into action trying to help her as panic began to break out.

"I think I seen some trees movin' up there," Beanpole had said, pointing to where Zeke was making his escape. "I'll see ya later."

With that he had worked his way through the crowd. When Cam hollered for everybody to drop down and stay in place, he paused, but since few people were obeying that order, he scurried on. Beanpole had grown up knowing his family's Cherokee heritage, and prided himself on living up to his Cherokee name, *Wolf*. Whoever the shooter was, he would never know he was being shadowed.

He had followed Zeke silently, keeping his distance, following the creek. At the falls Beanpole saw him duck into some brush and emerge wearing different clothes. He watched him climb up to the top of the ledge, then disappear. He would pick up the trail the next day.

So it was, on Sunday morning Beanpole told Gus before they left for church, "I think this was a professional hit man. I watched how he handled himself. He's tough, walked a mile upstream through them rapids." He told about seeing him change clothes and climb to the top of the thirty-foot ledge, then disappear. "Guy's strong. Knew what he was doin', and where he was goin'."

"You plannin' to tell Cam Bordain 'bout that?"

"Not yet. They got some state police in there with dogs. Let 'em have their fun. You remember that area up above the falls...some Boy Scouts up in D.C. was gonna build 'em a campground there an' they cleared a lot o' timber...but they run outa money or somethin' and didn't finish the job. I'll bet that sniper knew about that and stashed a ride amongst all that old brush. I plan to go up there and check it out."

"Me and Burly's goin' to church today, see what's doin' with th' preacher. I know he and Cindy Barker helped Abi Durango before she went to the hospital."

Beanpole wrinkled his brow and scuffed his foot. "Yeah...I prob'ly been wrong about him."

♦ ♦ ♦

That conversation lingered in Beanpole's mind as he drove up to the old campground site, parked and walked to the ledge. A thought struck him. *Maybe that guy didn't drive outa here at all. Maybe he had a boat hidden along the shore and used that to go out across the lake.* He looked for evidence in the tall grasses and mud along the shore that would indicate a boat had been stored or launched. He found nothing.

Walking back to the crest of the waterfall he heard the faint sound of men moving through the brush. The searchers would soon be at the falls, which would lead them to where he was. Time to leave. He backtracked to his truck, then spent some time looking closely at the piles of rotting timber. Suddenly something on the ground caught his attention...a tire tread mark. There was only one...a motorcycle? Too large to be a scooter. He examined the brush pile more carefully and could see that branches had been moved around.

"Ah," he said to himself. "He had a motorcycle stashed here." *That means he got across the West Virginia line pretty quick. Think I'll drive around and see if I see anything suspicious.*

◆ ◆ ◆

After the service at Strong's Creek, Grant and Elaine took the kids to the Valley Farmer's Kitchen for lunch. A lot of people from the congregation were there and people got to talking about the service and the pipeline situation. Brad had made it back from his Rooster Holler experience in time for church, but this extra ritual was pressing his patience. He wanted to get home to clean up his car before his movie date later.

He nudged his dad's shoulder. "Uh, Dad, I got some things to do...we gonna leave pretty soon?"

Grant was talking to Carrie Glossner. "Excuse me," he said, turning his attention to his son. "What's so urgent, son?"

"Oh, you know, I need to clean up my car for my date tonight."

Grant raised his eyebrows. "We'll go pretty soon. I'm talkin' with Mrs. Glossner right now."

Brad looked at her. "Sorry I interrupted."

She waved her hand. "Oh, that's okay." She looked at Grant. "You go ahead. We can finish this later."

Hearing the interaction, Elaine touched her husband's arm. "Maybe we should go now, hon. I've got stuff to do, too."

Grant smiled, pushed his chair back and stood up. "I know when I'm outvoted." Brad's younger sister,

Margie, seemed to be in a whisper and giggle contest with some other girls. "Sounds like y'all are havin' too much fun," said Elaine as she interrupted them. "Your dad and brother need to leave now."

Margie excused herself and they all left the restaurant. As soon as he changed clothes, Brad pulled his car onto the grass beside the garage and began emptying things out. His dad walked up. "Wow, I didn't know you could fit this much stuff in that little bug."

Brad was running the vacuum inside. He stood up and turned it off. Grant saw the old gas can Zeke had given him. "Where'd you get this, Brad?" He picked it up and sniffed it. "Did you run out of gas someplace?"

"Oh, yeah…a guy helped me out and forgot to take his gas can. I was gonna put it in the garage."

Grant looked at him quizzically. "When was this?"

"Oh, this morning, when I went to run the track at school."

"Well, where were you? I mean, Coop's Pit Stop is practically next door to the school. Did you walk over there for gas?"

"Uh, it wasn't right there. I just asked the guy whose house I was in front of and he had some gas and gave it to me."

Brad had begun to mix car wash detergent and water in a bucket. Grant turned off the water. "Son, something's not right here. Who helped you?"

"Some old guy I've seen around town. Don't know his name."

Grant persisted. "I want to take this back to the guy and thank him for helping you. Where does he live?"

After an increasingly strained conversation, Brad admitted where it was.

"Rooster Holler? What on earth were you doin' up there? That's way up past the track at school. Rumor has it there's some moonshine being made up that way, and who knows what else. That's why I don't want you going there."

Brad finally came clean and told his dad what he'd been doing. "I'm sorry, Dad. I didn't think you'd approve."

"You're right, but I do understand. We'll talk about that later. Come on, let's take my truck and we'll take this back to the man. I can't think who he would be. You don't know his name?"

"No. He lives up a long lane in a kinda shabby little house with a shed out back where he had a gas tank. He pumped out some gas and told me not to bother him again. He said his land was posted."

Wheels spun in Grant's mind. "That might be old Zeke Stoner...you should've recognized him. He's kind of a handyman around town. Sometimes does stuff at church. Some of the men around town kid him about making moonshine all the time."

They got into Grant's pickup and started out. "I thought moonshine was illegal," said Brad.

"It is...it's also immoral. To the law it's a tax revenue thing. I don't know why, but with Zeke they don't take it seriously...but I do." He gave his son a hard look, "And you'd better, too."

Brad squirmed. "I didn't see nothin' like that goin' on. It was just him, and an old rusty truck sittin' in the yard. It did feel weird being around that guy, though, and I was glad to leave."

They had just gotten to Rooster Holler Road where it turned up from the main highway at Coop's Pit Stop. Grant pulled in, turned around, and headed back home.

"Aren't you going up to Mr. Stoner's?"

"Second thought. I really don't think I want to do that. It's *you* I need to deal with, not him."

They rode the rest of the way home in silence. When they got in the house, Grant spelled the whole thing out to Elaine, who looked shocked. Then he turned to Brad.

"I'm disappointed in your judgement. I understand what you were doing, and I want you to learn something from this. For starters, give me your car keys."

Brad fumbled for them nervously, then handed them over.

"Now, for the next month, you're grounded. That means no movies tonight. No dates. I want you to spend the time you would have spent doing things you'd rather do, researching moonshine—what it is, why it's illegal, what usually happens to people who engage in it. I want you to do a report on it and print it out for me. Understand?"

Brad gulped, looked at the floor, then at his mother as she said, "Grant, don't you think that's a little rough. Nothing happened, really."

"I guess Stoner's somebody I've always felt wary being around. I want Brad to think through what we know about his shadow side. When he finishes, he and I will talk about this."

Brad hung his head and went up to his room. Life at the Mackabee house returned to normal for the rest of the day.

TWENTY-SIX

Billy heard about Brad's run-in with Zeke Stoner when Grant came to his office Monday asking him to pray for his son and the choices he was making as a teenager. "Maybe I've given Brad too much freedom. I told him not to go up Rooster Holler Road, but of course, since it's just past the school and around the corner, that's where he went."

"So, what are you saying...did he get into some kind of trouble?"

"Well, he got in trouble with me, but it's not so much *what* happened, as *who* happened." Grant told him about Brad running out of gas and Stoner helping him on the one hand, while threatening him on the other hand if he ever set foot on his property again. "I know you had a run-in with 'im when you first came here. I see the man as bein' a little weird. Anyway, please pray that Brad and his buddies don't go scoutin' around his place."

"I can understand your concern. My experience with Zeke Stoner was more humorous, really, than anything else...but it was weird—like he didn't know how to keep within the boundaries of normal behavior. How did he threaten Brad?"

"Said he'd call me and the sheriff if he came back up there. I think what scared Brad wasn't so much what he said as his tone of voice and his rough appearance. He said it was like maybe the man hadn't slept well and was on edge."

"Well, I guess that could be it. Anyway, Brad put the situation in your hands now, so let's pray about it...and I'd suggest you might mention it to Cam Bordain."

"What could he do? He's got enough on his mind with this shooting at the protest rally and trying to hunt down who did it. Why bother him with somethin' like this?"

"I just think Cam cares about people, no matter what else is going on. Can't hurt." They prayed together and then Grant left. Billy sat at his desk and tried to picture the times he'd been around Zeke Stoner. Oscar had seen to it the man didn't hang out around the rental house anymore. *Moonshine. They say Stoner makes moonshine and sometimes shares it with people he chooses. That would be enough reason for Grant not to want Brad hanging around him.* Billy put it in the back of his mind and went on about his business. He still had a lot to do preparing for Easter Sunday.

♦ ♦ ♦

Monday morning Beanpole went over to Mama Jean's house, entering through the back door. "It's Waya, Mama Jean—I didn't wanna startle ya."

She answered from the front room, "I seen ya drive up, which is unusual for you. What's goin' on?"

Stepping inside he said, "I know you heard 'bout that shootin' up at Bear Trail Pass...somebody shot that woman who organized a tree-settin' protest." He paused.

"Don't tell me you're involved in that?"

"Well, in a way, I am. I'm tryin' to find out who done it." He told her about tracking the man as he went up the creek and then past the falls. "I'm headin' back there today and I want ya to say a blessin' over me."

Mama Jean studied his eyes intently. "How come ya feel so strong about this shootin'? It was part of a pipeline protest and you've been big on that."

"This time somebody got hurt, and I don't take to that. Besides, it seems to be somebody who ain't got no interest in Frog Hollow. From reports I hear, the law thinks this was done by somebody outside the area, but I don't think so. He knew what he was doin', true, like a professional would. Trouble is, he seems to know the land too well. I wanna find out what's behind it and then I'll tell the sheriff 'bout whatever I find out."

Mama Jean sensed the passion flowing from his spirit. "I've lost a lot of folks in my day, and you're one of the few kin I have left, Waya. I don't want ya getting killed or hurt." She had him kneel with her as she sang a chant for wisdom, strength and safety over him.

When she finished he felt his inner strength had been enhanced. He would not fail. He thanked her, asked her to keep praying for the Great Spirit to guide and protect him, then left. In his spirit he pictured an old weathered building, not abandoned exactly, but not used much. Was this where the man lived? Was it a hideout? Or was it someplace out of the way that he was using temporarily?

As he drove around the vicinity where he thought the shooter might have gone, Beanpole felt frustrated. He'd seen a couple of dilapidated old houses with kudzu growing up the walls, rotting wood, and windows broken out. Not much likelihood of someone living or hiding out in such places. He wished he could get a clear mental image of what he was looking for. When he finally decided to go back to Strong's Creek, his spirit was taunted by a tingling sense of incompleteness. He pulled into a gas station and prayed. *Maybe somebody here saw this guy.*

It was a small cinderblock building on a gravel lot with two gas pumps out front, and a pay-by-the-minute air compressor. He decided to pretend he needed air in a tire and lacked the proper change. Stepping inside he found himself surrounded by floor to ceiling shelves along the walls, and floor display racks offering candy, snacks, household staples, auto supplies, hats, gloves, soft drinks, beer and bottled water. He got a cup of coffee from the self-service rack, then stepped over to the counter where an overweight older man with a heavy grey beard, and a goofy smile, looked him over.

"Ya lost, stranger?"

Beanpole introduced himself. "Naw, I just need some quarters to use yer air pump...and this here coffee."

As the man took his money he said, "Ain't seen ya 'round these parts before. Y'all new here?"

Beanpole took a guess at the make of motorcycle he was looking for. "I'm just lookin' fer a buddy said he was comin' up this-a-way on his Harley last Sat'day. He was 'sposed to call me, but he didn't, and he don't answer his cell phone. Y'all ain't seen nobody looked like that the last coupl'a days, have ya?"

"Not that I recollect. We don't cotton much to motorcycles 'round chere, noways."

"Well, thanks anyhow." Beanpole took a sip of his coffee, which was bitter, but he didn't let on. "Good coffee," he said with a tip of his paper cup toward the man.

He laughed. "Surprised at that. It's been six hours since I made it."

Beanpole ambled out to his truck, which he'd parked by the compressor, and went through the motions of checking his tires, then drove off. Not ten minutes later he rounded a bend and noticed an old barn set back a short lane on a neglected lot tucked into a stand of cedar trees. He hit the brakes and slowed down. Strangely, there were several tire imprints in the muddy red clay at the entrance to the lane. Beanpole felt a nudge in his spirit. *What's this?* He continued up the road until he found a place to turn around, then drove slowly back past the barn. The rusty roof, rotting siding, everything about it said it was decaying, but not gone yet.

The wooded lot led back around the bend where it ended at a corn field with a wide entrance clearing and a closed gate. He pulled in there, slipped between the strands of barbed wire that marked the wooded boundary, and made his way carefully back through the woods toward the barn. He approached it from the back where he noticed a double door that appeared to be in good condition. Squatting in the brush he studied the structure. There was no sense of life to the place.

"Now, somebody's been here," he said to himself, noticing the tall, weedy grass had been disturbed. On instinct he pulled a small halogen flashlight from his pocket, then shone it down the well shaft. It was full of weeds, broken branches and old leaves.

"That stuff's fresh," he muttered. "Somethin's hidden down there." His light beam wouldn't penetrate the debris enough to identify anything. Curious about the old barn now, Beanpole walked up to the door where he saw fragmented tire imprints--two different types of tread. More than one vehicle had recently entered the building.

He listened carefully, then opened one door panel expecting a rusty screech. It didn't happen. Stepping inside he was surprised to see a pile of hay bales in one corner. *Strange. These look like fresh bales.* He went over and dug his hand into the folds, expecting to find mildew. It felt like hay fresh enough to feed livestock. The bales still carried a remnant of the fresh hay odor. He stepped back. *Something's been covered up by this hay.*

As he was about to pull some bales away to investigate, he noticed a dark shadow on the dry dirt floor. *What's this?* He knelt and touched it with his finger. It was fresh. He sniffed it. *Motor oil.*

I don't know what I've found here, but I think its time to leave. Unless I miss my guess, that motorcycle's behind that hay. If it is, I don't want to compromise any evidence.

Outside, as he was leaving, he noticed another motor oil patch where the vehicle that had been inside had apparently sat outside for some period. *That might be a pretty bad oil leak...just might cause a breakdown.*

Beanpole worked his way back to his truck, then drove back to Strong's Creek where he stopped by Coop's for some gas. He inserted his credit card, selected the grade of gas, put the pump nozzle in his fill pipe and relaxed as he set it to cut off automatically. He looked around.

Whoa. What's this? Sheriff Cam Bordain had just pulled up in front of the store. As soon as he'd finished filling his tank, Beanpole went inside where the TV was broadcasting the weather. The sheriff had just bought a cup of coffee and was watching the screen.

"With the combination of warm and cold air masses, and this strong low-pressure system moving eastward from the Midwest, Limestone County and surrounding areas are ripe for heavy thunderstorms." The forecaster showed a map of widespread storm systems with abundant lighting strikes and circulation cells. Boxes outlined in red showed areas where severe thunderstorm watches were in effect. "This whole system should impact our area by sometime Thursday. Be prepared for high winds, and lightning. We'll keep you informed as the system develops."

Having noticed a buildup of heavy cumulous clouds as he was driving back from West Virginia, Beanpole was not surprised. As he pondered the storm Cam Bordain happened to catch his eye.

"Well, Beanpole. Don't see you outside Frog Hollow very often. Were you up at the protest rally last Saturday?"

"Me an' the boys was there...terrible thing, that shootin'."

"So, where were you when this came down?"

Beanpole told him about tracking the perpetrator and what he'd seen. "I knew you guys would be hot on his trail, but I wanted to see what I could uncover myself."

Cam's expression changed from friendly to guarded. "You really need to leave that stuff to us. We've got the state police and federal authorities involved. We've tracked the shooter right to where you tracked him. Our conclusion is that this is a hired gun from somewhere, obviously targeting protestors, not the pipeline itself. Most likely this guy's completely out of our area by now, but there are national alerts out."

Beanpole nodded. "I'm glad I ran into you because today I found out some more stuff you'll be interested in." He proceeded to tell Cam about the old barn and all the details. "My guess is he's not so far away...just wants it to look that way. Don't know why, or who might be behind it, but it looks well-planned to me. If you go dig around in that barn I think you'll find the motorcycle...and who knows what's down in that well."

Cam thanked Beanpole. "Appreciate all this. Now, it's time for you to step back. I'll call the West Virginia police and we'll find this place. Can you give me directions?"

Beanpole drew him a map, then they shook hands, and both left the store.

♦ ♦ ♦

Billy met Cindy for lunch Monday at a quaint shop on Village Lane known for its sandwiches, soups and salads that was located around the corner from the urgent care center. The walls were lined with photographs of local scenes, and customers ordered from a central kiosk, then took a numbered placard so their food could be delivered to the table. After they ordered Cindy spotted a table in the back of the room. They got their drinks, then sat down to await their meal.

"Do you come in here often?" asked Billy.

"Sometimes, but it's a little pricey. Still, the best light lunch in town."

Billy took in the room's hustle. "It seems like everybody knows everybody else in here."

"Mostly, they do." Cindy smiled, "After all, Strong's Creek is a small town. As you can see this place is very popular."

The buzz of dozens of conversations charged the room with energy and excitement. "I'm not so sure this is the best place to talk," said Billy.

"If you mean it lacks privacy, yes it does, but notice—everybody is focused on their own group and their own conversations. It's probably the best place to talk."

Sooner than he expected their food arrived. "Wow, you're right...this is fantastic," said Billy biting into his sandwich.

Cindy nodded. "So, what did you want to talk about?"

"Well, you grew up here and seem to know most peoples' backgrounds. I was just curious about Zeke Stoner."

"Zeke Stoner? What brings him to mind? He's not even on the list of people I thought you might be asking about."

Billy laughed apologetically. "Actually, you're right, except his name came up earlier today and he seems kind of mysterious...almost like he's part of the scenery around town, but maybe not very real to people."

Cindy frowned. "Well, I guess I'm like everybody else. I sort of see him around, but I really don't know him. If he didn't work for Oscar Bender, I doubt if he'd even come in to the village that often.".

"Of course, you know I had a run-in with him when I first arrived at Strong's Creek."

She nodded. "You told me."

"Well, there has to be more to him than what he exhibited that day."

"Actually, he's not a local. He seemed to show up while I was away at nursing school, so he's probably been here, maybe, ten years. I don't know where he came from. He does seem to look out for older folks, yet there are rumors about him up in Rooster Holler where he lives. He likes to put on like he's an old mountaineer, but I'm not convinced. I do know most people don't want their kids around him."

"Has he ever done anything to harm anyone?"

"Not that I've ever heard. He's just a loner."

Billy turned that over in his mind. "I guess some folks are just like that...really isolated...and maybe happy that way. I was just curious about him."

Cindy gave him a dismissive look. "Is that why you invited me to lunch?"

"Oh, no...it was just something in the back of my mind." They finished their sandwiches and Billy took her hands in his. He found himself immersed in the depth of her blue eyes. He squeezed her hands. "I just wanted to be with you."

She squeezed back. "Good. I like that."

"Are we still on for supper at your place tomorrow?"

"Absolutely."

TWENTY-SEVEN

Tuesday morning Billy made a courtesy call to Abi at the hospital. She was recovering quickly and thanked him and Cindy for their attention to her needs. While he was in town, it seemed a good idea to check in with Fletch Waverley, so he went by the office.

"I wish I'd known you were coming," said Fletch. "Unfortunately, I'm expecting some people for a committee meeting in a few minutes. What's on your mind?"

"I just want to bring you up to date on the protest situation." He told about Abi's progress and that he had stepped back when her pastor stepped in. "This shooting really was a fluke. I think it has impacted her thinking about the risk involved."

"She's not really your concern, William. The question is, what effect is all of this having on your churches? What about those men who attacked you...where are they in all of this?"

"Actually, two of them were in church Sunday. I think they're as shaken by it as anybody else. I haven't talked to them."

"Maybe it's time you did."

Billy considered that. "Perhaps it is."

The conversation ended abruptly as the people Fletch was expecting arrived. On his way to Cindy's for supper, Billy noticed how the unusually warm day was beginning to cool off. Heavy clouds and a chilling breeze were moving in. *Looks like a storm brewing,* he thought as he drove up Josef Lane. He remembered the possibility of late day thunderstorms had been predicted.

Cindy met him at the door still dressed from work, her blue eyes smiling with a warmth that tried to mask her exhaustion. Billy had known her long enough now to read her facial expressions. They kissed. "Are you okay? You look tired."

With a characteristic toss of her head she said light heartedly, "I guess I am. Just got in from the clinic a few minutes ago. We were so busy today I thought I was back at the hospital workin' in the ER. I'm afraid I haven't even started fixin' supper."

Taking off his coat, Billy put his arm around her shoulder and they walked toward the kitchen. "Let's do it together, what do you say?"

"Good idea...gives me a chance to see your domestic side."

"My domestic side?" He laughed. "I guess I do all right in that department, that is, I'm not one of those guys who just heats up frozen dinners. I picked up a few pointers here and there from Mom, however, cooking only for myself kinda narrows things down."

"Tell me about it." She rummaged in the refrigerator. "Do you like ham?"

"Sure."

"Earlene gave me a few slices the other day." She pulled the ham out and undid the plastic wrapping. "I can make up a glaze and we can broil this. I have some cole slaw and potato salad, too."

"Sounds good. What do you want me to do?"

She smiled. "Just keep me company."

It seemed like no time at all until they were sitting down eating their quickly-prepared meal. Outside the wind was picking up, creating an occasional whistling sound around the windows. As they finished eating Billy said, "Sounds like we're gonna get some heavy winds with this storm. Why don't I secure things out on the deck, then I'll help you with the dishes?"

"Thanks."

Thunder rumbled loudly as he secured the deck furnishings. Just as he finished there was a loud boom and large raindrops began pummeling him. He went back into the house. "This looks bad. Are you gonna be all right here?"

"Thanks for caring, but I've lived through quite a few storms since I got this place. Due to Earlene's generosity, I even have a generator if the power goes out. Maybe you'd better go on home before it gets worse."

"I hate to leave you by yourself..." said Billy hesitantly. "I could stay awhile until this passes."

She kissed him. "Thanks. I appreciate that. If I need help, Aunt Earlene's just up the road. You probably need to be at the house in case one of your parishioner's needs you."

"Yeah, you're right." He kissed her and squeezed her hand. "I love you."

In a voice warm enough to toast his spirits, Cindy replied, "I love you, too." For a moment the whole world seemed to stop as they embraced. Standing just inside the front door they were startled by a sudden strong flash of lightning, followed almost instantly with a menacing crash."

They both flinched. "That sounded too close for comfort," said Cindy. "Maybe I will go up to Earlene's."

Spurred by the lightning strike, they said good night and Billy went home. When he got to the house he noticed a large tree had blown down across the road, its root ball visible with every lightning flash. Billy checked the house and found no damage. He lit a fire in the fireplace then sat down. The plight of people living along the creek and in the hollow came to mind. *Lord, calm our fears and keep us all safe.* He smiled thinking about Cindy and the supper they'd shared. Suddenly a tirade of thunderous booms seemed to swallow up everything. Billy shivered, then a loud crashing sound came from the back of the house. *Oh, oh. Better check that out.*

In the guest bedroom the end of a tree limb had broken through the window. Rain was pouring in, soaking a rug that had just been donated by one of the church members. Billy grabbed some towels and sheets from the linen closet and began mopping up the water, realizing he had to go outside and do something to stop it from coming in. Grabbing his raincoat and a hat, he jumped into action.

The limb was from a tall oak, and the heaviest end had buried itself in the ground. He would need help to move it. Going back inside he rummaged through a storage closet in the mud room, finding a folded tarpaulin in the back. *Zeke must have left this after he cleaned up from the break-in.*

Already soaked to the skin, he managed to get an eight-foot ladder and the tarp out to the window, climbed up and busied himself finding ways to anchor it. Using a hammer, nails and some plywood pieces that he also found, he managed to protect the window from further damage. *It ain't pretty...hope it does the job.*

Back inside he continued mopping and cleaning up. Suddenly he noticed the sound of heavy rain had ceased. He stepped outside. The atmosphere felt like a surreal vacuum. Light rain was still falling, but the wind had stopped. Back inside he showered and put on dry clothes, then tossed the wet things in the washer and turned it on. He noticed the time—nearly ten o'clock. He turned on the late news.

"First tonight, we have news about a major storm that has moved into the area, hitting the community of Strong's Creek especially hard." Video scenes people had sent to the station from their cell phones told the whole story. Billy felt blessed that he'd only had one tree limb to deal with. One house in the center of town was shown just after an historic tree had blown over, crashing through the roof. "So far, we've heard of only minor injuries...no deaths. The storm seems to be moving on now. Let's go to our meteorologist for more details."

The camera switched to a man standing in front of a regional map showing where flash floods, lightning strikes, and closed roads were located. Outside the house Billy heard sirens as police, fire and rescue units responded to needs all around town.

"We've been watching this tropical depression move up the coast for the last two days," the meteorologist went on. "This morning it took a turn our computer models hadn't predicted, moving inland and racing into the mountains of Virginia where we're hearing about damage like you've just seen. The good news is this storm cell is moving away. Its circulation bore the imprint of possible tornado activity, but that concern has now ended." He pointed to features on the map. "The bad news is this depression is linking up with a cold front that is bumping into a warm air mass, creating the possibility for further cells to develop. The chance for strong thunderstorms, and possibly tornados, will stay with us for a few days. We'll keep you informed."

Billy turned off the TV and called Cindy's cell. "We're fine," she said. "I'm at Aunt Earlene's. You should have seen the lighting show through her great room window. It was spectacular. There was a lot of wind, but so far we've seen no damage."

After the call Billy leaned back, closed his eyes, pondering this relationship that was so new, yet so deep. *I told her I love her...and she said the same. Thank you, Lord, for this person you've put in my life.* The storm's imprint took second place as he went to bed.

♦ ♦ ♦

Wednesday morning the storm damage was evident throughout town. Numerous trees were down, and crews were clearing streets and helping people do makeshift repairs. The air was damp and cool, with blustery winds, and a turbulent cloud cover. Billy talked to Cindy as she headed to work, anticipating a long day at the clinic. He decided his first task was to report the damage to the rental house. He called Carrie and told her, then called Oscar Bender.

He explained that he had tried to move the heavy tree limb but couldn't do it alone. "I don't know how well my patch-up job will last if we get more wind. You probably need to send somebody over to do it right."

"Zeke could probably fix it...if I could find 'im. Maybe he had trouble at 'is own place—ain't been able to reach 'im yet this mornin'."

"Do you have somebody else? I mean, all we really gotta do right now is move that limb and board up the window properly."

"No, Zeke's my man...besides, ever'body in town's fixin' up their own stuff, and I hear the sheriff's organizin' folks to put sand bags down here in the lower part of town where too much rain can cause floodin'. Didn't have no damage here at the store yesterday, but I need to git hold of some o' them sandbags jest in case. I sure wish Zeke would come on in."

"Well, it's your house, Oscar. I understand what you're dealing with, and I'll pray for you. If it's any help, I called Carrie...thought maybe she'd know somebody who could take care of this if you can't find Zeke."

"Oh, what'd ya do that fer? That woman'll be the death o' me yet." Billy heard Oscar heave a sigh. "Okay, I'm sure yer gonna be busy with yer church folks today. I'll git it done somehow."

When Billy hung up, Clint and Lottie went through his mind. He knew the storm had hit in West Virginia, too. He called.

"We was jest wonderin' 'bout ya, Sonny," said Clint. "Heard on the TV that y'all got the worst o' that storm last night. We was fixin' to call ya."

Billy explained how things were. "Trouble is, they're forecasting more to come...especially rain. They're putting out sandbags in the low-lying areas around town. I'd like to help with that, but I also need to be checking on some of my people, especially the older ones."

"That sounds serious, all right. I'd say leave the sandbags to other folks and git y'self out there with your church people. Listen, since you've got that damage at yer house, maybe me an' Lottie'd best stay here this weekend and visit after this is over."

Billy was disappointed. He'd been looking forward to introducing them to people in the churches. "I think you're probably right, Pop. If we get the kind of rain I've been hearing about, the roads might not be safe anyway."

"Oh, one more thing, Son. We been hearin' 'bout them tree sitters near y'all. Ya got any idea how they done with the storm?"

"Actually, I hadn't thought about it. I'm sure the news people will be out there runnin' that story down. The pass where they are is a good thirty miles from here."

Clint put Lottie on the phone and after talking briefly, they all hung up. Billy was in his study at the house and just sat for a few moments. An empty, powerless feeling washed over him. He felt a little bit like he had after the ambush on Frog Hollow Road when he first arrived. *What am I doing here? I feel so overwhelmed...what difference can I make for anybody?*

He put his face in his hands and leaned forward with his elbows on the desk. *Lord, help me.* His inner tension began to subside. He pictured Cindy, Earlene and so many others he cared about, who also cared about him. *Thank you, Lord, for your gracious love. Show me the way forward. Help me to be present positively with people, no matter what happens.* Feeling stronger, he got up and drove down to Main Street Church to start work on the sunrise service. Easter was just a few days away.

Holly and her husband, Bernie, were both at the church when he got there. "Wow, I'm surprised to see y'all got in here this mornin'."

"Oh, it takes more than thunderstorms to slow us down," said Bernie with a snicker.

"Don't listen to him," said Holly. "He likes to minimize things. We don't have too much to worry about as high as we are, but people in the ravine sometimes have problems from storms."

"Yeah," said Bernie. "That dry creek out at the Plunket place can rise up real bad. Couple of times I've seen Miz Mazzie get stranded out there for a few days."

"I hadn't thought about that. Maybe I need to check on her today."

"You'd better do it soon, cause if we get more rain you might not be able to get in there."

"How does she manage when the creek's up?"

"Oh, she's full of old country self-sufficiency. She's got everything she needs...just sits out heavy rain and snow storms. She'll be okay."

Bernie used one of the classrooms to set up his tablet and work on a writing project, while Billy and Holly worked on the details for the sunrise service, as well as the regular service on Easter. They finished their work and Billy went home for lunch. The latest weather report said abnormally heavy rain would move in by late afternoon. He had no time to waste.

◆ ◆ ◆

While driving to Frog Hollow he thought not only of Miz Mazzie, but also Myrtle Giles, whose asthma had turned into a deeper pulmonary issue that required oxygen. *If the power goes out, she's going to be in trouble.* Then there was Mama Jean. He thought the old Cherokee woman would be equal to any challenge, but he needed to be sure she was still willing to speak during the sunrise service. The threat of torrential rain fueled him with a sense of urgency.

The road down into the ravine was muddy. He slipped into four-wheel drive to keep his traction. When he reached the creek, it wasn't dry. The previous night's rain had created a stream he was afraid to drive through. It was wide, but also rocky, and the current was rapid. Glad that he'd changed into jeans and an old pair of boots before setting out, he left the wrangler on high ground and waded across the creek, then up the muddy lane to the house.

At the porch he hesitated. *Now how am I going to go in there with all this mud on my boots and pants?* Uncertain, he knocked on the door. It opened almost immediately. "Hello, preacher. Glad to see ya. Come on in the house."

"Let me take off these muddy boots...."

"Don't worry 'bout that. We're used to mud around here. I had Flo put an old rug right inside the door in case we had to go outside fer somethin'. Leave 'em right there."

"Take off them wet socks, too. I got a pair o' dry ones that oughta fit ya. Flo...bring the preacher a pair o' them ole socks we got in the storage chest...and bring a coupl'a them old towels, too."

Within minutes Flo appeared with the socks, and Mazzie invited Billy over by the stove where she had a fire going. "Put them towels on that chair and have a seat. A body could get pneumonia outside on a day like this."

"Flo...bring the preacher some hot coffee."

Billy and Flo both did as instructed. He was amazed at Mazzie's simple hospitality. She sat down in her favorite chair and looked him over. "What'cha doin' out here in this weather?"

"Uh, listen, don't go to any trouble. No need to make coffee."

"Already made. I seen ya comin' up from the creek and knowed ya was gonna be wet and cold. I had Flo put the kettle on right away."

Even as she spoke, Flo came in with coffee, cream and sugar...and some molasses cookies. "Just some cream, no sugar," said Billy as he took the cup and a cookie. Flo set the rest down on a small table and disappeared. Billy bit into the cookie. It was delicious. "This is wonderful."

"I always fix something for my guests. Now, ya ain't answered my question. Why'd ya come all th' way out here with another storm brewin'?"

Billy ate another cookie and took a sip of coffee. "I just came to see if you needed anything, but I think you're well prepared for most anything that comes along."

Mazzie smiled. "Where's that young woman came with ya last time—Cindy Barker?"

"Ah, Cindy is at work. They have a lot going on at the clinic right now."

"She's a fine woman. Had a bad time of it a few years ago, but she done made somethin' of herself. I watched y'all two last time ya was here...she's kinda got a hankerin' fer ya."

Billy felt embarrassed. This was not the conversation he meant to have. "Actually, she told me that herself...and it's mutual. I think the world of her. We both appreciate your prayers, Miz Mazzie. Now, I'm dried out enough to get on my way. I need to check on Myrtle Giles and some other folks. Thanks again for your hospitality."

"Keep the socks," said Mazzie. "Thanks for spendin' a few minutes with an old lady whose time is about up."

Billy made his way back down the muddy lane and across the raging little creek, then drove around to the Giles house. Barney's truck wasn't there. He walked up to the front door and knocked. No answer. He went around to the back door where a note inside a clear plastic bag tacked on the door frame said, "Gone to town."

"Of course," Billy muttered to himself. He remembered Earlene telling him Barney always left a note on the back door when he and Myrtle went somewhere. He pulled out his phone and looked up the speed dial for Barney's cell. After a few rings a recording asked him to leave his name and number. "It's Pastor Upshur. Just stopped by your house to see if y'all need anything with this storm moving in."

He left his cell number, then called Cindy at work. "I'm in the hollow. Came to check on Barney and Myrtle but they're not here...."

"They just left here," she said. "All the dampness has caused Myrtle's asthma to flare up. They're going to the hospital in Peakview where she can be monitored and get her lungs cleared."

Billy felt relieved, but also regretted missing them. "Thanks, hon. I was concerned about them if the power was to go out." He looked at his watch: 4:15 p.m. "It just started to rain. I think I'll run to the hospital and check on her."

"I don't want to tell you not to go, but I hope you'll think about it a minute. We're getting reports warning us about as much as four to six inches of rain with high winds, and flash flooding. Myrtle will be safe there and Barney will probably stay right in the room with her. Why don't you call them later?"

This is serious. "Thanks. You're right about that. Listen, how late are you working?"

"I'll be on duty probably until this storm passes. If you're worried about me getting home, don't. I can stay on here all night if I need to."

"That's what I was wondering about. That makes me feel a lot better." He told her about visiting Miz Mazzie, and about her prayers for the two of them. "She's something else."

Cindy laughed. "Good ole Mazzie. Ya gotta love 'er."

While he was talking to Cindy, Billy noticed the uptick in storm intensity. Strong winds were causing the tree branches to dance as waves of heavy rain surged across the landscape in sheets. He made his way carefully around the ravine and up to Frog Hollow Road without incident. Water from the rapidly rising Strong's Creek occasionally flooded portions of the roadway, causing him to steer carefully. The highway into town was a little better, and traffic was light. Back at the house he parked in front then went around back to see if the tree limb had been moved. It hadn't.

"Zeke Stoner," he muttered. It looked like his patch work was holding up, which proved to be true when he got inside. Just as he turned on the TV for a weather report, the power went off. He lit some lanterns he'd prepared and left on the kitchen counter earlier in the day. They gave a warm glow that contrasted with the fury raging outside. He ate a snack supper, then prayed and turned in. His last thought before sleeping was, *I hope those tree sitters survive this. Be with them, Lord.*

TWENTY-EIGHT

Mama Jean wanted to be at her house despite the raging storm, but Waya had arranged for her to stay with her friend, Twila, whose house was on higher ground.

"I know he means well, but I need to be there to pray for everybody's safety."

Twila understood the spirit that flowed within Mama Jean. She knew this wasn't just stubbornness—it was conviction. At the same time, she listened to the news and knew the ferocity of what was coming. She was prepared in every way she knew to go through whatever might lie ahead.

Twila took charge. "Nobody ain't goin' out in this rain lessen they hafta, and you really don't hafta. They's even talkin' 'bout tornados and all kinds o' stuff. Best we stay hunkered down here."

Mama Jean knew she was right and went to the bedroom Twila had set up for her. She closed her eyes, withdrawing spiritually, feeling the pulsebeat of the storm outside, listening for its message. Sensing an aura of death and destruction hovering over the hollow, she said a prayer, then lay back on the small bed.

She thought of Waya who was with Gus and Burly. They'd said they were going out to check on the tree sitters at Bear Trail Pass. She worried about that. The pass was so isolated, anything could happen, and nobody would know about it. She said a prayer for all of them, wishing they would stop fighting against the inevitable.

Her meditation was interrupted by the clamor of hard rain and hail hammering the metal roof above her. The harsh wind whistled as though it was a wintry blizzard instead of an April storm. She shivered. Pastor Upshur came into her mind. She'd been expecting him to come back after he asked her to speak during the sunrise service, but so far, he hadn't. Easter was but a few days away, yet at the moment it seemed to be light years distant.

A rumble began outside, low at first, then gaining momentum. The house shook. She pulled aside the curtain and looked out. The sky was almost black as night. Angry clouds twisted and turned green, yellow and purple. Suddenly a section of cloud formed what looked like a vacuum tube that suddenly changed form, spawning a dark funnel-shaped projection that touched the ground. Explosive booms made it sound like a freight train was running right through the house. She was speechless as an uprooted tree, cinder blocks, pieces of wood, old tires, tools from the old shed out back, seemed to whirl upward then sail forcefully back to earth.

Twila burst into the room, "Get down. Get under the bed."

Mama Jean plunged down with Twila as they heard something crash into the house. They both screamed. It sounded like the roof itself was about to blow away. The women huddled under a quilt they'd pulled off the bed.

Suddenly the turmoil ceased. An eerie stillness crept into the atmosphere. The two women held their breath, pushed away the quilt, looking at each other.

"What's going on?" said Mama Jean.

After a moment Twila answered. "I...I think that was a tornado."

The two women slowly got up and took in the condition of the room. Things were disheveled. There was a gaping hole in the ceiling and it felt like the floor was slanting. Twila gasped as she went to the window.

"Oh, no."

"What? What's wrong?"

"The trees...garden...fence...it's...it's all gone."

Mama Jean joined her. It looked like a war zone. They exchanged glances and without a word went into the main part of the house. One wall was ruptured as though a cannon ball had gone through it. A table, chairs, bookcase—everything that had been on that wall was gone. Everything else had been tossed around. Shards of glass and broken dishes littered the floor. Twila opened the front door and sucked in her breath again.

"The porch is gone." A piece of metal roofing was jammed into the denuded branches of a large tree near the house that had somehow withstood the wind's fury. Next to it was a gaping hole where another large tree had been ripped up and moved, roots and all. Her car was nowhere to be seen. Mama Jean stepped into the muddy yard with her and they turned to look at the house. It was lopsided. Some twisted metal roofing formed a grotesque statue where a gable had been. The house was right on the edge of a swath of debris, stripped of soil right down to the limestone strata, that looked to be at least a hundred yards wide.

Mama Jean had seen the unharnessed power of nature before, but never like this. It had been horrible—all of this in just a few seconds, yet here they were, alive, untouched. She and Twila helped each other back to the house where they collapsed on the couch that miraculously hadn't even been touched. Mama Jean lifted her arms and her voice in a chant of thanksgiving to her Savior that they had been spared.

Then Waya came to mind. She felt helpless as tears burst forth, yet in her spirit she knew he was somehow all right. Neither of the women had a cell phone since the signals didn't carry well in the mountainous terrain. Twila picked up the telephone, but it was dead. The electricity was out. They suddenly had no car, and the road was probably blocked anyway.

Strangely the refrigerator was still standing. Twila had made some lemonade just before the storm hit. She got up and opened the fridge door. There It was, intact in its pitcher. She opened a cabinet that appeared to be hanging on the wall by a thread, pulled out two plastic cups that were exactly where they should have been. She and Mama Jean sat down again in limbo, drinking lemonade and eating some cookies that also had survived. Mama Jean began singing a prayer chant. She saw Twila put her hands to her face, her eyes wide, her skin pale.

Twila moaned and began rocking back and forth, tears gushing. "What are we gonna do?"

"I'm gonna keep singin'," said Mama Jean, "and prayin'."

She put an arm around Twila's shoulder. "I know God saved us for a purpose. He will send somebody here before dark."

♦ ♦ ♦

The Frog Hollow Boys knew nothing about the tornado. They arrived at the protest site soon after three SOM guys brought in supplies, relieving two who had spent the night in a tent. After the shooting incident Cam Bordain had kept a deputy there, but once it was determined the shooter had left the area, that ended.

"Sure makes ya wonder what good all this is doin' since they ain't nobody out here 'cept us now," said Gus. "As far as I know, they ain't even been no TV people out here."

"That's true enough," said one of the SOM guys. "We still doing what we set out to do...ya see they ain't in here cuttin' trees."

One of the other guys laughed. "Ya shoulda seen 'em yesterday mornin'. They was a whole crew come rollin' in to start work. They fired up their equipment and a bunch of 'em came down here and said they was gonna move us outa their way."

"So, what happened?"

"We called the sheriff, and he got on the phone with their boss. After that they pulled back and worked on loadin' some o' the timber stacked out there on trucks and hauled it away."

"Yeah," said one of the sitters. "That rain last night muddied things up a lot, so that's prob'ly why they ain't here now." He pointed to the sky, "Looks like we got us a lot more weather buildin' up. Ya won't see them guys today."

Gus looked at the darkening clouds. "Yeah, I heard we 'sposed to git a lot more heavy rain. Kinda looks to me like it could start any time."

The men went about resupplying the sitters while one of them grilled burgers on a portable gas-fired camp stove. The Frog Hollow Boys helped secure the equipment for another downpour, then they took a lunch break.

"I ain't been here since Monday," said Gus. "Surprised me to see they still got a deputy out at the main highway."

"Reckon they jest don't want no surprises."

One of the men produced a phone Cam had left that was connected to his office in case they needed anything. "We ain't needed it yet...and we ain't gonna. If we ask him fer help, next thing ya know we be arrested and that be th' end o' ever'thin' we been workin' fer."

After lunch the Frog Hollow Boys said they needed to get back to town. "Anything else we can do fer y'all?"

"I know this contradicts what I said a while ago but tell that deputy to check on us back here if th' storm gits real bad. With all them trees they done cut, t'ain't much left to hold the water back. We could have us a flood."

"You an' Burly go on," said Beanpole. "Think I might stay here jest in case they is some trouble."

Gus and Burly exchanged glances. "How ya gonna git back?" asked Burly.

'I'll figger that out later...jest tell Mama Jean where I'm at."

As the two men started to leave, the sky darkened, and thunder began to roll. "Maybe we oughta move the tent back in the woods farther," said Beanpole. "A real strong wind could take it down where it is now."

Even as they moved it the wind became stronger. "Man, that's got a bite to it," said one of the men pulling his rain gear on tighter. The sky began to exhibit misty colors dancing in thickening clouds. Lightning flashed, and thunder exploded sharply. The rain intensified.

"You guys okay up there?" shouted Beanpole as what seemed like a wall of rain drenched them, interspersed with hail stones, some as large as quarters. The cleared area began to look like a shallow lake with islands of tree stumps and brush piles. The rain ebbed as high velocity straight-line winds hit the tree sitters full force. The tent containing supplies strained at its ropes until they snapped, and it was blown away.

The men were trying to recover some of what they'd lost when drenching rain started in again. Trees with their roots weakened in the soaked soil began to fall. Beanpole tried to help a man whose feet had slid out from under him in the mud when a tree nearly hit them, its fall halted by the branches of other trees. He heard the men in the trees yell as their tarpaulins were blown away and their platforms began to break up.

Then it happened. Both trees seemed to come down at the same time, throwing their occupants into the midst of the other trees that were succumbing to the wind's force. Beanpole located the men, both of whom were injured. One had a broken leg, the other a crushed shoulder where a tree had fallen on him.

They used what first aid supplies they could find, pulled the men out of the debris, and tried to call for help but got no response. Remembering his combat years decades earlier, Beanpole helped them fashion crude stretchers, then they battled the storm to get the men up onto the ridge where they had more protection. Everyone huddled together until the raging storm subsided.

They tried the police phone again and got through. "We've got two men down here, and we've transferred up onto a ridge. Need medical help."

"I copy that," said the dispatcher. "Sheriff Bordain's gettin' in touch with the state police now requesting a med evac chopper. He wants to know exactly where you are and the conditions on the ground."

The SOM leader gave them the information they needed, then turned to the men. "Looks like good news and bad news. There will be two choppers, one for the injured guys, and one for us...they'll be arresting us now that the tree stand is down."

"No surprise there. We done what we could," said one of the men. It was a harsh ending to a protest rally that had gone sour from the very beginning.

Beanpole felt crushed. "Even the weather's agin us," he mumbled to himself. "At least nobody died."

♦ ♦ ♦

When Zeke Stoner went outside to check for damage to his property from the previous night's severe thunderstorm, he felt relieved. No trees had fallen near the house and the buildings seemed to be okay. There was no roof damage or broken windows. Since more heavy rain was called for, he pulled his truck down to the shed to fill the gas tank. It was sluggish when he put it in gear and let out the clutch. That seemed strange, but it was getting old and he hadn't driven it since coming in from Bear Trail Pass.

After gassing up he checked the other fluids. "What th' heck," he said out loud. There was barely any engine oil showing on the dipstick. "When did this happen? Could have froze up the motor."

He poured some oil in the fill pipe then pulled the truck into the shed and up onto a ramp he'd built for oil changes. It didn't take long to discover a sharp dent in the oil pan with a small gash that had caused the leak. *Wonder how long that's been there.* He remembered hitting something under the truck at one point in West Virginia. He had meant to check it out. "Dang it, that's just what I don't need with a storm comin' in. Oscar'll prob'ly be callin' me to fix stuff." He knew he had what he'd need to repair it, but it would take some time. He set to work.

Hearing the wind and rain firing up, he went outside to check out his old generator in case the power failed, then closed the door firmly and went back to work. He had just gotten the oil pan off the truck and begun assessing how he might repair the damage when the storm picked up strength. Looking out the window he saw how dark the sky had become. "This is bad," he muttered as he dropped his tools, sprinted to the door, hitting the light switch as he went out. A strong gust blew some loose boards he'd had leaning against the shed so they nearly hit him. Large hail stones pounded him as he made a dash for the house and the protection of his basement.

Tornado. The word popped into his mind. "Can't be," he muttered, "not around here." The roar of the wind increased with explosive force. As he got to his porch the funnel cloud hit the woods, tearing trees out of the ground and sending debris flying. He'd just gotten in the door when everything exploded. He tried to dive for cover, but the storm force literally picked him up, pulled him tumbling upward right through the roof as it disintegrated, hurled him several hundred yards, then shot his body into the ground amidst a flurry of trees that were breaking apart. It all happened in a matter of seconds.

Zeke Stoner was dead before his body hit the ground, his skull shattered, and his torso twisted around the base of a fence post that had somehow stayed in place.

♦ ♦ ♦

Cam Bordain kept up with weather bulletins regularly. Because he'd been personally involved with the manhunt that had now expanded into West Virginia, he was at the Strong's Creek substation when the tornado alert came in. The word, "tornado," sounded out of place. He'd rarely heard of such in the mountains, but he knew they could strike anywhere unexpectedly. He told his dispatcher to follow their emergency plan. "I'll secure things here and be over there as quickly as possible."

The wind and rain had just begun to increase, and the sky had a weird cast to it he'd never seen before. Running with his emergency lights and siren on, he stayed on the radio while he drove. By the time he reached the bridge over Strong's Creek he had his wipers on high and still struggled to see through the sheets of rain. Accident reports crackled over the radio and he gave thanks for lighter than usual traffic where he was.

Suddenly he came to a stop. The creek was over the road and washing across the bridge with a strong current. There were other roads to Peakview that wound around through the hills and woods, but he wasn't sure what shape they'd be in. As he called in to report the situation he saw a car coming toward the bridge on the other side, obviously expecting to drive through the flood. Almost before he could speak the car was swept up and plunged over the side, wallowing in the confused current. He could see a woman inside frantically trying to get out.

He wanted to wade out to the vehicle but knew he would probably never make it. The rain was falling so heavily he lost sight of the car as he called the fire station for assistance. More weather reports were coming in. He heard about a tornado apparently touching down, then skipping over the town, hitting again out in the Rooster Holler vicinity.

He got one of his deputies on the scene at the creek, then turned around and headed back into town. He decided the best way to assess things locally was to stop by Coop's Pit Stop—the town's gathering place.

"Anybody been up in the holler yet?" said Cam to a dozen men watching TV weather reports.

"We was jest talkin' 'bout that," said one of the men.

"I hear it's bad up there. They's a ditch tore plumb through the road, trees and stuff all over the place."

The storm had subsided considerably at this point. "I'm gonna need boots on the ground," said Cam. "How many of y'all are up to given' me a hand with this? Thankfully they ain't too many folks live up there, but as ya know, the ones that do are spread out pretty thin. It's gonna take some effort, but if there are injured folks, we need to find 'em quick. Once the weather settles enough, we can get a chopper in if we need to."

All the men volunteered. Cam laid out a map on the counter and they divided up into teams to trace out the various lanes and roadways, then set out to work the plan they had devised. Cam and another man named Jeff headed up Rooster Holler Road, past the school and on toward the bluff. Cam fielded calls between different teams while keeping an eye out for damage. Suddenly they came to a small crowd that had gathered where the road had been washed out. A state police cruiser was there, and he checked in with them. They had the situation in hand.

"Hey, ain't that Zeke Stoner's lane," said Jeff. Cam could hardly believe it. Trees were toppled every which way, the fence gone, ground torn up and debris from who knows where caught in clusters across the landscape. He could see up toward the house, except it didn't appear to be there.

"Got a bad feelin' 'bout this." Cam pulled the Interceptor up off the road where the lane was supposed to be. "We gonna have to walk in." He reported the situation to the others, then got out some equipment and the two men began making their way up the remnant of the lane.

"Over there...ain't that Zeke's old truck upside down?"

"Danged if it ain't." They went across to where it was, but there was no sign of Zeke in or around the truck. "The man's a little strange, but I wouldn't wish him any harm. Maybe we'll find him wanderin' around here someplace in a daze."

Making their way through the rubble they came across the remains of Zeke's house and shed. "Strange how tornados tear some things up and others seem to hardly be touched." While the walls were mostly gone, there was enough left to outline the structure of the small building. The scene was unnerving with clothing, furniture, a bathtub upside down in the yard, building materials mingled with parts of trees that were strewn everywhere.

"Now that's strange," said Cam, looking at the front door still hinged to the frame, standing alone.

"Hey, look over here...this is a closet, standing in one piece, door closed, walls intact. Maybe that's why they tell people to get into a closet during a tornado."

Cam went over and tried the doorknob. "This thing's locked.

Jeff stepped back with a strange expression on his face. "Do ya think maybe Stoner's inside there...maybe he took shelter there?"

Cam pushed against the closet, but it wouldn't budge. "Could be. He grabbed a crowbar and took a whack at the wallboard along the side of the closet. It splintered. He grabbed a piece and pulled away a large section, then suddenly stepped back.

"What?" said Jeff. "Did ya find 'im?"

"Nobody in there...but there is a circular stairway, you know, built around a pole. This place has a basement."

They got to work wrecking the closet, then went cautiously down the stairs. "Zeke, you down here? It's Sheriff Bordain."

No answer.

When both men were down they looked around the room which appeared to be totally self-contained. "I wonder why the man didn't come down here?" said Cam. "He was set up with food, water, a place to cook, a cooler, even a toilet and shower. Wonder what was in his mind?"

"Maybe this computer over here could tell us somethin' if we knew how to get into it."

"He even has a safe down here." Cam tried to open it. "We'll get the state forensic people to go over all of this." He paused and scratched his head. "So where is Stoner?"

Cam made his way back down the lane to his vehicle and called in a detailed report. As he finished one of the men from another team came up to him. "Sheriff, we found a body about a quarter-mile over there." He pointed in the direction. "It's in pretty bad shape...maybe we oughta throw a tarp or somethin' over it."

Cam went with him. It was Zeke Stoner. "Wonder how he got way down here? Do ya reckon the tornado picked 'im up and threw 'im over here?"

"That's what it looks like."

♦ ♦ ♦

Billy had told Cindy Wednesday morning that he was going into the ravine to check on some of the people in the thunderstorm's aftermath. He had made several stops and then went by to Barney and Myrtle's place. He felt relieved that they weren't there because that probably meant she was still in the hospital at Peakview.

Before he could leave, the storm hit with such fury he decided to wait it out in his Wrangler. At one point the wind rocked the vehicle so severely he thought it was going to be lifted off the ground, but nothing happened. He thought of Cindy, Clint and Lottie. *Lord, am I going to make it?*

He sensed a calm inner assurance. *Just wait. You'll be all right.*

When he tried to leave he found the road blocked by a large tree that had fallen across it. The rain had stopped. As he weighed the situation a couple of trucks pulled up behind him. Several men jumped out with chain saws and equipment. "Hey preacher, what y'all doin' ou'chere with this storm an' all?"

Billy explained he'd been visiting people to pray with them and see if they needed help, since so many were elderly. "That reminds me, I was gonna check on Miz Mazzie, but I never got that far. Y'all know anything about her?""

The men had fanned out and were beginning to remove branches, so they could cut the trunk into pieces. One shouted to him over the buzz of the saws. "Ya ain't too far from 'er place, but I doubt ya can git across that little creek. With all this rain it's more like a small river now."

"Maybe I'd better try that tomorrow. I went up there yesterday and nearly drowned."

The men laughed. "Yer okay, fer a preacher," they shouted.

It didn't take long for them to finish clearing the road. Billy drove up to Frog Hollow Church next. He was surprised to see no trees down. Outside of ponding water and a lot of mud, you could hardly tell there had been a storm. He went inside the church and knelt at the altar in prayer. "Lord, there are a lot of good people in this hollow who are getting, older and I know this storm is hard for them. Be with Miz Mazzie and Flo." He named others and concluded, "Please grant us healing, wisdom and strength for what lies ahead now."

When he came out of the church he looked up toward the next ridge at Earlene's house. He couldn't tell if she had any trees down. He thought of Cindy.

It was when he came off the ridge toward Strong's Creek that he had second thoughts about getting home. The creek was running wild, muddy water bearing parts of trees spilling out from its high banks onto the road in several places. He decided he could probably make it if he was careful and went slowly. *Lord don't let me meet anybody coming the other way 'cause I don't know what we'd do.* It took a while, but he finally got to the surfaced road.

A little later at the main highway he came upon the flooded bridge, thankful he didn't have to cross it. The police had blocked off the impacted areas with volunteer deputies directing traffic around the obstructions. It was getting late and the rain had not resumed, so more people were out and about.

When he reached the house there was water standing in the front yard, but it didn't appear to have gotten up to the foundation. He slipped into four-wheel drive and nursed the Wrangler around to the back. The tree limb was still jammed into the back window, but it looked like his repairs were still intact. *Guess Oscar never did run down Zeke. Ahh...maybe he was helping somebody else.*

When Billy got inside the house, his tension released like air from a balloon. Before doing anything else, he went into his study and sank into his chair, closed his eyes, and relaxed. When he looked up he saw the message light on the phone blinking. He checked it out.

"Hi, hon. Hope you're okay. Missed hearing from you but I know you were up in the hollow. We've been busy like crazy here, but I'll be getting off at six...finally. Not sure I can get to my house tonight. In case you didn't know, there was a tornado up on Rooster Holler Road. Zeke Stoner's place was destroyed, and they found his body out in the woods. So sad. Call me when you can."

Billy sat there, stunned. *Zeke Stoner dead.* He sank back in the chair and cried over this strange man he'd never been able to understand. *Receive his soul in your mercy, Lord.* He sat in silence for a few minutes, then picked up the phone and called Cindy back.

"I'm so glad you're okay," she said. "With all the phones and electricity and wi-fi out, I've been anxious about you."

"I've missed you, too. What a day. How soon do you get off?"

"Just about to leave now. Let's get supper over at the diner, what do you say?"

"Sounds like what I was about to ask you. Give me a few minutes to shower and clean up, and I'll meet you there."

Thank you for Cindy, Lord. I don't know what either of us would do without the other right now.

TWENTY-NINE

Thursday morning the sun blazed across a clear, blue sky. Billy was awakened by the sound of chain saws where crews were cleaning up storm damage. He had slept soundly after seeing Cindy home safely. They had both been relieved to find she had little damage at her place. Rubbing his eyes and stretching, he checked the time—nine o'clock. He hastily shaved and showered, then as he sat down for breakfast, turned on the TV where reporter Ray Brinkle's ten o'clock update had just begun.

"New developments today with the EverMore Pipeline. Strong straight-line winds estimated at nearly 100 miles per hour swept through Bear Trail Pass yesterday, taking down a large number of trees, including those occupied by tree-sitting protestors. Both men who had occupied the tree stands were hospitalized with non-life-threatening injuries. Protest supporters were credited with preventing further injuries and calling in emergency services. At the same time, several protestors were arrested and released on their own recognizance at a preliminary hearing.

"EverMore Energy has announced a temporary work stoppage while storm damages are assessed, including conditions at Frog Hollow where a tornado reportedly touched down briefly yesterday. The isolated community is next in line along the pipeline's proposed path.

"Yesterday was difficult for the Strong's Creek community as well. Another tornado struck a home in the Rooster Holler area, killing the resident and destroying his house. In an ironic twist, State Police say the victim is a person of interest in the recent shooting of SOM leader, Abi Durango, at Bear Trail Pass. A forensic team is on site evaluating evidence of an unknown nature found in the rubble. We will keep you informed as this story unfolds.

"The National Weather Service estimates that both tornados were rated E/F3, with winds possibly as high as 165 miles per hour. Weather experts believe it was the same tornado touching down in Frog Hollow, then skipping across the village of Strong's Creek, touching down again on Rooster Holler Road. So far, a lot of property damage has been reported, but only one death and an untold number of injuries."

Billy was dumbstruck as he watched the video scenes and listened to the report. He wasn't sure which houses in Frog Hollow were involved, but it appeared Mama Jean's was not one of them. He was especially interested in the scenes on Rooster Holler Road, remembering Cindy telling him Zeke was dead. *What a strange guy...what would he have had to do with the Bear Trail Pass shooting? You never know about people.*

Billy turned off the TV, deciding to drop by the sheriff's office, then go on to Frog Hollow. Although telephone service had been restored, no one had called him. He reached for the phone to call Cindy first, to see how she was. It rang just as he reached for it.

"Hello?"

"William, this is Fletch Waverley. I've been hearing news reports about a tornado over there. Are you okay?"

"Good morning, Dr. Waverley. We did have a very active storm here and I was just leaving for Frog Hollow when you called."

"Can you get in there? It sounds really bad."

"Yes. I was there when it happened, but I wasn't where the worst damage occurred."

"You were there? Why...I mean didn't you know the storm was dangerous?"

"Yes, Sir. That's why I went...to check on our older folks. The tornado itself affected a small area, but there were a lot of trees down. Strong's Creek was flooded when I came back, but they had things under control."

"I heard about the creek...they rescued a woman whose car was swept away."

"I heard about that. It was dangerous. A lot of damage in a very short time."

"What about your sunrise service Sunday? Were your churches damaged? Are you still planning to have that?"

"As far as I know, no damage to the churches. I haven't had time to check with folks yet, but I'm sure we'll proceed as planned on Sunday."

"Well, you take care of yourself, and keep me posted. Let me know if you need missional help from the district."

After he hung up with Fletch, Billy went ahead with his call to Cindy. "Good morning how are you doing?"

She sounded groggy. "Well, I'm up." She yawned. "How about you?"

He told her about the newscast, which she hadn't heard, and about Fletch's call. "You know, I think we need to have a prayer meeting, maybe organize some way to respond where people need help. I'm going to call Grant, Carrie, Earlene, and some others. Then I'm going into the ravine to check things out."

Cindy perked up. "Oh, I'm glad to hear that about the prayer meeting. I'm sure we could get a lot of people together for that....Hey, listen, do you mind if I go along when you visit?"

"Of course not...but are you sure? I mean, you had two long non-stop days in the clinic, and I know you were beat last night."

"Yeah, but I'm okay, and I know all these people. It's like we're all family. I'm off today, and hopefully Sunday, too. Do you want me to meet you at church?"

Billy felt a warm flush of anticipation. "No need to go there...I'll just come get you. Probably in an hour or so, say between eleven and twelve."

"Sounds good. See you then."

When he hung up, Billy called Grant and the others. They all agreed to the meeting. "Since Frog Hollow got hit the worst, preacher, you go on up there and we'll look in on folks in town," said Carrie.

"Thanks for the help. Let's meet at Main Street Church at seven this evening—will that work?"

They all agreed.

◆ ◆ ◆

First, he dropped by the sheriff's office to get information about damage in the area, and to see if there were any closed roads. As he talked to the receptionist, Cam stepped out of his office. "Oh, Pastor

Upshur, I was going to call you this morning. Do you have a couple of minutes to step into my office?"

Billy was surprised. "Sure...I just came by to ask for your help."

Cam closed the door. "Have a seat. What kind of help do you need?"

Billy explained he was heading to Frog Hollow and wondered what the state of damage to expect. "I'm especially concerned about Miz Mazzie and Flo. I saw them after the first big thunderstorm and nearly got washed away crossin' that creek. I *know* it'll be even worse now."

Cam nodded, and Billy went on.

"I believe Myrtle Giles is still in the hospital. Do you know anything about Mama Jean?"

"Beanpole's takin' care of that situation. He was arrested with the protestors yesterday, but I knew he wasn't part of it, so they didn't book him. Are you an' him gittin' along now?"

Billy nodded. "We're good."

"Well, you might wanna stop by...oh, she's at Twila's...do you know her?"

"Friend of Mama Jean's—helps her out. Met her once."

"What ya don't know is they was both inside Twila's house when that first tornado all but wiped it out. When Beanpole found 'em they was sittin' on a couch in the middle of rubble that used to be Twila's house, and they was drinkin' lemonade and prayin.' I'd say them prayers was answered."

Billy could picture the scene. "The shock of all that would be enough to take them down. I'll drop by there."

"We sent the EMT's out there, and they said Twila's in a state of shock, so they've taken her to Peakview. Mama Jean's house is where ya need to go. It wasn't even scratched. Beanpole took 'er there."

Billy started to get up. "Thanks, you've been helpful. Oh, you said you were about to call me when I showed up here?"

Cam paused, "Yeah...I guess it ain't none of my business, but anyway...Ya know old Zeke Stoner was killed by that other tornado over at his place."

"Yes...he was such a strange guy...very sad."

"Well, what's sadder yet, he ain't got no kin folk, at least not around here. The state police wanted to put 'im in a John Doe grave, but I been holdin' our fer more. I know it looks like he done some really bad stuff none of us woulda ever suspected...still, we knew 'im and he done a lot of good, too. Anyway, I wondered if ya could do a little service fer 'im, and maybe we can get up some money to buy a plat out there at the Frog Hollow graveyard." Cam paused. "I know that's a lot to ask."

"Wow...I'm a little overwhelmed with all of this. Now...first things first, God loves us even when we do terrible things." Cam looked at him like he wasn't sure where Billy was going. "Whatever happened in his life is between him and God, but he still deserves the dignity of a decent burial. My sadness is that he apparently never found his way out of whatever he was involved in."

"It's been on the news...they think he's the shooter that took down Abi Durango."

"The shooter? I heard he might've been involved, *but the shooter?* That doesn't square with the man I saw around town."

"Don't square with what I seen of 'im neither."

"But, why would he do such a thing?"

"For hire, I'm sure. He had all kinds a stuff in a basement safe. Ya wouldn't believe how much money. They was records showed he's been a 'gun for hire' ya might say, ever since 'e got outa the army. Apparently, he's jest been puttin' on a face he wanted us to see to keep himself safe."

Billy tried to wrap his brain around this. "So, who hired him? It couldn't have been the pipeline protestors...it had to be somebody who wants the pipeline to go through."

"Seems that way. All of that's out of my hands now. The state police and feds are takin' that on. You and me may never know what they come up with."

"Well, yes, of course I'll do a service, and I'll see what it takes to get a burial plat. Just let me know when you want to do this."

Cam stood up, and Billy followed suit. "We can't do nothin' 'bout that 'til the coroner releases the body, and then we'll have to go through the state police. Might even be a few weeks."

Billy shook his hand, and then left.

♦ ♦ ♦

Cindy greeted him with a kiss when he got to her house. "I was gettin' worried about you."

"I'm sorry. I should have called you. I got hung up with Cam Bordain." He told her what he knew about people in the ravine, and then about Zeke...and Cam's request.

"And you're going to do that?" She stepped back and looked at him with an expression he couldn't read.

Oh, oh. Maybe I don't know Cindy as well as I thought. Well, better to find this out now. "How do you feel about that?"

Her expression softened. "I think it's great. Don't think I've ever seen a preacher that would've said yes to that...I'm not too sure it won't cause you some grief around town. Folks seem to back away from people who do things like that."

Billy shifted his weight. "So did I...until now. Somehow all the stuff that's been going on around here these last few weeks has opened me to hear God in a different way. Here's what I think, if God creates each of us to be unique persons, and he tells us he loves us, then his love doesn't stop because we close our ears or ignore him. We can bury his body with dignity and trust that God is taking care of his soul."

Cindy took a couple more steps away from Billy, then swung around to face him. "And you think people will attend that funeral service? I doubt it. I would be surprised if anybody came."

"I know, but it doesn't require a congregation. It's something between God, Zeke and me...and anyone who does attend. I know Cam will be there."

Cindy softened and stepped back toward him. She smiled. "As you can tell, I'm struggling with this, but I'll be there." She pointed to her watch, "Now, it's gettin' late...whom should we visit?"

"Hmm...maybe we should just go down there and let the Spirit lead?"

"I'm for that."

Billy told her his concerns about Miz Mazzie, and they got as near the creek as they could, but it was still too rough to cross. Their next stop was Twila's house, and the shock of the damage was overpowering. They both fought back tears. People from town, friends and neighbors were all pitching in to sort through things and clean up the mess. Billy asked everyone to stop for a moment while he led them in a prayer thanking God for her survival, and asking for healing in her spirit.

"Cam said Mama Jean's back in her house. I heard on the news that the pipeline has been stopped for now. I'd like to drop by there."

When they arrived Mama Jean had a number of people with her, including all three of the Frog Hollow Boys. Billy swallowed hard when he saw them. *Okay, Lord, I'm trusting you with this.* It was Beanpole who came over to them. "Preacher, and Miz Cindy, glad y'all come by. Mama Jean's in here." He motioned to the living room and ushered them inside. Several who had been talking with her eased their way out of the room.

"Pastor Upshur, I prayed ya would come today. We been through a lot, me and God, and he somehow kept me safe. I'm concerned about Twila...ya know she's...."

"I know she's in shock. We're praying for her."

"Thanks, I appreciate that. So, what about this sunrise service...are ya still havin' it?"

"Absolutely." They talked about their plans and Mama Jean said she was looking forward to it. Cindy noticed the time.

"Didn't you say you wanted to go to Peakview to check on the Giles's?"

"Oh." Billy suddenly remembered the prayer meeting. "You know, maybe I can do that in the morning. I almost forgot the prayer meeting at Main Street tonight."

"Y'all havin' a prayer meetin?" said Mama Jean.

"Yes. We all need to pull together after these storms. We'd love to have you join us."

Mama Jean took his hand. "Thanks, but my days of goin' to meetin's at night is done. We havin' our own prayer meetin' right here. This house was saved and Waya and his friends say they gonna move it up where Twila's was. We all gonna be all right."

"Don't know why we didn't think of that instead of fightin' the pipeline," said Beanpole as he, Gus and Burly stepped into the room. "Makes a whole lot more sense than gettin' folks stirred up about somethin' we prob'ly can't stop nohow."

Gus and Burly nodded. "Abi Durango gettin' shot, and then them two tree sitters gettin' hurt...well, it jest made us think we gotta take care o' ourselves and our neighbors. Time we jest let be what'll be and go on livin'," said Gus.

"And, we're sorry we done treated ya so bad back when ya first come here, preacher. Glad we didn't hurt ya none."

Billy embraced all three men, then he and Cindy joined hands with them and Mama Jean in a prayer circle. Billy thanked God that good things were coming from difficult situations. "Show us new ways to be your people."

It was six-thirty when they drove up out of the ravine. "Let's eat supper after the prayer meeting," said Cindy. "This is all too good to be true, and I don't want it to stop."

Billy squeezed her hand. "You're right. I feel that way too."

THIRTY

When they got to Main Street Church Billy was surprised to find a cheese dip, ham biscuits, apple pie, & coffee set out on a table. Over a dozen people had gathered, including Earlene, Holly and Bernie from Frog Hollow.

"Y'all come on in and help yourselves to some food. We thought ya might not have had a chance to eat supper."

"Wow, this is something else," said Cindy. "We've just come from Mama Jean's, and you're right, we didn't have time to stop."

Earlene came over to them with a quizzical expression. "I stopped by your house on the way over here...wondered where you were."

Billy and Cindy knew people were beginning to be aware how often they were together. They exchanged glances, then filled their paper plates with food. Cindy thanked her aunt for caring. Carrie called the group to order just as Grant came in.

"Sorry I'm late, they're workin' on the bridge at Strong's Creek so I was delayed getting in from work."

"Git y'self some vittals," said Carrie. "Preacher, tell us what's goin' on in the hollow."

Billy filled them in on the details, then glanced toward Cindy, who seemed to know what he was going to say. "Somebody told me when I first arrived that there wasn't much chance the Frog Hollow Boys would 'get religion,' as it was said. Well, praise God, I believe they have. They've offered to move Mama Jean's house up on the ridge and put their efforts into that instead of fighting the pipeline."

The room was silent for a moment as people glanced around to see if they'd heard correctly, then applause broke out. "That's wonderful," said Carrie. "It's a miracle."

Somebody said, "Well, I'll be dogged. If y'all had told me I'd be hearin' this, I'd of said ya was plum crazy. I think this calls for prayers of thanksgivin'. I don't live in the hollow, but I know takin' away Mama Jean's house caused a lotta anger. Them boys fought hard to keep it from happenin'. Do ya reckon the storm was God's way of gettin' everybody's attention onto other stuff?"

It was a comment that could derail everybody into a discussion of the pipeline's pros and cons. Billy didn't want to go there, but he knew the comment needed a reply. "It looks that way, doesn't it? The thing is, the tornados have caused death, injury and destruction. Somehow, I just don't think God works that way. He doesn't send one hardship to counter another, but when things like this happen, God is with us. So yes, I think he wants to redirect our attention."

Grant stood up. "Now hold on, preacher, one of them storms killed a man who was mean and dangerous...somebody who hid behind all of us to cover up his dirty work. You tellin' me this ain't God's judgment?"

"Grant, I hear what you're saying, and no, I don't think God sent a tornado to do in Zeke Stoner. The man did that to himself. Sure, like all of you, I'm angry that Stoner used us as some kind of front to hide behind. I think his sins found him out, but if we're honest, we all have stuff we hide, or regret, or just haven't figured out in our lives. God loves us anyway, and if we turn that stuff over to him, he can show us a healthier way to live. If we don't, well...it looks like Zeke didn't do that."

Holly spoke up. "This whole thing is shocking because it puts the issue right on our own doorstep. How many of us really tried to get to know him? Here we celebrate God's transforming love all the time in worship, then we don't take it to somebody like Zeke."

Grant replied, "I think you're right, Holly. We could talk about that all night, but it's gettin' late and we need to get back to what we came here to pray about—how to help folks recover from this storm. Aside from Stoner's place, the worst damage was in Frog Hollow. Other than Mama Jean's situation, what kind of help do folks need there?"

"They need our prayers, and they're gonna need money and manpower," said Bernie. Here's an opportunity to unite our churches around something good. I'll try to find out some particulars."

"Now, that's good thinkin," said Carrie. "Grant let's you an' me git together and work out a way to involve people. Bein' that this Sunday's Easter, we couldn't find a better time to put out the challenge."

"Well, sure, if y'all agree, but aren't we movin' a little fast? He looked toward Billy. "Preacher, don't this need to git approved by the board?"

"Yes, to both things. I'm impressed with what we're talkin' about. There really isn't a lot of time to think about this, but we can get a buzz going so people are on board."

Billy paused. "There is one other thing I need to talk about."

Grant looked puzzled. "What's that?"

"It's about Zeke Stoner...."

"What, we back to him?"

"Well, here's the thing. Zeke was pretty much a loner. They've been able to trace him back to a small town in Kentucky, but there don't seem to be any living relatives. His real name, by the way, was Rodney Smeltzer."

People exchanged looks around the table. "I like Zeke Stoner better," said Bernie.

"Be that as it may, and regardless of what he did, there's no place to send the body for burial. I've got an idea...can we donate a burial plot at Frog Hollow?"

Grant shook his head. "Wait a minute...I'm still tryin' to get over the shock that he was an assassin, now you want me to help bury the guy?"

Billy held up the palms of his hands. "I hear what you're saying but giving him a graveside service and a burial place doesn't endorse what he did. Instead, it says God's love is greater even than this. Judgement is God's to do. He calls us to love one another, even when it's tough. I told the sheriff I'd do a graveside service and I'd like for y'all to stand with me."

For a few moments the room was silent as people studied their table tops.

Carrie spoke up. "We said we was gonna have a prayer meetin' here tonight. So, let's do it."

Billy asked them to join hands as he led a prayer for God's Spirit to reveal a clear path forward. People shared their emotions in sentence prayers, then he closed with a petition. "Lord, you know how hard it is for us to see clearly in the fog of feelings we haven't worked out yet. Light a path with your Spirit, and we will follow."

The tension eased.

"I'll do it," said Carrie. "I can't undo the harm this man caused, but I can forgive him. If I don't do that, then I can't affirm God's love that offers us all redemption and hope."

Grant responded, "You're right, Carrie. I'll help with that."

Earlene stepped up. "Count me in, too, and I'll work out the details with the cemetery committee."

Billy thanked them, then Carrie said with a twinkle in her eye, "Preacher, somebody mentioned you and Cindy have been seen together a lot lately." She raised her eyebrows playfully.

The room went still as people pondered where this was going.

Carrie went on, "I jest wanted to say, I've known Cindy since she was a young-un. She does a lot for folks around here and we love her." She smiled, "Maybe this ain't the right time or place to say it, but I think y'all two fit together right well."

People cheered, and Cindy came to stand with Billy. "Y'all are somethin' else." She squeezed his hand, "I think a lot of this guy, and we have been workin' together on things. If anything comes out of it, y'all will be the first to know."

Billy squeezed her hand in return. "I agree with Cindy." Looking into her eyes he felt the love they had discovered for each other. "I believe God has put us together out of our own needs, and our desire to serve him."

It was a positive note on which to end the meeting.

♦ ♦ ♦

Billy was swamped with work Friday and Cindy put in a full shift at the clinic. That evening they had a supper date at the Valley Farmer's Kitchen. The weather had warmed during the afternoon but then cooled off. They were shown to an upholstered booth toward the back of the restaurant where they sat side-by-side. Her blue and white striped pullover, silver loop earrings and loosely combed auburn hair created an aura of casual relaxation that drew him to her like a magnet. They gave their order to the waitress then leaned back. He put his arm around her shoulder as they gazed into each other's eyes.

"I love you," he whispered.

"I love you, too."

They kissed, only to be interrupted by the server with their drinks. "Oops, didn't mean to interrupt."

Pulling apart and laughing, Cindy said, "That's okay."

"So, looks like we're creating a bit of a stir," said Billy as they waited for their food.

Cindy laughed. "You mean Aunt Earlene yesterday? I should have been expecting it. She's been trying to pry me for information about us, and I've been playing coy. As I've said before, she always finds a way to get what she wants."

Billy ran his fingers over her hand, then looked into her eyes. "I think her niece does, too."

Cindy pulled back in mock afront. "What? You think I set a trap for you?"

They both laughed. "No, I think we were meant to find each other. You've really been good for me, and I love being with you, no matter what we're doing."

During the meal they discussed the happenings of the day, and what they'd been through together. After supper they lingered at the table with coffee. "Do you realize I didn't even know you existed ten weeks ago!"

Billy recalled the first time he saw her at Earlene's house. "You brought fresh air into that room when you took on Barney's attitude. Somehow I think I knew you and I were going to fall in love that very moment."

"Did you?" She faked afront, then put her arm around his neck. "So did I"

The world stood still. Billy knew he never wanted to be without her. "It has only been a few weeks, but I never want this to end...you and me, I mean." He paused. "Let's get married."

It had come out, just like that. They pulled together in a euphoric embrace.

"When?" whispered Cindy in his ear.

"How about June?"

"Yes!"

They pulled apart and he looked deeply into her eyes. "Let's be sure. You know I've got three years of seminary ahead of me, and from what I've been through here, being a student pastor can be very demanding."

"Why would you need to do that? Why not go on to school and then get back into serving a church after you graduate?"

He looked down. "That would be great, but money is the problem. It takes a lot of it to get a graduate degree."

She pulled his face up and kissed him. "I'm an RN. I've got a house we can sell. I can get a job in Richmond tomorrow, if I want to. We'll just do this together." She paused and backed off. "Unless you intend to stay here at the Strong's Creek Circuit?"

Billy sighed. "No, believe me, this has been a terrific experience, but it's too intense. I feel good about where things are going, but if you're willing to be the breadwinner for a while, I'd far rather do school full time. What I've learned here will always be a filter through which to process what I learn."

When Billy drove her home, they kissed at the back door. "You've made me the happiest man in the world tonight. Still, it's awfully fast. You said you could sell this house...I wouldn't want you to do that."

She squeezed his hand. "We can decide things like that later. Let's pray about this the next couple of days. You have a lot to do getting ready for Sunday, and I have long days at the clinic. If we still feel like we do right now at church on Sunday, then we'll do it. Okay?"

"Good idea," said Billy and they kissed goodnight.

THIRTY-ONE

A complication emerged Saturday morning when the creek dried enough for Miz Mazzie's neighbors to get in and check on her. They discovered a tree had fallen into the kitchen area of the house, causing a lot of damage. She was on the floor in the living room, dead. An autopsy would confirm what the EMT's suspected...she had died from a heart attack. The troubling part was that Flo was nowhere to be found. She had apparently run off in fear.

The neighbors had called both Billy and Cam Bordain. After going over the situation the sheriff put out a missing person report on Flo, then they contacted her son. It was a sad note for the tightly-knit Frog Hollow community on top of the long-festering pipeline struggle, topped now by destruction from a tornado. Billy felt peoples' grief and determination as he visited among them, lifting their needs in prayer.

As if that weren't enough, Fletch Waverley called. "I know I said I'd be at your sunrise service tomorrow, but something has come up and I won't be able to make it."

Billy was just as glad since Fletch always seemed to inject a sour note. At the same time, he had hoped to introduce Cindy and tell him about their plans. "I'm sorry you can't come...we'll miss you. I had wanted to talk to you about a couple of things."

Instantly on guard, Fletch said, "Oh? We just talked the other day. What's happened now?"

"Nothing bad, at least from my perspective. I'll tell you what's going on, but I really need to see you in your office next week."

They set a date on the calendar. "So, what's this about?"

"I'll give it to you short and straight. I've found the most wonderful woman I've ever known at Frog Hollow and we're going to be married in June."

Fletch was completely silent for a moment. "Have you been messing around with some woman over there? I can't believe it...you know, you can't marry someone in the church you serve and continue as pastor there? It's against the rules."

"No problem. I plan to resign effective June first."

"You what?"

"I said I am resigning effective June first. Cindy and I will be moving to Richmond and I'll go to seminary full time, then put in for an assignment when I graduate."

"I must say, this is sudden."

"Yes, I know. That's why I want to talk to you next week. There are some big changes happening that I'll spell out in detail when I see you. I do want to thank you for giving me this opportunity to experience the ministry. It has been filled with unbelievable challenges, and it has deepened my calling. So, thank you for that."

Fletch was almost lost for words but accepted the resignation. After he hung up, Billy had a flash of concern. *Whoa, I moved too fast. Cindy and I were going to wait until tomorrow to set this up for sure. Well, Lord, it's in your hands.*

Billy spent the rest of the day completing his Easter sermon, then met Cindy at her house for supper. While helping her clean up after the meal he said. "I got a little carried away today, hon...and, well, I let the cat out of the bag."

She was washing cookware and stopped, dried her hands and turned toward him. "What?"

"I'm sorry...I told Fletch Waverley about our plans to get married...and I resigned effective the first of June." He felt shame at having broken their agreement to wait for Sunday.

She shrugged her shoulders. "Oh, is that all?"

"Yes...isn't that enough?"

She laughed and put her arms around his neck. "I'm flattered that you couldn't hold it back. Now I have a confession...neither could I. After we finish in here I was going to tell you I put in a call to a friend in Richmond and asked her to scout out job openings. Of course, she was thrilled when I told her why I was asking. She can't wait to meet you."

They both broke out laughing. "So much for waiting. I feel like God's giving us his blessing, so let's announce our engagement at the services in the morning. We can talk about the other details later."

They kissed.

"Thanks for bringing love back into my life."

♦ ♦ ♦

Heavy dew coated the landscape at Frog Hollow Church as Billy arrived early on Easter morning. Earlene and Ralphie were already there. The forecast called for gradual warming and a mostly sunny day. They were carrying chairs out to the cemetery when Holly and Bernie arrived with the portable keyboard and sound system. By six-forty-five they had everything in place. Inside the church Carrie and Cindy had breakfast fixings set up and coffee was brewing.

The sun's rays began to glow across the ridges as Billy stood to begin the service. He had counted at least fifty people with more continuing to arrive. He called out a greeting using the words of Isaiah 49:13: *"Sing for joy, O heavens, and exult, O earth; break forth, O mountains, into singing! For the Lord has comforted his people, and will have compassion on his suffering ones."*

"Good morning. We welcome you to this Easter Sunrise Service. The sun is rising, and with it the promise of God's blessings for a new day." More people arrived as they sang Charles Wesley's hymn, "Christ the Lord Is Risen Today." Song birds warbled with the joyful sound. Billy noticed Oscar Bender drive up and unload extra lawn chairs to accommodate the overflow.

After the hymn, Grant read the familiar scripture about the women finding the tomb empty where Jesus had been buried, then his appearance to them. The Main Street Choir, fully robed, sang an anthem. The stress they'd all been through in recent days seemed to evaporate as the sun gradually filled the sky with its brilliance.

Beanpole helped Mama Jean up to the podium to a stir of mixed reaction among the congregation. Some who knew her applauded. Others who had only heard of her were less enthusiastic. Billy introduced her as a woman of rich faith from her Cherokee roots who had been in her friend's house when the tornado destroyed it. "She is a member of this church, a Medicine Woman, or healer, in her tribal tradition, and I've asked her to share her faith this morning."

Strong of voice, Mama Jean told about the faith she'd received from her ancestors, and how she had found Christ and now worshipped him. "I want to witness by singing a hymn you know well, first in Cherokee and then in English." With clear tones she sang, *"OOH NAY THLA NAH, HEE OO WAY GEE' E GAH GWOO YAH HAY EE. NAW GWOO JOE SAH, WE YOU LOW SAY, E GAH GWOO YAH HO NAH."* It was to the tune of John Newton's hymn, Amazing Grace, which she then sang in English.

Mama Jean went on, "Over many years I have used my house as a place of healing, peace and hope for people in our community. So many have found the Great Spirit of Almighty God there, then when the pipeline was changed to avoid this place where we are now, it was set to go right through my house.

"Now a new blessing has come. My nephew Waya and others are going to move my house to a safe place, and God will hallow that ground for his use. I don't know if the pipeline is evil, but much evil has surrounded it. Now I know God is in control even of that. I believe it is time to step out of that fight. God calls us to live in his Spirit wherever we are, no matter what happens around us.

"This week the Great Spirit took away the pipeline's threat. The wind removed trees and blew down houses. None of us were harmed. The wind has set us free to be Gods people of peace, love and spiritual strength. God will judge the souls of those who do evil, and he will bless those who walk in his way." She closed singing a brief chant of praise.

It was both a thrilling and humbling experience. Billy could feel the warmth and acceptance that filled the air. He preached a brief message, then Ralphie led the congregation in singing Alfred Ackley's hymn, "He Lives."

"I want to thank you for coming this morning," said Billy. "What a powerful celebration for Easter morning. Jesus rose from the grave as our Savior, and by God's grace we will rise from the destruction we have experienced."

People began to sing spontaneously, "Alleluia, Alleluia," joining hands in praise.

"Thank you, Lord, for the eternal power of your Spirit through which your blessings flow. Praise God and go in peace."

A joyful buzz of fellowship began to fill the room.

"One more thing," he hollered, and the buzz abated. "Please go inside the church and have breakfast. We face great challenges repairing tornado damage, and as Mama Jean said, moving her house. Grant Mackabee and Earlene Josef have information about ways you can help with these tasks."

Most of the people stayed for breakfast. Billy used the occasion to make some other announcements. He mentioned Mazzie Plunket's death. "We will have a memorial service to honor her life as soon as details can be worked out. Please be in prayer for her niece, Flo, who has some special needs, and lived with her. She seems to have run away after the storm. Sheriff Bordain and the state police are searching for her. Please pray that she is safe and will soon be found."

Billy called Carrie and Cindy to his side. "Now, I want y'all to give a big hand to these two who arranged this breakfast." The people clapped and called out their thanks. Billy took Cindy's hand and spoke above the crowd.

"One more thing...Cindy Barker and I want to make an announcement." The buzz in the room subsided again as everyone looked toward them. "This is the most wonderful woman I have ever met..."

Cindy interrupted. "What he wants to say is that I'm about to change my name to Cindy Upshur. We're going to get married in June, and you're all invited to the wedding."

The room swelled with excitement. Billy was overwhelmed with the love and support people expressed. He and Cindy barely had time to make the Main Street service, but they did...and made the same announcement there. Finally, when all the excitement was over, they got into the Wrangler and headed out of town. It was something they'd planned the day before. They headed for Clint and Lottie's house in Healing Waters, West Virginia.

As they drove up through the National Forest Billy pulled off on a wide piece of the road's shoulder. He took Cindy across the road to an observation area looking out at the splendor of God's creation. He told her about having stopped there before.

This time it was different. The trees on the mountain ridges seemed to dance for joy. The fractured young pastor who had yelled at God in anger among these same trees three months earlier had been transformed.

He was whole.

A new person.

And he had Cindy.

Whether or not the pipeline ever got completed no longer mattered—it had been a vessel of change that would bless him the rest of his life.

AUTHOR'S END NOTE

Fracking is a hydraulic process by which oil and natural gas is extracted from deep-rock formations by injecting fluid and other mediums like sand into a wellbore. Opponents of the process cite potential adverse impacts on the environment—water and air pollution, noise pollution, and the possibility of triggering earthquakes. Proponents speak of long-term energy stability and job creation.

In Virginia there are two controversial pipelines under construction that would carry natural gas from fracking sites through the state to new markets. Public reactions have created numerous challenges and delays.

This story is not about either of these projects or the companies involved, but rather explores relational situations that could occur in such an environment. It is a story involving both suspense and romance with an overarching message of redemption and hope.

Whatever might be your reaction to the story, I hope you will take time to compose a review of the book—what you experienced in reading it, how well or poorly you think it was written, and any reflections you may have. Your review will help others who may consider reading it.

Made in the USA
Middletown, DE
05 January 2023